Lucy Shaw
Wants More

Lucy Shaw Wants More
Published by The Conrad Press in the United Kingdom 2019

Tel: +44(0)1227 472 874
www.theconradpress.com
info@theconradpress.com

ISBN 978-1-911546-53-5

Typesetting and Cover Design by: Charlotte Mouncey, www.bookstyle.co.uk
The Conrad Press logo was designed by Maria Priestley.

Printed and bound in Great Britain
by Clays Ltd, Elcograf S.p.A

Lucy Shaw Wants More

JO BAVINGTON-JONES

For Sam, always my rock, and not so little anymore.
And for Gwynne and Kathy, my pillars of love and support.

The heart wants what it wants – or else it does not care –
Emily Dickinson

CHAPTER 1

Where was I?

'The name's Shaw. Lucy Shaw. Licensed to spill.'

As I announce this to an empty kitchen, I'm spinning my feet around on the Lino and taking up a shooting stance with a roll of kitchen towel in my hands. As I spin, I slip and crash into the door frame. Hearing the bang, Alfie, my Old English Sheepdog, looks up from his bed in the adjoining utility room, a look of resigned disgust on his doggy face. I can almost hear him saying, 'Oh dear! What has she done now?' before sighing and going back to sleep with a pitying grunt.

Rubbing my shoulder where it's hit the wood, I turn back to the kitchen worktop, with a sigh to match the dog's, unravelling kitchen towel sheets as I go. I've spilt a mug of tea and the puddle is now dripping onto the floor. As I watch the paper towels suck up the liquid, I have a bit of a déjà vu moment: about this time yesterday I'd been doing something similar – I'd made a cup of coffee. Without the cup. I'd got a mug ready, one spoonful of sugar in it, popped a coffee pod into the Tassimo machine and waited for the green light to indicate it was ready. So far so good. Light went green, I pushed start. Mm, there's that lovely fresh coffee aroma... Unfortunately, dappy cow here hadn't put the mug on the machine and the coffee was pouring all over the side.

I'm not always this dopey. Honest. There are just certain times of the month when I suffer from clumsy-itis and absent-mindedness. Yes, you know what I'm talking about: PMS. PMT. Pass my shotgun. Pity me time. Call it what you will. It turns me into someone else, and we don't get on very well. This *other* person gets tearful and short-tempered, and her spatial awareness goes awry. She should probably take to her bed for a week, and she certainly shouldn't get behind the wheel of a car. She has bruises on her arms and legs from door frames jumping out at her, and furniture mysteriously moving. She's a bit of a nightmare.

Obviously it's not her fault, it's those pesky little things called hormones, but that doesn't make her any easier to live with. I reckon Adam only accepted the forbidden fruit from Eve because she was pre-menstrual – he probably thought the wrath of God would be preferable.

Anyway, *she's* in residence at the moment, and I can only apologise.

Let me tell you a bit about the real me. The real Lucy Shaw.

Well, perhaps the most important thing to know is that my surname is, unintentionally, ironic. I really ought to be called Lucy Unsure. For those of you who've already met me, you'll know that I've spent most of my adult life searching for the secret to happiness. And mostly failing. I'm one of those people who always want what they haven't got, and contrarily, once they have it, no longer want it. It's a most dissatisfactory way to live and one which I have come to realise I must fight against. I'm just not sure how.

Anyway, here I am, forty-four years old, still married to my saintly and long-suffering husband, Paul, aka Mr. Half-a-Job, and mum to six-year-old budding maths genius, Tom. I'm not sure if either of them is responsible for the smattering of greys I now have in my shoulder-length golden-brown hair, but every time I look in the mirror in the morning, a new batch has appeared. It's as if an evil hair fairy, a 'hairy' if you will, comes in the night and paints a few more strands. My green eyes still have a sparkle in them, but they are definitely now framed by a few more lines. I'm not ready to get old, but the inevitability of ageing now stares back at me from the mirror. All the tell-tale signs are there, from little brown age spots on the backs of my hands, to the crepiness beginning to show on my neck and décolletage. One of these days, my mother is going to be looking back at me.

I'm still a stay-at-home mum and my days are mostly rather dull: school run, dog walk, potter and procrastinate and pick, school run... You get the gist. Paul's an IT Project Manager and now works from home full-time, which isn't ideal as he now knows exactly what I do, or rather don't do, during the day. Tom, my bright little blue-eyed boy, is in his third year of primary school and is my raison d'étre. Life's light relief comes mainly from my get-togethers with the other mums from school. We meet regularly to moan and confide and reassure. Knowing that they have similar problems and sadnesses makes life all the more bearable. I had one such catch up the following day.

CHAPTER 2

Mum's the word

The air still feels full of summer as I walk to the tearoom in the park the next morning. It's early September and I've just dropped Tom at school and am very much looking forward to catching up with the other mums for the first time in ages. We often don't see each other during the long summer holiday – everyone's away at different times, and those six weeks just seem to disappear one way and another.

As is often the case, Clare has arrived first. I'm always early, but she's always super-early. Clare's become the closest to me out of all the mums and we enjoy those first few minutes on our own.

Clare's bagsied a table outside – another advantage of always being early – and she smiles as she sees me approaching.

'Lucy! It's so good to see you! Thank God they're back at school. I don't think I could've stood another day at home with Little Miss Attitude.'

I laugh. 'Chloe been giving you the run around again?'

'That's an understatement. Honestly, she's six going on sixteen. I dread to think what she'll be like when she really is a teenager.'

'I must admit, I don't envy you. I think girls mature faster than boys. Tom's still very much my little boy. Although I do get scary little glimpses of what's to come.'

Clare sighed. 'She does my head in, Lucy. The attitude I get from her – you wouldn't believe it.'

'She's just testing the boundaries. You cop the worst of it because you're the closest to her. She feels safe pushing you. It's almost a compliment,' I say, trying to make Clare feel better.

'Well it doesn't bloody well feel like one. Honestly, I could throttle her some days.'

'Oh dear! You just have to take a deep breath and count to ten. Be consistent. She'll come out the other side. Eventually!'

'Ten wouldn't be enough!' Clare sounds exasperated. 'Anyway, Mrs, enough of my woes. What's been going on with you? How're things at home?'

'Honest answer? Stagnant. Dull. Monotonous.' I sighed.

'Oh dear! No better then?'

My marriage has been on the wane for a while, and Clare's become my confidante. She really is like a sister to me.

'Nope. Honestly, the thought that this is it for the rest of my life depresses the hell out of me.'

'What are you going to do? Are you going to leave Paul?'

'I can't. I just can't. It would destroy him. And it would hurt Tom. I couldn't live with myself.'

'I wish I could help, Lucy.'

'You do! Trust me, without our chats I'd be a basket case by now. You're the only thing keeping me sane,' I said, pulling a face that would suggest otherwise.

Clare laughed and said: 'Things must be bad if you're relying on me for sanity,' as she pulled an equally mad face.

We're still laughing when the other mums start to arrive.

'Seriously, though, Lucy, you know I'm always here for you.'

'Thank you. That means a lot,' I reply, giving Clare's hand a squeeze.

13

CHAPTER 3

The 'M' word

Once the other mums, Sarah, Zoe and Charlie, are settled on the wooden bench seats, coffees steaming on the picnic table in between, we take turns to catch everyone up on our summer news.

'Thank God that's over!' is Charlie's opening remark, which she makes the second she sits heavily down and plonks her mug equally heavily onto the table, sploshing some of the cara-mel-coloured liquid onto the wood.

It's quite unusual for Charlie to blaspheme. Her life's normally pretty perfect. In fact, she's planning her wedding to her pretty perfect fiancé, so we're all surprised at her mini outburst.

I wonder who'll be the one to ask what's happened as I'm busy watching the trail of coffee meander across the table and drip between the slats onto the grass. I'm leaning my chin on my elbows and feeling kind of distant, caught up in my own pretty imperfect life. Sarah's the one to speak first.

'Oh dear! What on earth's happened? Spill.'

'She already has!' Zoe couldn't resist jumping in. 'Sorry, Charlie. Seriously, what has happened?'

'It's just this bloody wedding. Who knew planning the happiest day of your life could make you so bloody miserable?'

Hearing Charlie's words, and the tears and frustration in her voice, I realise I have to stop dwelling on my own problems and focus on someone else's. They're always so much easier to deal with aren't they?

'Let me guess...,' I say. 'Rich's parents?'

Charlie's future in-laws are challenging at the best of times. They have a habit of taking over and of making Charlie feel that she just isn't good enough for their precious son. I can only imagine how she feels as Paul's parents are brilliant.

'You guessed it, Luce. His bloody mother only rang the venue and told them we needed to cancel the booking as "we've decided to go elsewhere – somewhere a bit more upmarket"! Cheeky cow! How dare she?'

'No! What did Rich say about it?'

'What does he ever say? Absolutely nothing! He's too frightened of the old witch.'

'He really needs to man up, stand up to her and put your wishes first on this one, Charlie,' Zoe said.

'I wish! It's putting our relationship under a hell of a strain.'

'Maybe you should just say sod everyone else and elope.' This was my helpful suggestion.

'The way I'm feeling at the moment, I'm not even sure I want to get married.'

'If I were you, I'd just spend the money on a fantastic holiday. You could always buy a ring and change your name by deed poll.' Me again. I think I was saying what I wished I'd done.

'Might not be a bad idea. I dread to think of the fireworks we'd come back to though. I'm convinced Rich's mum is part dragon.'

'What about his dad?'

'He just goes along with whatever she says – anything for

a quiet life. All I ever hear him say is "yes, dear",' Charlie says with a sigh.

None of us really knows how to help her and we have to settle for saying we're here if she needs us.

'Thanks, lovelies – I appreciate it. It felt good to vent anyway. Now, enough of my problems, what's everyone else been up to over the summer?'

It seems as though everyone else has had a fairly uneventful summer, just keeping the kids occupied and counting down the days 'til they went back to school. It's sad that we now wish away our summers, I thought wistfully. There was a time when the long school summer holiday was longed for and celebrated – when we were young and those six weeks really were the best days of our lives.

After we've said our goodbyes and promised to meet up regularly, all agreeing that these sessions are like therapy, I walk back to the car with marriage on my mind.

CHAPTER 4

Marriage and me

Time spent driving on my own is valuable thinking time. Cocooned in the safety of my car, I can let my mind drift to whatever is bothering me. Today, especially after the conversation about Charlie's forthcoming nuptials, marriage is on my mind.

I already have one failed marriage behind me and it isn't something I'm proud of. Sadly, though, I'm not sure I've got it right second time either. In moments of complete honesty, to myself at least, I have to admit that I'm not happily married. I just pretend to be, in a performance worthy of an Oscar. A BAFTA at the very least. Bullshit Award for Terrific Acting, best female in a leading role. I try hard to be Paul's leading lady, but my heart just isn't in it anymore. The script had turned out to be absolute rubbish and the love story had turned into a bit of a disaster movie.

The worst part is that I'm the villain of the piece. My husband, Paul, hasn't really done anything wrong. I know he loves me and would do anything for me. I wish I felt the same, but I know that any love I had for him has shrivelled like an old prune. Of course, I rationalise that I haven't fallen out of love with him on purpose, but the guilt eats away at me nonetheless. I think my ovaries had fallen in love with Paul, and I'd hoped the rest of me would follow, but I don't think it ever happened. I was good at kidding myself. Buy now, pay later: that's my approach to marriage. I'd decided that I could keep on making the payments, but it was getting harder and harder to find the money.

I've made a conscious decision to make the marriage work: the alternative is too awful. I really believe that I'm the problem, and that any future relationship would go the same way. So, what's the point in leaving? Best thing for Paul and Tom is for me to stick it out, isn't it? It's just so hard pretending all the time and the strain's beginning to show; the mask slipping. Something has to change, but I've no idea what.

CHAPTER 5

The state of the union

The following morning sees me outside school with Tom, waiting for eight forty-five to arrive and the gates to open. Tom goesto my old primary school, but it looks a lot different than it had in my day. Fences and keypad protected gates surround the place: it bears rather too strong a resemblance to a prison, rather than a welcoming place of learning and play. I think it's a sad reflection on today's society and feel a bit glum as I wave Tom off a few minutes later.

I catch up with Clare as she trots back to her car, her step probably a little lighter now that she's free of her offspring for the day.

'Hi, Lucy. How's it going? You OK?'

'Hiya. Same old. Can't seem to shake off the miseries at the mo. How about you?'

'I'm OK. Another riveting day of walking the dog and doing housework. I think I may actually be addicted to vacuuming. I've started making patterns in the pile with the hoover. It's surprisingly satisfying. You should try it.'

'Ha! My ex used to do that. I always took great pleasure in running through his carpet artwork barefoot after he'd hoovered.'

'Nutter. Seriously, though, are you OK? You seemed pretty low yesterday.'

'I'm just in a funny place at the moment. Trying to work out what to do to make life more bearable – I don't think hoovering's gonna fix things for me.'

'What d'you mean? Hit the booze? Hit the husband?!' Clare laughed.

'Don't laugh. It hasn't come to that yet, but…' I said with mock seriousness. 'No, I thought if maybe I had something that was just about me – nothing to do with being Paul's wife or Tom's mum, then that might just make everything more bearable. Something I don't have to share. Something that makes me feel like Lucy again. I feel kind of lost. D'you know what I mean?'

'God, yes! I think any woman who's a wife and mother can identify with that. Marriage and motherhood are like identity theft! It's just disguised in ribbons and bows and cake so you don't see it coming until it's too late.'

'Ha! Nice simile! Marriage and motherhood: the smiling assassins!'

'At least we can laugh about it.'

'Well, it's that or cry, and I've done that far too much lately.'

'Let's have coffee just the two of us soon, Luce. Maybe we can come up with some ideas.'

'Thank you. I'd really like that.'

Exchanging a quick hug, Clare and I go our separate ways.

Opening the front door when I get home a few minutes later, I'm greeted by a very bouncy dog, all tail and teeth, so happy to see me as always. We have a routine these days and he knows that his walk's next on the agenda. I enjoy our walks, but they're solitary and give me far too much time to think about my unhappiness and the state of my marriage.

Grabbing Alfie's red lead from the hook by the front door, I shout a goodbye up the stairs to Paul in his spare room office and set off, heaving a sigh of relief as I close the door behind me.

Alfie and I have a favourite walk on dry days and he doesn't need me to tell him which direction to take. Nose sniffing the air, he trots along without a care in the world, stopping when he catches a whiff of something deserving of a sniff. The only decision he has to make is which tree to pee up.

'I'm definitely coming back as a dog,' I say to him, as he cocks his leg for the umpteenth time. 'You've got it sussed. Fed and walked and fussed over. Happy with your lot.'

I often talk to my dog as we walk. He pays little or no attention most of the time, his ears just pricking slightly if I use his name, in case a relevant instruction or titbit follows.

I continue, 'Mind you, if I came back as a dog, I'd probably be one of those poor starved and terrified ones you see on Facebook in Romanian rescue shelters. You know, the ones I scroll past really quickly because it's too upsetting. You're a lucky boy, Alfie.' Hearing his name, he looks up from the nettles he's sniffing. 'Yes, I know, I'm lucky too.' I'm not sure who I'm trying to convince. I should be happy, shouldn't I? I'm married to a man who loves me, am mum to a fantastic little boy, have a nice home and lifestyle. On paper I should be happy. That paper is one of those kid's drawings of a house, mum, dad, child and dog. With a big yellow sunshine in the top corner and an oversized flower in the bottom one. It's stuck to the fridge with some tacky fridge magnets brought back as souvenirs from holidays, a constant visual reminder of a happy little family unit.

But, when I look at that picture, the mum isn't smiling. Sure, there's a big, red crayon smile on her face, but it's not real. It's something she puts on in the morning. It's something she hides behind. A part of her disguise. No-one must suspect it's not real, and see the sadness beneath. No-one must suspect that she sometimes thinks about running away from her life. Without her smile, she'll be judged and found wanting. Without her smile, she'll no longer be loved. But that smile's so heavy to hold, day after day after day, when all she really wants to do is take it off for a while. Put it in a drawer, underneath some knickers and socks, and just have a rest from it.

Recognising that my mind's wandering down a dangerous path, I force myself to change direction. Nothing good will be found at the end of that path: just a cliff edge that I'm too scared to peer over, into the abyss below.

Slapping my hands against my jeans-clad legs, I call to Alfie. He comes bounding over and I ruffle his coat and tell him he's a good boy. This simple action brings me back from the cliff edge to safety once more and we continue on our walk. I take in grateful breaths of fresh air, tilting my face up to the sun and taking in the beautiful vistas all around me, every shade of green below a bright blue sky, the blessings of nature all around me. In those moments it feels good to be alive. But I know that all too easily my mind can take that *other* path and that the cliff edge is always there, just around that bend in the track.

CHAPTER 6

Well I never

Home again and Alfie is laid out on the cool tiles of the utility room, a slobbery puddle forming under his mouth from the big slurps of water just taken. He is content. It's now ten thirty and I know that Paul will be wanting a coffee. I make two mugs and take one upstairs. Paul is on a video call, so I tiptoe in and put the mug on the coaster on his desk, careful not to accidently appear in the meeting. I've done this before. In my nightie. I can never go to one of Paul's office parties again. He gives me a thumbs up to say thank you and I creep back out, closing the door behind me. Well, I might want to do something noisy, like hoover. Or scream.

I do neither of those things. Instead, I retrieve my mug of coffee from the kitchen and head to the lounge. With Paul tied up on the phone, it's safe to watch a little bit of daytime television, something I no longer have the luxury of doing very often now that Paul works from home. The guilt is simply too much. I must be busy doing housewifely things, earning my place in the household hierarchy. Today I think sod it. As an afterthought, I pop back to the kitchen and grab a packet of chocolate digestives which I'd hidden at the back of the larder cupboard. I switch on *This Morning*, hoping it's Phillip and Holly presenting today. I don't like their stand-ins nearly as much.

No effort is required of me. I lose myself in the programme, absent-mindedly munching my way through half a packet of biscuits. Items on cooking the perfect roast potato, and clothes to flatter every body shape. Round in my case after all the biccies. Then they start talking about something that catches my attention. Something that suddenly engages me. Something that really shouldn't. Philip is addressing a woman we only see from the back. And she's obviously wearing a wig. He's asking her about a website. It's a dating site. With a difference. It's apparently a site called Secret Affair, and it's for married people. I had no idea such a thing existed and it has piqued my curiosity. Turning the tele up a fraction, I twist the top on the biscuit packet and put it on the table with my now empty mug.

I'm a little bit gobsmacked as I listen to the be-wigged woman's tales of her illicit encounters with several married men, one of whom she had an affair with for over a year. She sounds shameless as she describes rendezvous in hotels, with champagne-fuelled sex and the occasional bit of mild S&M. Personally I'd prefer tea and M&M's, I think idly. Philip is trying his best not to show his disapproval. Holly is trying not to giggle. The woman is talking matter-of-factly about the time she almost got caught by her husband as she left a hotel after one such steamy session. Philip is asking her if she feels guilty. She says she doesn't. She says it saved her marriage. She says it made her feel alive again; a beautiful, desirable woman. It made her feel like *her* again.

That thought imprints itself on my subconscious, but any further enlightenment is brought to a halt by the sound of Paul's office door opening and his familiar cough. That smoker's cough I've started to hate. It makes me clench my jaw and think bad things. He's obviously coming down for a cigarette break. Quickly turning off the TV, I scurry into the kitchen, putting my mug in the washing-up bowl and the biscuits back in the cupboard. I feel like a naughty child, not wanting to be caught with my hand in the cookie jar. It's crazy. I resent it. But would Paul actually even care? I wonder. Is all this guilt of my own making? But now isn't the time for such philosophical musings. I must look busy. I must justify my existence.

But, as I pull a duster and can of polish from the cupboard under the sink, my mind returns to those words: "it made her feel like *her* again". I try to banish them but, as I dust and hoover, and think about what to do for dinner, they lurk and taunt and vex. I want to feel like *me* again. I want my identity back. I want this feeling of dissatisfaction to go away. Paul's voice, my husband's voice, breaks through my errant thoughts:

'Do you fancy takeaway for dinner, Luce?' he's asking.

'Um. Could do I s'pose.' I'm feeling guilty for the thoughts. I must make amends for them. 'Nah, I'll cook something. Maybe get a Chinese on Friday?' I must make it up to my family, so I will cook.

'OK, cool,' Paul says, easy going as ever. He hasn't noticed my feelings of guilt, even though I feel that they're screaming out of me. He puts his arms around my waist and gives me a squeeze before heading back upstairs to work, oblivious to the thoughts in his wife's brain which have now sunk to her gut and are curdling like sour milk.

CHAPTER 7

Shake it off

I feel like I've had a near miss and realise I must shake off the thoughts and feelings that are threatening my stability. I can't do anything that could hurt my family. I need to pull myself together. So, I give myself a good talking to and put the troubling thoughts back in their box, forcing the lid down like that of an overstuffed suitcase. I have to tuck a few escaping ends back in before the lid is fully on. But it's on. For now.

I'm back on script now and my crayon smile is back in place. I will be on my guard and careful not to let my mind wander to dangerous places. I must distract myself – it's always worked in the past, albeit only for a while. I need a project, a plan, something to keep me occupied, instead of preoccupied. I'm still trying to decide what to do as I get a Bonio for Alfie and make sandwiches for Paul's lunch. I'm still too full of biscuits to contemplate eating yet myself, but I need to do the dutiful wife thing. If it wasn't for all my nagging feelings of guilt, Paul would probably starve, I think with a wry smile.

'Shall we sit in the garden? It's gorgeous out.' Me to Paul as he comes into the kitchen.

'Definitely. I could do with some fresh air after a morning of moany old windbags.'

'Let me guess... the French contingent?' I chuckle.

26

'Who else?' Paul says as he settles himself at the picnic table. 'And it looks as though I'll have to endure them in person next month. Joy of joys.'

The company that Paul works for has its head office in Paris, and he's thus far managed to avoid a visit.

'Joie de joies, you mean,' I say with an exaggerated French accent. 'That's a bummer. But you never know, you might enjoy it when you get there.'

'I doubt that very much,' Paul snorted.

'Well, at least you get to stay in a nice hotel. Bit of French cuisine and an open bar. Can't be all bad? Obviously, it won't compare with the culinary delights I lay before you every night, but you can't have everything.' I'm trying to make him feel better about the trip. Should I say that I'll miss him? Or would that be too much? I'm already secretly excited about having some time alone in the house. I can't tell you how exhausting it is to constantly say the opposite of what I'm actually thinking. It's really very tiring indeed and it will be utter bliss to switch off the whole mouth/brain system for a while.

'I'll miss you and Tom though. I hate leaving you guys,' Paul, interrupting my reverie.

Me, guilty. 'I know. We'll miss you too, but it'll fly by and you'll be back before you know it.' Reassuring.

'Yeah, I s'pose so. It's a shame I can't take you with me to the city of romance. You'd love it. Maybe another time I can swing it for you to come too.'

The brain/mouth thing again. My brain's thinking, 'I don't want to go to the city of romance with you,' and my mouth's saying, 'that would be lovely'. Another surge of guilt pushes up through me and I think what an ungrateful cow I am. I reach over and put my hand over Paul's and apply a little reassuring pressure, and mentally check that my smile is in place.

Withdrawing my hand, I change the subject and we spend the next twenty or so minutes talking about what needs doing in the garden. It's a safe topic and a distraction. The garden is much longer than it is wide, but we've made the best of it with a winding path and planting that meanders snake-like alongside until it reaches a decking area and summerhouse at the far end. Paul and I wander up the path, stopping to look at plants along the way, discussing what works, what we could improve. I'm more of a gardener than Paul, but he takes an interest and digs a hole when asked. He's lit another cigarette and is blowing the smoke away from me, but it still makes me clench my jaw. Don't say anything Lucy. Remember that non-smoking Paul is impossible to live with. (Previous attempts by Paul to give up smoking had almost ended in whatever-the-word-is-for-killing-your-husband.)

We're nearing the far end, and my favourite bit, of the garden and I can't help but smile for real as I see the chalky-blue summerhouse which looks a bit like a giant beach hut. It definitely has a bit of a seaside theme going on, with mini lighthouse solar lights strung across the front and a collection of beach-finds arranged on the deck. There are also strings of driftwood and holey pebbles hanging from the eaves. A trip to any beach always results in pocketsful of irresistible bits and bobs being brought home, and many of them find homes in the garden. Inside the summerhouse I have a little table and a chair where I sometimes sit and try to be artsy and craftsy with bits of sea glass and pottery, their edges smoothed by time and tide.

The deck itself is fenced on both sides, but the fence has

completely disappeared under lush green foliage. Two years previously, I'd planted a passionflower and it had spread like wildfire along the fence, over the summerhouse and back down the other side. It had obviously been planted in just the right place and it had thrived and blossomed with flowers the colour of clotted cream, rich and fruitful and unstoppable. The flowers were turning now and the tendrilly vines were pregnant with burgeoning fruits, which would ultimately become fat and ripe and orange, until they plopped onto the deck, too heavy to hang on any longer.

I can never see this passionflower without marvelling at its lust for life, whilst simultaneously feeling a sad sort of irony that this of all plants should be thriving in my garden. Unlike the plant, I don't feel I've been planted in just the right spot, and passion is sorely lacking in my life. Paul deserves passion, I think, as I glance round at him, still puffing on his cigarette. I'm just not sure I can give it to him.

Thankfully, to Paul, the passionflower is just that: a flower. Paul's world is black and white. Or in this case, green and cream. But I exist in the grey bit in between – the bit Paul doesn't believe exists. I see shades of green, and almost black, in the leaves, and hues of blue in the creamy flowers.

Paul looks at his watch. 'Time to get back to the windbags.'

'No rest for the wicked, eh?' I say. But he's not wicked, is he? I am.

We walk back to the house in silence. As Paul heads back upstairs to his office, I call after him: 'I'll bring you up a cuppa before I pick up Tom.' The dutiful wife thing. The big red crayon smile.

CHAPTER 8

What's for Dinner?

I'm now cursing myself for turning down Paul's suggestion of takeout for dinner. I'm standing at the kitchen sink looking down the long expanse of green lawn, idly watching a magpie dunking something big and white into the bird bath. It's probably a hard lump of stale bread brought from a neighbour's garden to be soaked and softened and made edible, although sometimes I find bits of white cardboard mistaken for bread, and subsequently abandoned in disgust.

'Good morning, Mr. Magpie. How are your wife and children?' It's not morning and I don't know if it's a 'he', but I've said those words to every lone magpie I've seen for as long as I can remember. Just in case one really is for sorrow. A funny little habit learned in childhood I suppose.

I'm wondering what to do for dinner and feeling less than inspired. As I continue to watch the magpie pecking in a most satisfied manner at what has obviously turned out to be bread this time, I remember that one of Paul's favourite puddings is of the bread and butter variety. I hardly ever make a proper old-fashioned pudding, so making it will also serve as a penance for my less than saintly thoughts about my marriage. I can't actually remember how to make it, so I pull my phone from my back jeans pocket and do a quick search for a recipe, wondering as I type what we ever did before mobile phones and the internet. Typically, I don't have all the necessary ingredients.

A trip to the supermarket is the last thing I feel like, but it can't be helped.

'Tea!' I say to Paul as I plonk one in a very long line of mugs of tea on his desk. 'Got to pop to Tesco's – doing bread and butter pudding tonight and got no cinnamon. Or sultanas. Or white bread, actually. I'll be back after school.'

'Ooh what's the occasion? You never do puddings.' Damn. Why did he have to say that?

'Oh no reason really. Ask Mr. Magpie!' I say with an enigmatic wave of my hand as I hurry out the door.

'Nutter!' comes the call from behind.

'You don't know the half of it,' I mutter as I jog down the stairs, trying not to see the dust that has gathered at the edges of the striped treads.

Grabbing my handbag and some reusable shopping bags I pick up my car keys from the hall table, resisting the urge to draw something rude in the dust – oops missed more than a bit during my staged housework earlier – I leave the house with my usual sigh of relief.

Ten minutes later and I'm at the trolleys in the supermarket carpark, ferreting fruitlessly through my purse, bag and pockets for a one-pound coin. I know, I know, I should have one of those token thingies on my key ring – I just have the clip left from the last one which got stuck in a trolley. With a sigh, I resign myself to lugging a basket round the shop.

It doesn't take long to pick up the ingredients for the pudding, but I still don't know what we're going to have for main. I decide it's OK to cheat as I'm making pudding, and I head to the 'Finest' aisle and grab two portions of bourbon-pulled pork and mash along with some bung-in-the-microwave veggies. Tom has just developed a taste for pepperoni pizza so it's a cheese-stuffed crust pizza for him. There's ice cream in the freezer for his pudding as he will turn his nose up at bread and butter pudding: it has dead flies in, aka sultanas.

Checking my watch, I still have time to spare, so I pop back to the toy section. Tom is collecting a particular series of Power Ranger figures and I can't resist checking to see if they have any he doesn't. I'm in luck and I add the toy to my basket before heading to the self-service check-out. I'm not going to analyse why I'm spoiling my son. I don't need to. I already know the answer.

Fifteen or so minutes later and I'm waiting at the school gates with Clare. It's her turn to have a bit of a moan. School runs are like mini therapy sessions for us both.

'Honestly, why do I bother? I think Greg thinks I just sit on my bum all day and do nothing! Neither of them shows me any appreciation for what I do for them both. They just take it for granted that the house will be clean and tidy, clothes washed, ironed and put away, meals on the table. Just once I would like a thank you or some recognition for what I do. Is that really too much to ask?' Clare is feeling more than a little unappreciated.

'No, of course it's not. You work very hard to look after Greg and Chloe – you do loads more than me every day. Maybe you should stop doing as much – let them see what happens then.'

'I don't know, Lucy, I don't know if I can – it's my job after all, isn't it?'

'Well, yes, I s'pose so, but wouldn't you expect some recognition or thanks for a job well done if you went out to work?'

'I guess so. I don't think either of them realises the sacrifices I've made – giving up my career to stay at home has been really hard, harder than I ever imagined. Sometimes I wish I hadn't left work to have Chloe. It's always me who has to compromise.'

'I hear you! I've often wondered if giving up work was the right decision. It felt like it at the time, but now… Can you talk to Greg about how you're feeling?'

Clare sighs. 'I don't know. It'll probably just cause a massive row. As it is I'm always trying to keep the peace between Greg and Chloe.'

'Hmmm… they are both quite hot-headed aren't they? Can't be easy.'

'I'll probably just blow like a ruddy volcano one of these days. I can feel the pressure building!'

'Maybe that wouldn't be a bad thing? Give them both a bit of a shock.'

'Yeah, but I'd feel lousy and guilty afterwards.'

'Feeling guilty seems to come with being a wife and mum, I'm afraid. It does in my case anyway.' I've spotted the kids coming towards us, so we need to wrap up our chat. 'You know you can rant at me anytime, anyway. It might help a bit – being able to vent.'

'Oh it does, Lucy, you'll never know how much.' Clare gives me a big smile before turning and waving at Chloe. Thankfully, Chloe is smiling too so at least Clare is going home with a happy six-year-old rather than a stroppy teenager.

Tom runs over to me and thrusts his book bag in my hands. 'Hi, Mum, can we go to the shop for sweets?'

'Yes, of course. As soon as you say the magic word.' I may feel like spoiling him, but he still needs to remember his manners.

33

'Pleeeeaaassseeee!'

How can I refuse this beautiful boy? 'I've got a surprise for you in the car too.'

We're soon home and Tom is excitedly taking his new green Ranger out of its packaging. Happy son. Project *Happy Husband* is underway in the kitchen, and a bread and butter pudding is all ready to go in the oven.

Paul's well on the way to being happy about ninety minutes later, having enjoyed the finest Tesco's have to offer. I've just cleared the plates and am back in the kitchen to get pudding.

'Et voila! Upside down pudding,' I announce as I walk back into the dining room.

Paul looks confused. 'I thought you were doing bread and butter?'

'I was. I am. I dropped it getting it out of the oven. Sorry! I rescued most of it.'

Paul laughs. 'It doesn't matter. I'm sure it'll still taste lovely.'

After dinner, I send Paul and Tom off to the playroom: 'I'll clear up – you two go and play. Tom, show Dad what you got today.' I need a few minutes to myself to calm the sea of thoughts crashing round my head. I have to stop trying so hard – I feel like I'm going a bit mad – and it's only a matter of time before Paul notices. I use the simple task of loading the dishwasher to ground myself once more.

For the next ten days, life plods on, same old same old, but I know I'm simply marking time until Paul goes away. Then, for four days and nights, the red crayon smile is being erased. I can't wait.

CHAPTER 9

Marble run

That's it. I've finally lost my grip on reality. I was only hanging on by my fingernails before. My marbles have gone the same way as the plot. I need to confide in someone and there's only one someone who fits the bill: Clare. She won't believe what I've gone and done. I certainly don't. Paul's been gone a day, after hugs and we'll miss yous from me and Tom. Only one of us was sincere.

Are you free for coffee sometime soon? Like today? No pressure. I press send and the text message disappears off into the ether, probably bumping into the plot and a marble or two as it goes. Putting the phone down on the desk next to me, I hope Clare is her usual efficient self and replies at once.

She does. *You're in luck – free this afternoon before pick up.*

Yay! You're a star! Half one at the garden centre?

Perfect. You're buying! See you later.

I look at my phone for the time. It's already gone eleven, so I don't have too long to wait before I can unburden myself. Thinking about what I have to tell Clare is making me nervous and a sharp pain pierces my temple. Stress. *Does it serve me right?* I wonder, as I rub the side of my head where the arrow of pain struck. I'm worried my friend will think badly of me; will judge me. Another arrow. But I know I need to talk to someone and there really is no one else I can trust with this. I have to believe she will understand. Sympathise even.

There are, as usual, a million and one things that need doing around the house and garden, but I find myself flitting between rooms, between jobs, and not really accomplishing anything. I know I should have some lunch before heading out, but for once food is the last thing on my mind. I think anything I tried to swallow would get stuck in my throat, like a lump of held back emotion. I decide to leave early – I can wander around the garden centre before Clare arrives. She's always early anyway. Feeling a little better to be doing something proactive, I run a brush through my hair, grab a pink cardigan that vaguely goes with my t-shirt – it's still too mild to need a jacket – and head out. It's a ten-minute drive through the nearby countryside and I can't help but smile as I drive with the windows down, sunglasses on and Heart 80s playing on the radio. It still feels like summer and the songs of my teens never fail to lift my spirits. I'm singing along to Haircut 100 and it's starting to feel like a fantastic day.

Part of me wishes I could just keep driving as the sign for the garden centre looms into view. It's easy to pretend everything's OK that way. With a sigh, I flick the indicator and turn into the driveway, trying to dodge the ever-present potholes. It didn't matter how often they resurfaced the drive, the potholes soon came back. Idly, I thought the driveway might be a fitting metaphor for my marriage. The potholes are back with a vengeance despite my best efforts to patch them over.

Once I've parked the car (badly), I choose the entrance that heads directly to the outdoor plants and meander through the flowers and shrubs without really seeing them. I'm aware of them, of course, but unable to focus. My mind is very much elsewhere. But it's passing the time. I mooch through the other departments, idly stopping to look at bird feeders and some rather splendid wellies with spaniels on. How Paul would laugh at me if I went home with them, I think. Paul. My husband's unexpected and unwelcome appearance in my thoughts sends my hand to my temple once again. 'For God's sake, Lucy, sort yourself out,' I find myself muttering, still rubbing the patch of skin by my eye. I'm glad there are no other customers nearby to see me acting like a bit of a nutter.

Deciding that the best thing to do is wait for Clare in the café, I head over to the double doors and push my way in, relieved to see it's pretty quiet and that our favourite sofas are unoccupied. I quickly text Clare to tell her where I am before ordering a cup of Earl Grey. I should probably have chamomile for my frayed nerves I suppose, but I can't stand the stuff. I'd have to be down to my last nerve to resort to tea that tastes like slightly perfumed grass. Currently I still have enough nerves left for them to jangle.

It's not long before the doors open and Clare appears. She spots me and gives me a big grin and a wave. I respond with a grimace and the pretence of tearing my hair out. She's laughing as she sits down opposite me: 'Right then, missus, what have you been up to?'

'Let me get you a drink and then I will reveal all. Tea?'

'Please. Don't forget the extra sugars!'

'As if. It never ceases to amaze me that you are so slim when you take about four sugars in your tea. Most unfair by the way.'

'Yeah, but I live on sodding lettuce the rest of the time to make up for it,' Clare replied whilst doing a pretty good rabbit impression.

Laughing, I head over to the counter to order her cuppa, and a second Earl Grey for me. For once I don't have any trouble resisting the array of dome-covered cakes on display. As I wait for the drinks, I turn to Clare, echoing her rabbit face: 'Carrot cake, Bugs?' The question's actually redundant as Clare never has cake. She has an iron will where calories are concerned – apart from the ones that go in her tea. It's one of the many things I admire in her.

The second I'm re-seated, Clare pipes up: 'Spill.'

'OK, but promise you won't think badly of me?'

'I don't think there's anything you could say that would make me think badly of you. Unless you were shagging Greg. You know you can tell me anything. I'd never judge you.'

'I hope you still feel like that after I've told you,' I say, swallowing a mouthful of tea. 'Right, here goes… I've joined a dating site.'

'O… K… er, wasn't expecting that. Happy to roll with it for a minute though… don't you have to be single to do internet dating? How's that gonna work… you know, having a husband already?'

Clare seems surprisingly unfazed by my revelation, much to my relief. And I wasn't struck down by lightning or anything. So far so good.

'That's the thing though, it's not a singles dating site – it's for married people looking to have an affair. It's actually called Secret Affair. I saw it on *This Morning*.'

'Bugger me with a broomstick sideways!' was Clare's response. 'I had no idea that sort of thing even existed. Cool!'

'Cool? I thought you'd be shocked.'

'Very little shocks me really, Lucy. I wasn't always happily married either you know. I've had my share of extramaritals.'

'Ooh, you kept that quiet. Cool!'

'Ha ha! Yep, I'm not the straight-laced prude people take me for. Thankfully, I'm happy now, but I totally understand your position. Been there, done that, didn't keep the t-shirt – bit of a giveaway.'

'God, what a relief. Thanks, Clare, for understanding and not thinking I'm a right slut!'

'I didn't say you're not a slut,' Clare said with a wink. 'Tell me more about this site then.'

'Well, I suppose it's pretty much the same as any other dating site, except you don't use your own photo for obvious reasons. You have to create a profile – you know, a bit about you and what you're looking for – and then you can search all the men's profiles to try and find a match.'

'But how do you know what the men look like?'

'You do put real photos up, but they're password protected, so you can control who sees your pics. And you can search by location to find local matches. Some of it's a bit naff – you can send virtual gifts like flowers and chocolates and stuff like that. And there are thousands of people on there. It's a real eye opener.'

'Sounds quite exciting – I might join it myself next time I find the loo seat up at home.'

I know Clare's only joking, but her words give me some reassurance that I'm not an evil cow after all.

'It is exciting. I do get a thrill every time I log on and there's a message waiting. The excitement definitely outweighs the guilt – not sure what that says about me?'

'It says you're human, Lucy, that's all. Just a woman looking for something to make her feel alive again.'

'That's it, Clare! I desperately want to feel really alive, feel like the old me again.'

'So, how far have you got? Have you arranged to meet anyone yet?'

'No, not yet. I'm still window shopping for now, while I get my head around the whole thing. I'm not doing this lightly. It is fun though, and it makes me feel good.'

'Well, I expect a blow by blow account of everything that happens from here on in.'

'Maybe not everything, eh? I don't kiss and tell.'

'Mm... actually you're right, you can spare me the gory details. A brief summary will suffice.'

'Or a summary of briefs, as it were,' I say with a giggle.

'All I ask, Lucy, is that you don't take any risks, and that you tell me where and when if you do arrange a meeting. I'm going to worry anyway, but at least someone will know where you are.'

I hadn't thought about how my exploits would affect Clare and feel a stab of remorse at my selfishness. 'Oh God, please don't worry about me – I promise to be careful. Chances are I'll chicken out anyway.'

'Well, whatever happens, you know I'm here for you,' Clare said, reaching across the table and giving my hand a squeeze. 'I know how unhappy you are, Lucy, and life really is too bloody short. Get out there and have some fun. If you're careful no one needs to get hurt.'

'Thank you. It means so much to have your support and understanding.'

'No need to thank me – I can't wait to hear what happens next.' Clare's looking at her watch as she finishes her sentence. 'Time to collect the little darlings.'

'God, that came round quickly.'

'Time flies when you're talking fun. I have to say I'm even a little bit jealous of what lies ahead for you. I'll be living vicariously through you from now on. Brighten my dull little existence.'

'Well, watch this space,' I say as we make our way out of the café and back to the cars. We exchange a quick hug and leave in convoy for the school.

CHAPTER 10

The cat's away

I follow Clare out of the car park and think about the conversation we've just had. I'm so relieved that Clare understands.
She's surprised me with the revelation about her first, unsuc-
cessful marriage and it's made me feel better about my own
situation. It feels good to have an ally. After I'd made my disclo-
sure about the dating site, Clare had wanted to know all the
details and I'd been happy to oblige.

'So, what did you put in your profile?'

'It's all a bit naff to be honest, but I can change it, add to
it as I go along. I said something like "married mum of one
looking for more than the school run and walking the dog" and
"wanting to get my spark back and to want someone again".
Then I had to describe myself a bit – you have to pick between
things like "average", "athletic", "curvy" for your build. Didn't
know what to put so I went for curvy. You have to fill out stuff
like hair and eye colour, height, birthday – you know, general
details about yourself. And then what you're looking for in
a partner.'

'… in crime!' Clare interjected.

'Don't! I feel like a criminal already!'

'Only teasing. Go on. What did you say you're looking for?'

'Said I'm looking for tall, dark and handsome but will

probably fall for someone short, bald and interesting-looking! Thought it might be a good ice-breaker. Good sense of humour, kind, intelligent, not arrogant. I thought about putting honest to be ironic. Oh, and non-smoker of course.'

'Ooh I'd date him! Do you have to pay to join?' Clare, practical as ever.

'No, the men have to pay but not the women. I think it's to make sure there are enough women on there and to make it easier for women to keep it all hidden from their husbands – you know with joint bank accounts and not having your own income, stuff like that. I think you can pay if you want to upgrade your account, but I haven't really looked into that yet.'

'Sounds like a bloody good business idea if you ask me, they must make a fortune.'

'I guess so. I don't know how much it costs the men.'

'Well. I really hope you find what you're looking for on there. I'm excited for you.'

'Thank you. It's early days and I really don't know what's going to happen, but…' I drifted off, not knowing quite how to finish the sentence. Saying out loud that I'm excited at the prospect of potentially having an affair scared me.

CHAPTER 11

Is it bedtime yet?

It's Paul's second night in France and I'm eager to make the most of his absence by spending time on Secret Affair. The only thing stopping me is, of course, Tom who is telling me in surprising detail about his day. Normally my questions about what he's done during the day result in only one answer: 'Nothing.' Or sometimes, 'Can't remember.' Clare informs me that girls are different and she always gets a detailed account of every last little thing that has happened in her daughter's day. She says she's perfected the art of appearing to listen when in reality she's zoned out and is wondering what to cook for dinner.

Realising I'm doing the same, albeit not with thoughts of dinner, I force my attention back to Tom's animated little face. My heart does a little leap as a wave of pure love washes over me. God I love this boy. I feel a bit guilty for where my mind has been. Am I mad to even consider doing something that might jeopardise his future, his happiness?

'So then Jake threw the chair right across the room. It only just missed me by this much,' he says while illustrating his point by holding his thumb and forefinger tips up in front of his eye and squinting at the barely visible gap between them. I suppress a laugh, not wanting to detract from the seriousness of my little story teller. 'Mrs Price said he had to go to the head teacher's room which only happens to really naughty boys. And he went on the sad board again. I've never had a sad mark, Mummy.'

'That's because you are the best boy in the whole wide world and you make me proud every single day.' I put my arms around my son and hug him until he wriggles to be free. 'I love you, Tom Tom. Don't you ever forget it.'

'I love you too. What's for dinner?'

'Whatever you want,' I say laughing. Oh to have the simple problems of a six-year-old. 'And after dinner, we can play whatever you want.' My feelings of guilt are definitely benefitting Tom.

Unsurprisingly, Tom's choice for dinner is turkey dinosaurs. Another gourmet delight served up by yours truly. As he refuses to eat most cooked vegetables, I do at least get him to eat a raw carrot while his dinner's cooking. I bung an extra T-rex and a few more chips in for me, knowing that otherwise I probably won't end up eating tonight. We eat in front of the TV. I will not be winning any mother-of-the-year awards, but Tom is happy and that's really all that matters right now.

I try to remain patient with Tom for the remainder of the evening as we play Power Rangers Vs Transformers. I get told off innumerable times for getting things wrong and am relieved when bath time comes around and bedtime's that much closer.

Finally, Tom's tucked up in bed with a story tape to listen to and I'm free. I stand in the doorway for a few more seconds – just watching him, his blonde hair tousled by the hairdryer, cuddly black and white dog hugged tight to his chest. He's only recently stopped sucking his thumb in bed, but still his right thumb hovers near his mouth. My beautiful boy. Still my baby. 'Sweet dreams,' I whisper as I head back downstairs. The evening stretches ahead of me, full of potential and promise. I have that feeling of butterflies, of anticipation, that anything is possible.

I settle into my favourite seat on the sofa and pull the recliner handle, wriggling back onto the cushion. My laptop's on the seat next to me and I open it eagerly and switch it on, waiting impatiently for it to start up and load all the icons. As soon as the internet explorer pings on to the screen I click on 'open an incognito window' – I'm already learning the art of deception thanks to Phillip Schofield - and am soon back in the world of illicit encounters. My very own garden of Eden, bursting at the seams with forbidden fruit. My heart lifts when I see that I have seven new messages. Along with a virtual red rose and a yacht. I'm still not sure of the etiquette yet, but feel obliged to at least send a thank you message to the senders of these gifts.

Fingers trembling slightly, I click on the first unread message. It's from someone calling himself London Calling which already suggests we may not be geographically suited. I suppose I should tell you my username. I had toyed with Lucy Sure and Lucy Lawless but had rejected them on the grounds that they suggested I might be either easy or reckless. I consider myself to be neither of these things. Yet. So, I'd settled on Toe Dipper hoping to imply that I was just dipping my toe in to test the waters. God forbid any more pervy interpretations.

It's quite a short message: *Hi Dipper! Great profile. Would love to chat more. Hope to hear back from you. Jx*

Short and to the point, I think. I wonder what the J stands for. James perhaps. Or Jonathan. I like both those names. I click on his username to switch to his profile page. It says he's 55, Aquarius and works in financial services in London. He's also short. Too short and too old and definitely a non-starter as far as I'm concerned. Ever polite, though, I quickly compose a 'thanks, but no thanks' reply and hope that's the end of it.

Loading the second message, from GeorgeClooney1 – this guy's either supremely confident or delusional – I'm not prepared for the full-on nature of his words. This is not a man who wastes time on small talk. Or introductions for that matter. My face flushes as I read what he apparently wants to do to me. He hasn't even seen what I look like so I'm more than a little surprised. Talk about the direct approach. Maybe some women like it, but it's a big turn off for me. I decide not to reply to Mr. Clooney and hope that my silence speaks volumes.

With a sigh, trying not to be despondent, I click on the third message which is from KentishMan. I'm relieved to read the following: *Good evening. I hope my message finds you well. I came across your profile and it very much resonated with me – you sound delightful. I would love to have the opportunity to find out more about you, and perhaps I could be the one to give you your sparkle back? If you like what you read in my profile, I would love to hear from you. Respectfully yours, Rob x.* What a gent, I think as I click through to his profile, trying not to get my hopes up. His location says Surrey which is far from ideal and rather confusing given his username, but everything else sounds pretty much perfect – a tall, forty-six-year-old solicitor, with brown hair and eyes. Too good to be true? I wonder. I'm interested enough to find out more.

I decide to reply to KentishMan straight away - before nerves or guilt get in the way. *Hi Rob, and thank you for your lovely message. I very much enjoyed your profile. I do wonder though if geography is our enemy...? L.* Too formal? I wonder. Or too negative? I don't want to appear too eager and I'm certainly not brave enough to put my name or a kiss. Before I can change my mind, I press send. There's nothing else I can do now but wait to see if he replies.

Realising I haven't had a drink all evening, I head to the kitchen, returning with a large glass of cranberry juice. I only drink it at home these days because I'm tired of people looking at me sympathetically and mouthing 'UTI?' whenever I order it. I used to say, 'No, I just really like it,' and grit my teeth as they smiled and nodded, tapping their noses conspiratorially. Taking a couple of big glugs of the icy drink, I settle back down to read the remaining messages. I've only been gone a couple of minutes, but I have three new messages. As I scan my inbox, I see that one is from KentishMan. A tiny tingle goes down my spine – I really didn't expect to hear back from him at all, let alone so soon.

Hi L, so glad you took the time to reply to my message – thank you. Please don't let distance be a barrier as I'm happy to travel and my time is my own. Perhaps we can chat and get to know one another a bit better? Rob xx. Two kisses this time. And he still hasn't seen my photos. This forbidden contact with a stranger definitely excites me, and I ignore any creeping feelings of guilt. We're only chatting after all. No harm in that.

Abandoning the other messages, I reply to Rob: *I'd like that. Actually, I do have a question – your location and username do rather contradict themselves. Should I hear warning bells?! Lx.* One kiss. No name. No harm.

It's barely a minute before a reply pings back: *Ha ha! Well spotted, but no need to worry – I'm not being deceitful. I was born and raised in Kent but now live in Surrey. I split my time between Surrey and London for work. I will always consider myself a Kentish Man though. Are you a Kentish Lass? Rob xx.*

His explanation sounds believable. And he's not pushing me for my name or my password. I'm really starting to enjoy chatting with Rob and decide to give him the benefit of any doubts I have. *That makes sense – thanks for clearing that up! I am indeed a Kentish Lass. Born and bred. And my name's Lucy X.* A name. One big kiss. No harm.

Hi Lucy, it's really great to meet you. So, how are you finding the site? Have you been on here long? You definitely sound more normal than some of the women I've chatted to on here! Rob xx.

I only joined a couple of days ago – you're the first person I've really chatted to. I'm still finding my way around to be honest. Not sure what to expect. How about you? Lucy x. Name. A kiss. No harm.

I've been on here about a month. Had a couple of meetings over coffee, but they weren't for me. It's a bit of a minefield for us men let me tell you. I had one woman tell me she'd be needing an allowance! Rob xx.

I feel a tiny pang of jealousy that he's met other women. I know it's ridiculous, but I feel it all the same. *Good lord! Really?! That's outrageous. Well, I can assure you I'm not one of those women. It is a bizarre place though, isn't it? I still can't quite believe I'm on here. Lucy xx.* Two kisses. Am I upping the ante? No, it's still just harmless chat.

Yes, it is, but judging by the number of members, it's clearly meeting a popular need. And it's a strangely honest way of going about, in an odd sort of way. We're all in the same boat. Do you know what I mean? Rob xx.

I'm starting to. It's a sort of honesty amongst thieves, isn't it?

There's no need or indeed any point in lying. We all know why we're here. It's certainly been an education reading men's profiles. So many of them say the same thing – that they love their wives and would never leave them, but their physical needs aren't being met. They talk about a complete lack of affection – even down to a hug or a kiss. It's all terribly sad. Lucy xx. It's strange writing these words as I am one of those wives. I too am guilty of neglecting my husband's physical desires.

It's certainly true in my case, Lucy. My wife is, and always has been, my best friend, but we're more like brother and sister now. Every other aspect of our life together is good. I fought this for a long time, but I can't go without some form of physical affection from a woman for the rest of my life. Does that make me a bad person? I hope not. Rob xx.

We're really starting to open up to each other and forming a connection. It's crazy. And we still haven't even seen each other's photos. I wonder if I'm brave enough to suggest we exchange passwords? I decide I am and I ask Rob if he's happy to take this next step.

Happy to do so, Lucy. Mine is "seeme". Sadly though I have to log out now as my wife is due back from her book club any minute. I've really enjoyed chatting with you and I hope we can carry on getting to know each other very soon. Take care. Rob xxx. Three kisses…

Thank you. Mine's "pinkfizz". Be gentle, lie if you have to! I've really enjoyed chatting with you too. Bye for now. Lucy xx. Still holding back a third kiss. But revealing my face. Escalating.

I can't wait to see what Rob looks like and I eagerly enter the password he's given me on his profile page. My heart sinks. This is not the face I have imagined and he looks a lot older than forty-six…

50

CHAPTER 12

Romantic Fool

After the disappointment of seeing what Rob looks like I decide to take a break from the site to gather my thoughts; really think about what on earth I'm doing. After letting Alfie out in the garden for a wee, I refill my glass and take myself off for a soak in the bath.

Soon I'm sinking into vanilla-scented bubbles with a contented sigh. I've even turned off the light and lit a couple of lemongrass-scented candles and placed them on the tiles around the bath. Bliss! Tom was sleeping soundly when I popped my head in and I had turned off his story and tucked the covers around him, kissed my fingers and touched them to his forehead. I leave the bathroom door ajar just in case he stirs. And also so Alfie can let himself in as he often does – he likes to lie on the bathmat and keep me company. Now I can relax and let my mind wander where it will...

I have to admit that I really enjoyed chatting with Rob – I got a buzz from it and there's no point denying it. Am I being horribly shallow to now judge him based on his looks? Am I naïve to imagine that Mr. Tall, Dark and Handsome is waiting for me to click on his profile and he'll come running? I know from experience that attraction is a strange and inexplicable force and can happen when, on paper, you wouldn't expect it. My short, bald husband is a perfect example of that. Paul's appearance in my thoughts doesn't bring with it the expected twinge of guilt, which strikes me as odd. Am I already shamelessly committed to this path of infidelity?

I think back over my conversation with Rob. We've struck up a bizarrely open and honest relationship very quickly. Perhaps it's the shared secrecy of what we're doing that unites us. Or simply the anonymity of being safely hidden behind a computer screen. It is a strange sort of honesty, but it is honesty nonetheless. It's all a bit of a paradox, I conclude with a sigh. As I've never been in a situation like this before, I suppose it's normal to feel rather bemused by the whole thing: it's all rather surreal. And he mentioned his wife so openly – I even know she goes to a book club. But even so, she doesn't seem real to me. Everything feels at a distance, removed from my reality, but the reality is that I could be that woman; the one whose husband is looking for the company of another.

Maybe I haven't thought this through nearly enough. Can I honestly – oh the irony – contemplate being the *other woman*? Am I kidding myself that I could ever go through with meeting another woman's husband and maybe even pursuing a physical relationship with him? The betrayal against this imagined wife is somehow almost worse than the betrayal of my own husband. Sighing, I sink further into the steaming water and close my eyes.

The thoughts continue apace, however, and with no more clarity than before. They are whizzing around my head, colliding and bouncing off one another. It's useless to try and ignore them or think about something else – they will not be quieted and demand my full attention.

Taking a deep breath, I dive back into the melee and try to apply some logic to the matter. Things to consider... Do I really think I can have an affair with all its associated risks of being found out, people I love being hurt? Am I prepared to gamble on my marriage and possibly even the future happiness of my son? Will I be able to live with myself or will the shame and guilt eat away at me? What if I fall in love and I'm the one who's hurt? So many questions. My head is buzzing uselessly.

I suppose what it boils down to is can I live a lie?

Can I live a lie? This is the one. This is the thought that produces a silent tear, running in a rivulet down the contours of my face until I taste it in the corner of my mouth.

I'm already living a lie. This admission brings a lump to my throat and the threat of more tears. I can't give in to these though. I'm worried that once that particular dam bursts there will be no stopping. These would not be silent tears, but sobs which wracked my every fibre and threatened what little equanimity I had in my life. It's true though that my life, or at least my marriage to Paul, is not an honest one and that I am an actor in a reluctant role, playing to an audience; putting my all into my performance, but going to bed drained at the end of every day from the strain of the pretence.

I rub my fingers across my temples and try to calm the storm in my head. I can't afford to give in to the maelstrom that threatens: the damage could be irreparable. I swirl the thoughts like candyfloss onto a stick until one overall idea remains: what is one more lie in a life that IS a lie?

Before the candyfloss thought solidifies, I climb rapidly out of the bath, pulling the plug out as I go. Action is the only safe option right now and I busy myself with preparations for the night, getting myself and the house ready for sleep.

'Bedtime,' I say to Alfie, 'go to the loo,' standing by the open back door. It's dark now and a starry night. I lift my eyes to the night sky, looking for answers I know I will not find, as the dog disappears obediently off to do his business. He trots back in and lifts his eyes to the cupboard that contains the dog treats, waiting for his bedtime biscuit. A creature of habit, and simple ones at that. Lucky thing, I think, none of the complications of us humans.

'Come on then, boy, let's go to bed,' ruffling the fur on his head before turning to close and lock the back door. Paul normally locks up at night and doing this simple act makes me realise again that I'm not missing him.

By the time I reach my bedroom after checking that the front door is locked, Alfie is already sprawled across the middle of the bed. I can't help but laugh as he wouldn't dare do this if Paul was here. Like me, he's taking full advantage of Paul's absence. 'Cheeky sod!' I laugh, and he wags his stump of a tail, knowing full well what I mean.

'Bib bib, budge over.' There's not room for me to get into my side of the bed. Alfie grumbles but shifts his body over to Paul's side nonetheless. He's quickly resettled and before long will be sleeping soundly. I fear sleep will not come so easily to me and reach for the book I'm currently reading. Maybe a few pages spent with detective Harry Bosch on the streets of LA will help. It takes a few chapters, but reading does prove soporific and I welcome the blessed relief of sleep.

CHAPTER 13

The cold light of day

'Time to get up, sleepy boy.' I ruffle Tom's hair as I speak the words quietly in his ear. He's not one of those children who's up with the lark, and I hate having to wake him. This is one of the times when I do miss Paul, as he has no problem with rousing Tom from even the deepest sleep. He says I'm too soft. Maybe I am. Maybe it's a mum thing? Dads don't seem to be quite so emotional in their attachments to their children. The other mums often say their husbands are much less tender in their dealings with the children, and that it's the cause of many a falling-out.

Tom stirs as I continue to stroke his head. 'Good morning, my lovely boy. Time to get up.' He stretches and rubs his eyes.

'Mummy, is today family learning day?' Quickly awake.

'I'm afraid not – that's tomorrow.' He's been asking me this question every morning for the last few days, excited at the prospect of having me come into his class with the other parents for the afternoon.

'Oh. OK. I wish it was today.' He's disappointed, as he has been the past few mornings.

'Tomorrow will be here before you know it though. And we'll have lots of fun making you a kite.' Secretly though, I dread the family learning sessions which have become a regular feature at Tom's primary school, and they are the cause of much grumbling amongst us mums. I displayed a complete lack of creative ability where modelling a sea creature using willow sticks and tissue paper was concerned at the last such session, and am in no hurry to experience a similarly humiliating event. I suppose it will, however, be a distraction from the current train of my thoughts.

'Uniform's by your feet,' I tell Tom. 'Get dressed and I'll go and start breakfast. Would you like banana pancakes?' Tom's face lights up at the offer of his favourite breakfast.

'Yes! Please, Mummy. They're my favourite!'

'I know,' I reply with a smile. I never offer to make pancakes on a school day normally, but the lingering feelings of guilt are informing my actions. 'How many can you eat?'

'A hundred!' comes the reply.

'A hundred? You'll be the size of a house! How about three to start with and then we'll see what your tummy says?'

I head back downstairs to the kitchen, resisting the urge to help my young son get dressed. It's all too easy to do everything for him, but I know he must be able to do such things independently.

Busying myself with the morning routine is like sticking my finger in the leaky dike which holds back the rushing torrent of thoughts that have been so troubling of late. I know it's a temporary fix, but it's better than the alternative. I must keep busy, keep that hole plugged.

It's easy to make a six-year-old boy happy. Three banana pancakes later and it's a very contented Tom who goes happily into school at eight forty-five. The dog will be similarly content after his morning walk. I, on the other hand, am heading into

56

an autumn of discontent, with no idea of how to make things better. With the day stretching empty ahead of me, I recognise that I'm in the danger zone once more. Too much time on my hands. And my mind. But the dog needs walking, whether I feel like it or not, so I head for the hills.

I usually relish the walk: it's precious time to myself when Paul's at home. But with Paul away, it's time to think I could do without. And so I walk. And I think. And I wonder. I wonder if Paul is content. He always seems happy enough on the whole, but is he? Why do I assume that he is any more content than I, when his needs aren't being met? I know it's within my power to make him happy. The simple act of sex on a regular basis would be enough to make Paul happy. It might once have been a simple act between us, but now it felt as though a little piece of me died every time I relented and had dutiful sex.

I don't really know when, or why, my feelings towards Paul changed, but change they did. Thinking back, I suppose becoming a mother had something to do with it. The pregnancy, a traumatic emergency caesarean and the trials of being a new mum might all have contributed. I have asked myself if I would've stayed with Paul had I not fallen pregnant and I can't say with any confidence that I would. But I convinced myself I could make it work. The shocked joy I'd felt on discovering I was expecting the baby I'd been told by doctors I could never have, had no doubt clouded my judgment. That combined with whatever was going on with my hormones, I probably wasn't thinking straight at all.

My train of thought has carried me to the top of the hill and I realise I'm quite out of breath. Sitting down on a dryish patch of grass and hugging my knees, I look around for the dog, calling out so he knows where I am. He finishes what he's sniffing and lollops over to sit by me. We sit like that in companionable silence for a while, my hand resting on his back, until he gets bored and trots off in search of more good sniffs. I'm still not thinking straight seven years later. And I'm certainly not talking straight. Not to my husband at least.

Getting to my feet before I seize up, I brush the back of my jeans and carry on walking, taking deep, grateful breaths of the mild September air. The chill of autumn still hasn't arrived and I can't help but smile as I lift my face to the sun. I take in the vista spread before me, the rolling green hills merging into the darker woods below, the sky cloudless and bright, and suddenly I feel an intense burst of gratitude. 'I'm lucky.' I say the words aloud, almost subconsciously. They rather take me surprise and I stop to analyse them. Am I lucky? I ask myself. Looking around me again, I have to conclude that I am. I'm free to enjoy this beautiful landscape whenever I want to. I'm not cooped up in some overheated office or stuck in a job I hate. I have a lovely home, a husband who loves me and a happy, healthy son who thinks I'm wonderful. I have so much to be thankful for. I must count my blessings. I will count them. And I will do better. I will be the wife my husband deserves and I will live up to my son's belief.

And so, as I make my way back from the walk, I have talked myself out of the doldrums once more. I am determined that I can do better. I will do better. And I won't go back on that dating site. What was I thinking? How stupid am I? It's still working when I get home and I ignore the little voice niggling away in the back of my mind: 'Who are you kidding?' it's saying.

CHAPTER 14

That night

It's my third night without Paul and once Tom's in bed I settle myself on the sofa and flick through the channels in search of a programme to lose myself in. Nothing takes my fancy though, so I put a radio channel on instead – my music of choice at the moment is Eighties, and I am immediately transported back to my teens as the sound of Eurythmics' 'Sweet Dreams' fills the room. It's a song that takes me back to a school geography field trip to Holland, when the song was being played everywhere, and I'm back in a Wimpy in Amsterdam with some of my classmates. It seems a lifetime ago. Simpler times, happier times, I sigh.

But were they really? Were those teenage years really simpler? Happier? If I'm being really honest, they probably weren't. They were filled with angst and heartbreak. Everything was out of proportion and felt so acutely. If the boy you had a crush on didn't know you even existed, it felt like the end of the world and resulted in many a pitiful poem or picture. Somewhere in the attic I still have shoeboxes filled with notebooks and diaries, cards and silly mementoes of boys gone by.

I thought back then that with adulthood would come answers; that everything would be sorted. I'd be sorted. How wrong I had been. I feel just as angst-ridden as I ever did at fourteen, only now there's not just me and my feelings to consider; I have a husband and son whose happiness feels like my responsibility. I pretend to be happy so that they can be happy. It's a depressing thought and I try to push it to the back of my mind. I mentally write it on a piece of paper, seal that into an envelope, put the envelope in a box with the lid tightly closed and shove the box in the back of the wardrobe. Lately, though, the lid of my Pandora's box keeps popping open and the thought is back at the front of my mind. I don't want to address the thought because there is never a satisfactory outcome: in order for me to be happy, I have to sacrifice the happiness of others, don't I? It can't be done.

I'm definitely feeling rather forlorn this evening; the nostalgic music probably isn't helping. Mr. Mister 'Broken Wings' comes on and I can feel tears pricking at the corners of my eyes.

'Damn it!' The expletive bursts out of my mouth uncontrollably and even the dog lifts his head in surprise. He had been sleeping peacefully at my feet, but now heaves himself up and onto the sofa next to me, seeming to recognise that I need comfort.

'Sorry, boy, good boy,' as I stroke his back. 'I think tonight calls for wine. Won't be a minute.' With that I head for the fridge where I know a bottle of pink has been languishing for months. I rarely drink, but right now I need something to take the edge off. Pouring myself a generous glass of White Zinfandel – even my choice of pink wine wears a disguise - I head back to the lounge, collecting my laptop from the side as I go. Wine and social media are clearly the way to go tonight, and soon I'm logged into Facebook to see what exciting things are happening in other people's lives. The perfect distraction.

Well, I now know what several people had for dinner, have liked at least half a dozen hilarious pet videos, scrolled quickly past an animal cruelty post (that really would tip me over the edge tonight), and watched some random woman as she demonstrated how to properly apply make-up. Never gonna happen, I thought as she got out yet another sort of brush and started contouring her face with yet another shade of concealer. My foundation, when I bother to use it, will continue to be applied in the same way as my moisturiser – just spread around my face with my fingers. The Facebook woman would be horrified. It's just another way in which I clearly fail at life and as a woman, I conclude.

After taking a rather large glug of wine, I log into my email account – the secret one I use for Secret Affair. I'm ignoring the little voice in my head which is reminding me I said I wouldn't. I'm not, I tell it. I'm not going on the site, just checking my emails. As I type my password and press Enter, I realise I'm holding my breath in excited anticipation. If I have received any more messages, I will have notifications in my in-box. As the screen loads I can see a dozen or more unread messages and a shivery thrill runs down my spine. Each email just says who the message is from – it doesn't display the content. If I want to find out more, I will have to log onto the site itself.

So I do. Well, it's not doing anyone any harm, is it? I tell myself, taking another swig of my drink. It's only chatting. I know, I know, I'm delusional as ever. Never mind, eh? I reassure myself as the site loads and my excitement builds. As I wait for the screen to fill with content, I suddenly remember I haven't used an incognito window and a feeling of panic sinks from my chest to my belly. 'Bugger.' Another expletive leaves my lips. I make a mental note to delete the browsing history, still worried that I don't know how to keep my illicit activity hidden. I must be more careful in future.

My fear of discovery is, however, soon overtaken by my eagerness to read the messages I've received. One name catches my eye straight away: KentishMan. Rob. I click on his message, realising as I do so that he will have seen my photos since I was last here. I feel a twinge of nerves; I'm worried what he will say. I know it's stupid – it shouldn't matter a damn what he thinks of me. But, strangely, it does matter to me and it's with trepidation that I read his words:

Hello again, Lucy, and thanks for your password. No need to lie – you look lovely. A real breath of fresh air on here if I'm honest. I'm around tonight if you're free to chat. I'd love to get to know you some more – that's if my pics haven't scared you off! Rob xx.

My heart's beating a little faster right now. He thinks I look lovely. My ego swells a little. And then I remember. His pics. They had scared me off a bit and now I don't know what to say to him without hurting his feelings. I realise what a potential minefield the site is and how easily I could get myself in a pickle. I can't ignore him though – simple good manners won't let me do that. I think again about the bizarre nature of the site. I hit reply and start to type.

Hi Rob and thank you for your kind words. I hesitate. I have no idea what to say to him. *Of course your pics haven't scared me off, silly!* I feel like I'm digging a hole for myself, encouraging him when I should be putting him off. *I will confess to having a bit of a wobble about being on here though.* Nice! Make it a generalisation about the site rather than a specific about him. *I'm honestly not sure if it's right for me. Lucy x.* Back to one small kiss. I press send and wait. I don't have to wait long as a reply pings back a minute or so later.

Glad my ugly mug didn't send you running for the hills – I'm better in the flesh! I totally understand your reservations about being on here and I respect you all the more for it. An affair isn't for everyone. I hope we can keep chatting though. Rob xx.

I can't help but smile at his *running for the hills* remark, as I had indeed gone running for the hills that very morning. He sounds like such a nice man, so reasonable and understanding.

Thank you for understanding. I'd like to keep chatting to you too, but I can't make any promises of anything more. I think I need more time to see how this sits with me. But please don't stop looking for someone in the meantime. Lucy x.

No worries Lucy. I enjoy chatting with you regardless of what does or doesn't happen down the line. So, tell me more about what you're looking for. Rob xxx. Upping the ante with three kisses.

That's the million-dollar question! I guess I'm just looking for something to make me feel alive again. Something that's just for me – nothing to do with home and hearth. (I can't say husband and son – it makes it too real and I feel guilty.) *I want to want someone again. Does that make sense? Lx.* Not too much encouragement.

It makes perfect sense. I guess I'm coming at it from the other side – wanting to be wanted. My wife hasn't wanted me in a physical sense for a very long time. I can't spend the rest of my life like that – I want to feel close to a woman again, to have that physical contact. I don't want to leave my wife, but I can't live like a monk anymore. Rob xxx.

Rob's words hit home hard. Is this how Paul feels about me and our marriage? I wonder. It makes me feel uncomfortable to make the comparison. Could I blame him if he were to have an affair? After all, wouldn't I have driven him to it? Picking up my wineglass, I realise it's empty and pop to the kitchen to refill it. It's not like me at all, I think as I pour out another large glassful. But then nothing about any of this is like me: I'm chatting to a strange man about potentially cheating on my husband. It's definitely more than a one glass thing.

Setting my glass down on the coffee table, I return to my messages. Just while I've been chatting to Rob, five more messages have arrived as well as a virtual red rose and a diamond ring. I'm slightly tiddly by now and eager to look at the other messages. As much as I'm enjoying chatting to Rob, I'd like to discover who else is on the website.

It's hard, isn't it? Keeping a marriage alive. I don't want to hurt anyone, but if this is it for the rest of my life… Lx. I don't finish the sentence. I don't think I need to. Rob feels the same. I don't wait for Rob's reply. I select the first of my unread messages. It's from someone calling himself MrWrong:

Hi there, Toe Dipper. Great profile. Love to get to know you better. Password's 'bigboy', let me know what you think. Baz x.

If his password and name are anything to go by, I suspect I will not be impressed, but I dutifully click on Baz's profile nonetheless. I skim read his details: works in construction, smokes socially and lives in Essex. He's lost me at *smokes socially*, but I still enter his photo password out of curiosity and come face to tattooed-torso with Baz. That'll be a no then. I wonder if I should reply anyway, let him down gently. I decide not to as I really don't know what to say.

Another message has just come in from Rob, but I decide not to reply immediately and instead select the next unread message from HappyChappy321:

Dave hear. You sound luvley. Ide luv to give you your sparkle back. Hope to here from you. Xx. That'll be a no then. Sorry, Dave, but spelling's important to me. I still feel a bit mean as I delete the message.

Next comes DomSeeksSub. Like everyone else on the planet, I've read *Fifty Shades* and I know exactly what this means and it is not my cup of tea. I don't even bother reading his message.

Rob's message is still waiting for my attention:

Sounds very much as though we're in the same boat, doesn't it? Whatever you decide, I hope we can stay in touch, Lucy. Just talking with you has made me feel better than I have in ages. Rob xxx.

I pause to think about Rob's words. I feel the same; just chatting with him has made me feel good. Maybe this will be enough for me? Enough to make me feel better about the rest of my life. Maybe I don't have to actually have an affair to satisfy whatever's missing from my life.

Same here, I write back hurriedly, eager to get back to my other mystery messages. *It's really given me a lift. Thank you. x.*

The next message piques my interest. It's from LonelyArms which is a bit naff I suppose, but no more so than ToeDipper. The subject of the message reads *Come on in, the water's lovely.*

Hello there. Like you I'm just dipping my toe in to test the water before I take the plunge. Your profile resonated with me – you sound nice. And normal. And I mean that in the best possible way. I'm sure these must seem like shark-infested waters to you, but maybe I can be the one to dispel your fears, take your hand and jump right in beside you. Jx.

I know it's a bit cheesy, but I like the fact that he's tried to be original and played on my profile name. I'm interested enough to check out his profile:

Old-fashioned gent seeks old-fashioned affair with a lady who's not afraid to fall a little bit in love. Sane, solvent and willing to travel for the right woman, I'm not looking to disrupt your life, just make it a little bit better; to restore your sparkle and your smile. I'm tall, dark and I've been told handsome (although that was by my mother) and as I run my own consultancy business, my diary is my own.

It's the first profile I've read on here that mentions the L word and I'm a little taken aback. If I'm honest, I'd assumed that it was all about sex for the men and that they'd run a mile at the mention of love. I hadn't really thought about falling in love with someone, but could I realistically have an affair and NOT fall a little bit in love? I stop to think about what I'm actually looking for and I realise that I am looking for an old-fashioned love affair. I also realise that this could lead to me getting hurt, having my heart broken. Am I prepared to take that risk? Only one way to find out, I decide as I reach for my glass again...

CHAPTER 15

More of the same

I'm now propped up in bed, having pinched Paul's pillows to make myself comfortable, and my laptop is perched on my thighs. Alfie is lying across the foot of the bed, paws twitching as he dreams.

I logged out of Secret Affair before coming up to bed and worked out how to delete the browsing history, hoping that would be enough to hide what I've been up to. I'm now logged back in on an incognito tab and have just re-read LonelyArms' message. I can see that he's still online too.

Hello and thanks for your lovely message. I really enjoyed your profile too. You're right about the sharks! I haven't dipped my toe in too far for fear of having it bitten off! Lx. I match my sign-off to his, wondering what his name is and what he looks like. I know that he's forty-seven and a quantity surveyor from Surrey. If he's telling the truth. He's also a Scorpio like me.

While I'm waiting to see if J replies, I check out the next message. And promptly delete it. AllMan goes straight for the kill and I'm not sure some of the things he suggests are even physically possible. Or indeed legal. Well, Lucy, you wanted honest and you certainly got it that time. I get back on the bike as it were, and open the next one, hoping for something a tad more subtle.

Sledgehammer subtle. Delete! I think I'm blushing, but there's nobody here to see thankfully. Just as I'm about to click on the next message, a new one pops up and I'm excited to see it's from LonelyArms:

Thank you so much for taking the time to reply – you wouldn't believe how many women simply don't bother. I'm James, by the way, and I'm very pleased to meet you. X. I'm surprised to hear that not all his messages received responses as I really liked what I read about James. Maybe the L word scared some women too?

Hello, James, it's very nice to meet you too. I'm Lucy, I wrote, wondering what to say next. *Have you been on here long? I only joined a few days ago – not sure what to make of it all really! X.* He replies immediately:

Hello, Lucy. It's all a bit bonkers isn't it?! I joined about a week ago and was starting to think all the women on here were a bit mad until I came across your profile. You've given me hope! James xx.

Yes, the whole thing is pretty bonkers. I'm keeping an open mind, though. It's early days. Have you done anything like this before? Lucy x. I'm still holding back a second kiss. I still don't know what he looks like.

Confession time. I had an affair with a work colleague a couple of years ago. We had a wonderful year together and it just sort of fizzled out naturally. No one got hurt. I guess now I know that it can work, I want it again. I hope I haven't shocked you? James xxx.

I have no right to be shocked – I'm on here, after all. I know how hard it is to be married but still lonely. It will have to be a very special man to tempt me though – I'm not doing this lightly. Lucy x. Am I really doing this, I wonder? It feels as though whatever it is I'm doing is gaining momentum. It's starting to feel real, as if I might seriously be considering having an affair

68

with a married man. I should feel shocked, shouldn't I? But, as I analyse how I'm feeling, I have to be honest and say that the over-riding feeling is excitement. Shock and guilt have very much taken a back seat as I travel deeper into the realms of affair-dom. (But not affair-sub-dom!)

While I'm waiting for James to reply, I quickly read Rob's latest, feeling a little guilty at dropping him so abruptly. I'm relieved when he says that an old friend's popped round to see him and that he has to disappear for a while. I hurriedly return a *no problem, catch up soon*, before returning my attention to James, my mysterious tall, dark and handsome admirer. I hoped I wouldn't be disappointed when I saw his photo. I don't have long to wait:

Quite right too, Lucy. You shouldn't settle for anything less than perfect. Now, I'm not saying I'm perfect – you'll have to make up your own mind about that - but I'm happy to share my password with you. Please don't feel any pressure to reciprocate if you're not comfortable to yet. I'm happy just getting to know you better. My password is 'thesearms'. I hope you like what you see. James. Xxx.

I waste no time in entering the password and soon I am looking at a face that is indeed handsome, with hair that is indeed dark. His profile says he's six feet two. James is indeed tall, dark and handsome and I am indeed experiencing a slight flutter. There must be a catch, I think, as I continue to assess his features. This man is too good to be true. Of course, there's a catch, Lucy – he's married.

Your mother was right, I write back, *you are handsome. It's only right that I give you my password too. It's 'pinkfizz'. I'm probably far too girl-next-door for you – be honest with me, I won't be offended. Lucy x.* It's nerve wracking to think of James inputting my password and judging me on the way I look. What if I'm simply not his type? It's an anxious wait as I sit staring at the screen willing a new message to arrive. Thankfully I don't have to wait long:

You're beautiful. Just lovely. Thank you so much for trusting me with your password. I would love to meet you in person one day, if you'd like that. We could just meet for a coffee, perhaps? Somewhere of your choosing, naturally. It's important that you feel relaxed. There's no rush, though, we can just keep chatting for as long as you like, but I already know I want you, Lucy. James xxx.

As I read his words, I feel a flush come to my face and a flutter to my insides. He wants me. Just a few short minutes ago, this man didn't even know I existed. And now he's saying he wants me. My head is in a bit of a spin and I don't think it's entirely wine-induced. Maybe this is just how it happens on a dating site… no point pussy-footing around when everyone knows why they're here, I suppose. It's mad. But it's really happening. It's happening so fast that I start to feel a little scared. Not scared that it will happen, but scared that it won't. The admission shocks me. I want this.

CHAPTER 16

Flying high(ish)

I stayed up stupidly late chatting to James, and this morning I'm a bit of a zombie. There is absolutely no chance of Tom getting pancakes today. It'll be a miracle if I manage to get some cereal into a bowl to be honest. There is a strong possibility I will soon be pouring milk all over the kitchen worktop. This does not bode well for family learning this afternoon, when I have to be bright and breezy for the kite to stand any chance of getting off the ground.

James and I had chatted like old friends last night, about everything and nothing. Nothing being our respective spouses. Whereas Rob had spoken openly about his wife, James didn't mention his once, so I hadn't mentioned Paul. I don't know if it was a conscious decision on his part, but I could understand it. We were creating a little fantasy world in which only we two existed. Bringing real life into it would have shattered the illusion and made something which so far felt very special, feel sordid.

It's hard putting James to the back of my mind and focusing on the day ahead. Paul is due home today and I'm anxious about his return. Will my face give me away? I feel awful admitting to myself that I haven't missed him – not on an emotional level anyway. There has been the odd practical thing when I've wished he was around, and sharing the Tom load, but I haven't been counting the days 'til his return so I can fall into his arms. It's a sad admission and one that I'm not proud of, but it's an honest one. I'm not in love with my husband. I didn't fall out of love with him on purpose and I don't really know when or why it happened. But it did happen, and now I have to decide what to do about it. But not right now. Now I have to get one small boy to school, one dog walked, and one house clean and tidy before the dreaded kite making.

The first three things on my list are straightforward. At least when Paul arrives home this evening, it won't look as though I've done bugger all while he's been away. I've loaded up the slow cooker with a casserole for dinner – just need to bung in some dumplings later – and even tidied up Paul's office. I'm doing my best *proper* wife act and am in danger of overdoing it. Hopefully Paul will just think I've really missed him. I know it's a tangled web I'm weaving, but I can't go on as I have been. And, as I can't bear the thought of ending my marriage and breaking Paul's heart, I can only see the web getting bigger.

After a quick lunch of a tuna sandwich and a can of Coke (caffeine is most definitely the order of the day – I've already had three mugs of coffee) I gather up the materials I've collected as suitable for making a kite and set off for the school. I'm early, as ever, but it's the only way to guarantee a parking space not a million miles away. I'm not surprised when I pull up to see Clare's red Mini already parked – she's the only mum who's always earlier than me. She spots me in her rear view mirror and raises her hand to acknowledge me. When we're this early we sometimes sit in one or the other car together and have a quick catch up, so I hop out and go round to her passenger door:

'Hello! How's you? Looking forward to a fun afternoon with the little darlings?' I say with a grimace as I get in and shut the door.

'Oh yeah! Can't wait to make a tit of myself again as I demonstrate my complete lack of anything even verging on creative ability,' Clare replies with a grimace to match.

'Tell me about it. Do you remember the disastrous octopus? It was so bad. I was absolutely mortified. I tried blaming Tom, but I don't think anyone fell for it.'

'God, those sodding willow sticks that were meant to bend into shape. Half of mine snapped and the others kept pinging out of the ties. My goldfish looked more like a road traffic accident.'

'It wasn't that bad. Better than the monster from the deep I produced. Anyway, kite making's got to be easier,' I say, trying to sound more optimistic than I feel.

'Sod the kite making – I want to hear what you've been up to while the cat's been away. You do know I plan to live vicariously through you from now on?' Clare winked at me.

'Not much to tell, really,' I say, trying to play it down. I'm not quite ready to admit how excited I'm feeling about my online adventures. 'Just chatted to a couple of guys who seem nice. Early days. Still not sure if I can go the whole hog.'

'It must be exciting though? I will admit to being a teensy bit jealous.'

'It is, I guess. And a bit scary. I still can't imagine actually meeting someone. It's one thing chatting online, but...' I can't verbalise the actual reality of an illicit meeting with a strange man.

'Bound to be. I'd be a nervous wreck.' As Clare says this she's also looking at her watch. 'Bugger, we've got to go. Let's meet up for lunch soon so you can fill me in on all the details. I'm really excited for you.'

'Thanks, Clare. And thanks again for not judging me.'

'I'd never think badly of you, Lucy. If you think having an affair will give you something to help you stay married and no-one gets hurt, then I don't see what the problem is frankly.'

'Not everyone would be so understanding though.'

'Well, I get it and I'm here for you no matter what.'

'Thank you. That means a lot. Right, let's do this!'

As we walk the short distance to the school gates, the other parents start to arrive and we exchange waves and pull faces at one another, none of us particularly looking forward to the next couple of hours in an overheated classroom with thirty excited six-year-olds. Thanks to the vast quantities of caffeinated drinks I've had I'm actually feeling quite awake again, if a little frayed around the edges.

We're soon reunited with the kids and the tables are strewn with sticks and canes, paper and string, glue and tape and scissors as we all do our best to construct something that not only looks like a kite, but flies like one too. I'm not optimistic as I look around the room. Clare catches my eye and pulls a face and I try not to giggle. I make the shape of a dunce hat with my hands above my head and draw a capital D in the air. Tom isn't impressed.

'Mummy, will you concentrate? You're not supposed to be naughty or you'll go in the sad book.' I'm being told off by my six-year-old son and have to stifle another giggle.

'Sorry, sir, yes, sir,' I raise my hand in a mock salute, which is wasted on Tom. I think the can of Coke may have been a caffeine too far as I'm feeling mildly hysterical. For Tom's sake I need to take this seriously and I turn my attention to the two lightweight sticks we're trying to bind together to form a t-shape for the centre of the kite frame.

I've selected materials based solely on how light they are, my theory being the lighter the kite, the better the chance of getting it off the ground. As a result, it's never going to win a beauty contest, but it might just fly. A bit. The sticks are skinny green plant sticks and I'm recycling the cellophane wrappings from a bunch of flowers for the covering. It's clear with multi-coloured flowers dotted over it and Tom's not overly impressed.

'It's a bit girly, Mummy,' he says disappointedly when I take the stuff out of the bag.

'Well, I am a girl,' I offer up in my defence. He's not impressed. 'Just you wait – when ours is the only one that doesn't crash and burn, you won't mind a few flowers then!' As I say this I look around the room again and see that the weather outside has changed. It looks as though the wind has dropped and it's raining lightly. No chance of a crash and burn scenario then, just a soggy drag along the ground most likely. I point out the weather to Tom, still building my defence for the plastic flowers, and whisper to him:

'All the paper kites will get all wet and soggy, Tom. They'll probably just fall apart.'

Tom takes this in and then we giggle conspiratorially behind our hands.

'I can't wait to tell Daddy about it when he gets home later.'

Daddy. Paul. I don't want him in my head right now. 'I expect he's excited to hear all about it too. Right, what's next?' I say trying to close the daddy door. Soon, the kite is really taking shape. Thankfully, it's kite-shaped. We just need to add a tail now with a few twists of the cellophane attached at intervals, and we're done. Standing up and stretching, I look over to Clare where she and daughter Chloe look as though they're having a bit of an argument over something. Chloe, six going on sixteen, has very definite ideas of her own and Clare looks as wound up as the ball of string she's holding.

'Back in a minute, Tom. Just going to see if Clare and Chloe need a hand.'

'OK. I'll just tidy everything up.' Tom, six going on sixty.

'Thanks, superstar.' It's at moments like these I really appreciate how lucky I am with Tom. I manoeuvre my way around the classroom desks and mini-chairs:

'Ladies! Looking good! What a fab kite – gorgeous colours, Chloe.' Clare looks gratefully up at me. I can see she's at her wits' end with her argumentative daughter. 'Just got the tail to do now? Brilliant. I bet it'll fly like a bird.' Clare mutters under her breath: 'Yeah, a penguin.' Chloe doesn't hear and is pacified and smiling angelically. They just needed a mediator. I don't need to do or say anything more, so I give Clare's shoulder a squeeze: 'Hang in there. It's nearly over,' and head back to Tom who's sitting at a tidy desk twiddling the kite around.

'Right, everybody, five minutes more and we'll head to the top playground to fly your wonderful kites.' Tom's teacher sounds more optimistic than I feel. 'If you could return all the scissors to the pot before you go.' Was she worried an overly competitive parent might be tempted by an act of sabotage? I wonder, the mild hysteria making me giggle again. Tom glares at me. Serious face.

Thankfully by the time we get up to the playground, the

mizzle has fizzled out, but there's still not much wind. As usual there are some wonderful-looking creations from certain of the parents; great colourful confections, beautiful, beribboned pieces of art. Clare and I exchange looks of despair as we compare our less extravagant efforts. Our children don't help. Chloe is now standing with her arms folded and a face like thunder. And Tom is staring open-mouthed at a fabulous kite that looks like an eagle which one of the few dads here has constructed.

'Wow! Look at Jack's eagle. It's awesome!'

'Yes it looks amazing, doesn't it?' I say before whispering to Clare, 'Style over substance – I bet it flies like a rock.'

'I'm past caring. I just want the ordeal to be over so I can go home and have a glass of wine. Sod the yardarm.'

'Just remember, you're doing this for Chloe – to make her happy.'

Clare snorts: 'Pah! Does that look like a happy face to you?'

I can't help laughing as I look over at Chloe: 'Well, no, it's more of a "this is the worst day of my life" and "how dare you even breathe the same air as me" face, but in years to come she'll look back and smile and be grateful for you.'

Another snort. 'Well she can write and tell me how grateful she is from boarding school!'

I'm still laughing as Tom and I climb up the grass bank at the edge of the playground, which is quite steep and now slippery from the rain, but will hopefully give us the best chance of catching what little wind there is. I'm puffing a bit when we get to the top. I think I'm coming down from all the caffeine. We stand and watch as other kites get thrown into the air, kids running with them, parents shouting instructions. It's all a bit of a farce as kites are dragged along the ground, some leaving brightly coloured tissue paper in their wakes. Competitive parents are getting frustrated and cross, and children are getting upset. There will be tears before bedtime. And tears, as another kite rips on the concrete playground.

'Right, Tom, are you ready? You've got this. All you need to do is hold this bit and run in that direction,' I say pointing to the bottom of the kite and diagonally across and down the hill. There's no way I'm running anywhere and running the risk of falling arse over tits in front of everyone. I figure if he doesn't run straight down the hill, Tom stands a better chance of not falling over. So considerate. 'Then, when you get halfway down, sort of throw the kite into the air. I'll hold onto the string at the other end.' Talk about the blind leading the blind. I'd never flown a kite before – another bone to pick with my parents.

'OK? Go!' I shout, and Tom takes off down the hill shouting 'Geronimo!' as he goes. Several people close by look up on hearing his war cry. I can hardly bear to look. But then Tom lets go as instructed and our little flowery waterproof kite jolts a little before soaring for a few seconds. OK, so soaring might be a bit of an exaggeration, but it's in the air and it doesn't just drop like a stone. Tom has his arms in the air and is cheering, clearly over the moon, as the kite drifts gently back to earth.

As I re-join Tom on the playground, having warily descended the hill, I see that the kite hasn't survived the landing intact. Shoddy workmanship on my part no doubt. Thankfully Tom isn't bothered. In his eyes it's been a success and he's ecstatic. 'We did it, Mummy. It really flew. Jack's eagle didn't – it just sort of fell. Ours was the best!' Tom puts out his little hand for a high five. He's happy. So I'm happy. I realise in that moment that making this little boy happy means everything to me. I can never do anything to jeopardise that.

CHAPTER 17

Daddy's home

Tom and I walk back to the car with Clare and Chloe. Thankfully Tom hasn't reached the age where he thinks he hates girls, and walks on ahead with Chloe happily enough.

'So, Paul's back tonight then? How are you feeling about it?' Clare, sotto voce, looks at me questioningly.

'Not great, to be honest. I haven't missed him. And I'm starting to get a bit paranoid about him seeing through the act.' Equally quietly.

'It can't be easy. I don't envy you. Not that anyway. Are you free for lunch on Friday? You can use me as a sounding board if it helps.'

'I think so. I'll check the calendar when I get home and text you.'

We part company at our cars and I get in with a sigh at the thought of returning to real life once more. Tom instantly starts with happy chatter about what a brilliant afternoon it's been. He doesn't notice that I'm not really giving him my full attention and the occasional 'yes' or 'I know' satisfies him. I'm feeling tired again now, the late night's caught up with me, and a weight of sadness descends on me. If my emotions were a kite right now, they definitely wouldn't soar, but would drop to the earth and crumple in a heap of twisted sticks.

Once home, I send Tom upstairs to change out of his uniform. He runs off happily and a few minutes later I hear the TV come on in the playroom. When I take him in a drink and a snack he's playing happily with his action figures. He doesn't need me right now, so I take myself off to the garden for a few minutes. Alfie trots out after me. I sit at the table on the patio, head in my hands, and just stare. At nothing. I just stare into space. I don't know that I'm even thinking. I'm just overwhelmed with tiredness. Alfie puts his muzzle on my leg and looks up at me sadly – he's a barometer for my feelings and now knows I need comfort. Gradually I feel the patch of jeans under his jaw grow warm and damp with his doggy drool. Somehow I've got to get back in character for what lies ahead.

Heaving myself up from the chair – my body feels as exhausted as my mind – I head back indoors, telling Alfie that he's a good boy and ruffling his thick neck fur as I go. It's reward enough for him. I call to Tom in the playroom as I head for the stairs:

'I'm just going to have a shower, Tom.' I pause on the bottom stair, waiting for a response.

'OK.'

'Don't open the door to anyone unless it's someone you know, like Granny.' I wait again.

'I won't.' My obedient little soldier.

Reassured that Tom's OK for a while and won't be admitting any strange men to the premises (the irony isn't lost on me), I take myself off to the bathroom. I'm hoping a shower will revive me a bit. Besides, I need to shed the dog-be-dribbled jeans.

Fifteen minutes later and I'm back downstairs and feeling a little more with it. The citrus-scented shower gel worked its magic on my senses. Paul is due home in less than an hour and I still need to make the dumplings and get them in the slow cooker. Busying myself with domestic tasks helps me get back into character – not quite the domestic goddess, but a reasonable approximation. I lay the table with the matching cutlery and even open a bottle of red wine to breathe. 'Careful, Lucy,' I mutter to myself, 'he'll think he's come to the wrong house.' With nothing else to do but wait I head for the playroom to keep Tom company.

'Daddy will be home soon. Have you missed him?'

'Yes! Loads. I can't wait to tell him all about today and our awesome kite.'

'You'll be able to show him too. I took a video on my phone.' I've been holding back that bit of information to surprise him. To be honest I hadn't been optimistic about having anything worth filming, but our little sparrow of a kite had surprised us.

'Yes! Awesome!' Awesome's clearly his word of the day. I conclude he watches too much American TV. 'Do you think Daddy will bring me a present?'

'I'm sure he will, although he might not have had a chance to go to the shops.' I knew Paul would have bought him something, even if it was from the airport. 'You'll have to give him a big hug when he gets home – he'll really have missed you.'

'And you, Mummy. You'll have to give him a big hug too.'

'Yes, I will,' I say, giving Tom himself a big hug. I will have to hug my husband when he gets back. And tell him I missed him and I'm glad he's home. I will have to lie and hope that the mask doesn't slip, that I don't give myself away. For the sake of my son and his father, I will speak those lies, and another little piece of my heart will turn black.

It's not long before Alfie alerts us to the fact that his master's almost home. He's up at the window, stump wagging, before Paul's car has even pulled onto the drive.

'Daddy's home,' I tell Tom just as his keys turn in the front door.

'Daddy's home!' comes a shout from the hall as Paul comes in and dumps his bags on the floor.

Tom goes running, sock-clad feet sliding on the wooden floor. Alfie goes running, paws sliding as he struggles to get traction. I get to my feet, plaster a smile on my face and, taking a deep breath, make my way to where the three of them are now bundling excitedly on the hall floor. The laugh that escapes my lips is real; I can't help but feel joy at the sight.

'Welcome home,' I say. 'I think they're pleased to see you.'

Extricating himself from the bundle, Paul looks up at me: 'I hope you are too. I've missed you.'

'Yes, of course I am. We've all missed Daddy, haven't we Tom?' I reply, aware that I'm trying to generalise. I don't want this to be about me and Paul.

Paul steps towards me and embraces me. 'Maybe you can show me how much you've missed me later?' His breath smells of cigarettes.

I can't speak, so I just smile at him and pull away, changing the subject. 'Casserole for dinner. With dumplings. It should be just about ready.'

'Casserole. Yuck! You know I hate casserole.' I can always rely on Tom to run interference.

'Well, if you can eat a bit, you can have as much chocolate ice cream as you want for pudding. As it's a special occasion with Daddy being home,' I try to pacify him.

All I can think about during dinner is Paul wanting me to show him how much I've missed him. His words filled me with dread and I've been feeling anxious ever since. Thankfully, Tom is full of news and chatter and doing a great job of keeping Paul's attention.

'And then I let go and it went up really really high and it really flew like an eagle – not like Jack's eagle – but a proper one. And everyone said it was the best. Even with the flowers on it.'

'Sounds like you and Mummy did a great job,' Paul says, smiling at Tom and reaching over and giving my hand a squeeze.

I force myself to smile at him. 'It certainly went better than I expected. I put the success down to Tom's excellent running and throwing.' I try to turn Paul's attention back to his son, and away from me.

'Well, I'm very proud of you both. Show me that video again, Tom.'

While Tom proudly shows off his kite-flying skills, I clear the table. I still can't shake off the anxiety about bedtime. With the kitchen tidy once more and the dishwasher running, I go in search of Paul and Tom, and find them in the playroom. Tom is oohing and aahing over a model plane his Dad has bought him. I knew Paul wouldn't let him down.

'Wow, that's a nice plane. I bet it's just like the one Daddy flew in. Do you think if he'd looked out of the window he'd've seen your kite, Tom?'

Tom looks at me as if I'm not very bright and doesn't dignify the question with an answer. I change the subject. 'Bath tonight, Mr. Do you want to watch a DVD with Dad first?'

'Yes! Power Rangers!' Tom punches the air.

Paul groans. He's sat through this particular DVD far too many times already. 'Why don't we all snuggle up on the sofa and watch it?' he says. 'Then I'll bath you and read you a bedtime story.'

There's no way I can refuse, but at least Tom sits in the middle so I cuddle him, not Paul. Alfie grumbles that there's not room for him too, but then settles at my feet. I too have been forced to sit through this particular film more than once and I let my mind drift, paying little attention to the far-fetched action on the screen. It seems like no time at all and the credits are rolling. 'Right, bath time. I'll start running it.'

Soon I can hear laughter and splashing coming from the bathroom. I can guarantee there will be more water outside the bath than in it when I go in to clear up. I don't mind though as they're having fun together. I've laid clean pyjamas out on Tom's bed, closed the curtains and put his night light on.

'Don't forget to clean your teeth,' I say to Tom when I hear the water swirling down the plughole a little while later. He's out of the bath and leaning over to watch the mini whirlpool swirling round the plughole – it always fascinates him. Paul has draped a towel over Tom's back and is waiting patiently to dry him. He stifles a yawn, obviously tired from his trip.

'Someone needs an early night,' I say when I see how tired he is.

'Now you're talking,' he says, a lascivious look on his face.

Damn. Why did I say that? I'd only been thinking of sleep.

'Make sure he does his teeth properly.' Distraction is all I can think of. 'I've left his jarmies on his bed. I'll be downstairs – if you need anything just shout. Night night, Tom. Sweet dreams.' Blowing Tom a kiss I head back downstairs.

I stick the TV on, flicking through the channels for something to take my mind off the impending doom of an *early night*, and find an old episode of *Grand Designs* about to start. To be honest, I just zone out and before I know it an hour's passed and it's grown dark outside. It's nine o-clock and Paul hasn't reappeared.

Tiptoeing up the stairs, I head to Tom's room and poke my head in. There, fast asleep next to his little boy is Paul, book still open on his chest, arm around a sleeping Tom. It's a picture that can't fail to make my heart swell with love. And it does. But that love is tinged with sorrow.

I know I should wake Paul, but I don't. Instead I quickly get ready for bed myself. If Paul should wake and come into our bed, I will be sleeping soundly. Or at least pretending to…

CHAPTER 18

Don't be alarmed

When I wake the next morning, just before the alarm's due to go off, I turn to see Paul sleeping next to me. I turn away again quickly and press the off button on the alarm clock before it has a chance to sound, climbing out of bed as carefully and soundlessly as possible. I don't want to still be in bed when he wakes. It's awful, I know, but I can't bear the thought of him trying to take me in his arms and kiss me with that sour, smoky morning breath.

Retrieving my dressing gown from the hook on the back of the bedroom door, I tiptoe to the bathroom to go to the loo, making no sound as I close the door. So desperate am I to put off Paul's waking, that I don't flush the loo before creeping downstairs. I'm hoping to enjoy a cup of tea on my own – giving me time to collect my thoughts and put them in some sort of order before I have to get into character for the day.

I'm soon settled on the sofa with a mug of tea and my feet up on the coffee table. My mobile phone's in my dressing gown pocket and I can't resist a quick look at my secret emails. I switch on my phone and enter the four-digit code to unlock it, feeling a shiver of anticipation as my email account loads and messages start to appear. There is a dozen or so new messages, but I'm only really interested in one name and I'm not disappointed;

I have two new messages from LonelyArms and I experience a tightening in my tummy as I click on the link to take me to the website. I click on the first of James's messages:

Hi Lucy. Been thinking about you a lot since we chatted. Can't get you out of my head if I'm honest. Hope you're around to chat tonight. James xxx. But of course, I hadn't been around to chat as Paul had come home, I think regretfully. I click on the second message which is timed a couple of hours after the first, feeling a little worried that James will think I've been ignoring him:

I guess you're not around tonight – I can see you haven't been on-line so don't worry, I know you're not ignoring me! I realise it's not always possible to log on here. I check my messages regularly, so message any time and I'll respond as soon as I can. Hope you're OK. Thinking of you. James xxx.

The man is a mind-reader! I can't help but smile to myself as I sigh with relief. It's crazy how much I already value James's opinion of me, this man, this stranger. He seems to intuitively know I need reassurance, that I can't bear him to think badly of me. I'm not imagining it, am I? This genuine connection we seem to have?

He said to message any time, so I take him at his word and type a response:

Hi, James. So sorry I couldn't chat last night. Been thinking about you too. I really missed chatting to you last night. Crazy, eh?' Lucy xxx. Short and to the point. I still feel a little anxious at messaging him at a time when he's probably at home with his wife as I have no desire to be a home wrecker, but assume that he is careful about security. After all, he's done this sort of thing before so is probably a bit of an expert. This thought does give me pause, although I'm not sure why it bothers me.

I wonder about it for a while and come to the conclusion that some part of me wants to be the first; not one of a string of adulterous affairs. I know that makes little or no sense, but it does niggle at me nonetheless.

Having replied to James, I skim down the list of unread messages and see one from KentishMan – Rob. I'd sort of forgotten about Rob since James appeared on my radar, but I remember our early exchanges and feel a strange sort of loyalty towards him. I open his message:

Hi Lucy. How's it going? Have you been swept off your feet by Mr Tall, Dark and Handsome yet?! If so, I wish you luck. If not, I'd love to chat some more. I want to know everything about you. Hope to hear from you soon. Rob xxx.

Have I been swept off my feet by Mr Tall, Dark and Handsome? I can feel colour come to my cheeks as James's face swims into view. I'm certainly in danger of it, but I have no desire to confide this to Rob. Deciding that I would like to keep chatting to Rob, I type a short reply, aware that time is running away from me and I need to wake Paul and Tom.

Hi Rob. Apologies for the radio silence – not always easy to get on here, as I'm sure you know. No feet sweeping has occurred and I'd love to get to know you better too. Just to warn you messages may be rather spaced out though. Hope you have a good day. Lucy xx. The messages weren't the only spaced out things, of course.

Quickly logging out of the site, I tuck my phone back in my pocket and head to the kitchen to make tea for Paul and get a juice for Tom. Time to face the day.

'You should have woken me last night.' These are Paul's words when I shake him awake, putting his tea on the bedside table beside him.

'Sorry. You were so sound asleep - I didn't have the heart to.' Well, that was true – my heart definitely wasn't in it.

'I was looking forward to a cuddle. I really missed you this week.'

I should probably say 'me too', but I can't bring myself to, so instead I say sorry, again.

'Sorry. You just looked so peaceful...' I trail off, not knowing what to say. 'Must go and wake Tom up, or we'll never be ready for school.' As I leave the room I'm feeling sick with worry and guilt. How can I possibly keep up this charade of a life? I'm exhausted just at the thought of it.

The morning routine saves me from any more soul-searching. For a while at least. Paul is in his office by eight o'clock and Tom delivered to school for eight forty-five. I've brought Alfie on the school run with me, planning to head to the beach for our walk instead of the usual hills. I know full well that I'm doing it to put off going back home for as long as possible, but I don't know what else to do. I simply can't face Paul right now.

Clare and I walk back to the cars together as usual. I know she's dying to ask me about my illicit activities:

'Well?' she asks. 'What news?' She nudges me with her elbow.

'Um... dunno really. Still chatting to James and Rob. Think I kind of like James. Think I might actually be going a little bit insane...'

'Ooh, exciting! And how was last night with Paul coming home?'

'Awful. I can't bear him being anywhere near me. I found him asleep in Tom's room at nine o'clock and I just left him there and went to bed. What the hell am I going to do? I honestly don't know how to go on right now.' I could feel my voice crack as I said the words out loud. The thoughts were one thing, but verbalising them made my situation much more real. And even more hopeless.

'Oh dear. I am sorry, Lucy. I wish I could help.'

'Oh, you do, believe me. If I didn't have you to confide in, God only knows what state I'd be in.' I give Clare a grateful smile. We're back at the cars now. I open the hatchback for Alfie to jump in:

'Up! Good boy. Mind your head,' I say as I carefully lower the boot. 'We're off to the beach – hoping to blow the cobwebs away,' I tell Clare. 'And, of course, putting off going home.'

'Well, you know where I am. Any time. Call me.'

'Thanks, Clare. Means a lot. Have a good day and I'll see you after school.'

CHAPTER 19

Running away

As I drive out of the village, I feel like I'm running away. I suppose I am. Running away from my life. Just for a couple of hours. The late summer sunshine lingers on, and I drive with sunglasses on and the windows down. My hair blows carelessly around my face and in the rear view mirror I can see Alfie leaning over towards the open window, his fur forced backwards by the wind. He's sniffing the air appreciatively, excited to be off on an adventure. I turn up the car radio as the adverts come to an end, and Human League come on... 'Don't you want me, baby?'... I can't help singing along to another eighties anthem. The lyrics bring thoughts of Paul, unwelcome, to my mind. I push the thoughts, as I want to push Paul, away.

It's about a thirty-minute drive to the beach I've chosen. It's a very dog-friendly place with huge expanses of sand that Alfie loves, as well as being the best beach to find sea-glass. I've brought a bag with me in the hope of collecting as much of the sea-sanded stuff as I can find. I'm planning to spend some time in the summerhouse in the weeks to come, decorating picture frames with the coloured glass. Just another distraction technique, really; another way of not being in the house with Paul. A way of hiding from the truth of my life and keeping myself busy.

A rough track leads down to a few informal parking spaces and thankfully there is room for me to park, with only one other car here before me. I keep Alfie on the lead until we reach the beach itself, and he pulls at it, eager to go off exploring. I can see a couple of people off in the distance, but otherwise we have the beach to ourselves. I'm glad, as I really don't feel like interacting with anyone right now. As soon as I unclip his lead, Alfie's off, heading at once for the sea. The tide is out and leaving foamy streaks across the compacted sand.

I amble after the bounding hound, lifting my face to the sun and taking in deep, grateful lungfuls of the sea air. I can't help but feel better, invigorated and somehow calmed all at once. The sea has always had a restorative effect on me, and even now, with my mind in turmoil, it doesn't fail me. I stand and watch Alfie as he splashes joyfully in and out of the shallows. Pure, unadulterated joy. I'm kind of envious. I continue walking along the beach, just staying out of the reach of the waves, knowing that Alfie will adjust his course accordingly. He never strays far. But I'm thinking about straying. I'm thinking about adulterous joy.

After about ten minutes' walking, I turn up the beach towards one of the pebbly patches that drift now and then across the sand. The pebbles are all very small and I know that amongst them are lots of pieces of sea-glass waiting to be discovered. Once I find an area rich in glass, I sit down and start looking around for flashes of blue. There's always lots of clear or white glass and the brown and green's pretty common too. The most prized bits are dark blue and sometimes red and yellow. Every now and then I look up to check on the dog, but he's happily doing his own thing. I focus on the task at hand; it requires no thought and little effort and it's really quite soothing. It allows my mind to switch off for a while. All I have to do is shuffle along a few feet now and again when I've exhausted a patch.

My back starts to ache after a while so I stand up and stretch, roll my neck a couple of times and carry on along the beach, calling Alfie as I go and stepping over ancient and rotting breakwaters. I can now make out the rocky headland at the farthest point of the beach, jutting out into the sea, where we've often brought Tom to play in the rock pools. Memories of being here with Paul and Tom are bittersweet, reminding me what I have, and what I risk losing if I'm not careful. I wish I still felt about Paul the way I had at the beginning. I wish I understood why my feelings changed.

Reaching the end of the beach, I find a flattish rock and sit down. Alfie soon joins me and accepts a stroke and a few words before wandering off again. The people I'd seen on arrival have disappeared up one of the cliff paths and we've got the beach to ourselves. I'm overtaken by a feeling of calm, the like of which I've not felt for a while. My thoughts, which have been so scattered of late, suddenly coalesce. I know what I need to do.

CHAPTER 20

Decision

Taking my phone out of my pocket I realise I have no signal here on the shore, so I call the dog and set off purposefully to the car. I need to act before my courage evaporates.

Back at the car I give Alfie a drink, take off his lead and load him into the car. I still have no phone signal, so I set off back up the track to the road and civilisation where, hopefully, normal service will be resumed. I find a parking space in a residential road and am soon logged into Secret Affair. I don't bother looking at the growing list of unread messages. I know exactly what I want to do.

Let's meet. X. I type the words and hit send before I can chicken out. My heart's in my mouth. I've done it. No going back. Now all I can do is wait. Wait and see how James replies. If he replies. It's going to be an anxious wait and I know I'm going to have to resist checking my phone every other minute to see if he's replied.

Although I feel like a nervous wreck, the feeling's tinged with positivity; I've done something proactive, something to change my current situation, which has become more than untenable. Right or wrong, at least I've done something.

As I drive back home, a little seed of excitement has implanted itself in my mind. Whatever happens next, I'm going to embrace it. Or him. A real sense of optimism is returning and I suddenly become aware that I'm smiling. Really smiling. Not the red crayon smile that I've been sporting for so long. I feel lighter, no longer burdened down by the weight of my world. I realise that my shoulders are no longer up round my ears, the tension has drained away with the tide and been replaced with excited anticipation.

Pulling onto the drive some thirty minutes later, I open the front door and call out to Paul: 'I'm home – I'll bring you a coffee in a mo.' He may, of course, be in a meeting – in the past when I've stuck my head round his office door to ask if he wants a coffee, I've had responses from whoever he was video-conferencing with: 'White and two, please!' or 'Make mine a tea!' Paul doesn't mind though. He thought the time I inadvertently gate-crashed a meeting wearing my nightie was hilarious.

Hanging Alfie's lead on the hook by the door, I kick off my trainers and head to the kitchen. I'm humming the last song that played on the car stereo: 'In the Air Tonight' by Phil Collins, and I stop to beat out the drum solo on the worktop before filling the coffee machine and making two mugs of coffee.

'Your coffee, Sir,' I say to Paul as I place the mug carefully on his rather messy desk. 'Didn't take you long to mess up all my good work. I spent ages tidying up in here while you were away.' I'm not really cross. It's just something to say.

'Yep. You know me. Papers everywhere, can't find anything. That will never change.'

'I don't know how you can work like that – it would do my head in. Anyway, I'm going up to the summerhouse – I collected a load of glass at the beach and want to do something arty farty with it.'

'OK, I'll come and find you at lunchtime if you haven't reappeared. Don't glue your fingers together this time.'

'Oh ha ha. I only did that once. Mind you, I don't think my fingerprints ever recovered. Laters.'

'Laters. Thanks for the coffee.'

'Welcome.'

I gather up the bits I need, including a portable radio, my phone and coffee and am soon settled at the craft table in my bolt hole at the bottom of the garden. I'm surrounded by pots of sea-glass, all washed and sorted by colour. I'd recently bought four small seascapes in boxy white frames, just cheap and cheerful ones from The Range, and am planning to decorate the frames with the glass. I've tuned in the radio to Heart80s and they're playing The Communards' 'Never Can Say Goodbye'. Alfie has followed me and is now lying in a shady spot on the decking where the Passionflower grows with such abundance.

I've just selected the perfect starter piece for the corner of the frame and am unscrewing the top of the super glue when my phone beeps to announce I have a text message.

Hiya, just wanted to check you're OK. Was worried about you earlier. It's from Clare. Bless her.

Aw thanks! I'm actually doing better. The sea air must've helped.

That's good. Any gossip? I'm so bored today. I've just hoovered the lounge in concentric circles.

Ha ha! Well, sort of. I've told James – you know – LonelyArms – that I want to meet him! Eek!

Oh my God! Exciting. What did he say?

Nothing yet. I don't know if he's even seen my message.

Let me know if you hear anything. If you need me, I'll be

perfecting the art of hoover carpet design.

Nutter. Will do. Coffee and catch up as soon as you can drag yourself away from the housework?

God, yes please. I'm free tomorrow morning.

It's a date. Park after drop off?

Perfect. Look forward to it. xx

Me too xx. The prospect of sharing a gossipy session with Clare lifts my mood even more. It has also put James to the forefront of my mind again and I quickly check my messages: nothing. But I can see that he hasn't been online since I sent those reckless two words. Patience, Lucy, I tell myself and turn my attention back to the frame.

'Oy! Where's my lunch?' Paul's words reach me from halfway up the garden. I've managed to engross myself in my project for over an hour and am surprised.

'In the dog. He loves tuna sandwiches.'

'Come on, wench, I need feeding. I've been slaving over a hot desk all morning.'

'Oh so demanding,' I joke back. I know Paul's not really bothered that lunch isn't ready and waiting for him.

We walk back down the garden together with Alfie ambling along behind us. He's slept right through Bonio-time, no doubt the effect of the sea air and exercise.

'Let me wash my hands and I'll sort out a sandwich,' I tell Paul.

'Got glue on them, have we?' he jokes.

'No. Maybe. Yes. A bit. OK, quite a lot. Occupational hazard,' I retort.

Paul laughs. 'Speaking of which, I got a really nasty paper cut this morning. Can you kiss it better?'

'Give it here then,' I say, reaching out for his hand.

'It's not on my finger,' comes the reply, with a laugh as dirty as my hands.

'Pervert.'

Paul's still laughing and I realise how much I enjoy our banter. We'd lost it of late and it feels good to have a taste of it again.

'Yep. Give us a kiss.'

I don't stop to think for once and let Paul put his arms around me. I kiss him on the lips, just once. It's fine. But that's all. It doesn't make me want to kiss him harder. I pull out of his embrace and set about making lunch.

CHAPTER 21

Park life

The following morning brings the first sign that Autumn is just around the corner, with a very slight chill in the air and that mizzly rain that doesn't really make you wet. It's mid-September and we're well and truly back into school mode after the long summer break. Tom is settled and happy in his routine and Paul is focused on a big project at work, giving me plenty of time and space to myself.

Clare and I are sitting at our favourite table in the café at the park, having just dropped the kids at school.

'Well, I don't need to ask if you heard back from Mr. Lonely Arms,' she says. 'It's written all over your face.'

'I checked my messages in the loo last night – he says he can't wait to meet me. He's checking his diary for times next week. Oh my God, Clare, I can't believe I'm really doing this!'

'I can. You needed to do something, Lucy, and maybe, as mad as it seems, this is actually what you need. Providing you play by the rules, then nobody has to get hurt.'

'It's scary though! Going off to meet some strange man. I'm not sure I have the courage to do it.'

'You do. It's natural to be nervous – anyone would be. First anythings are scary. If you weren't nervous, I'd be nervous!'

'I guess so. It's all getting pretty real now. I've started thinking about the practicalities of it – Where to meet? What to wear without causing suspicion? What to tell Paul? I will admit I am excited though.'

'I'm excited for you. And a teensy bit jealous. Not that I'm not happy with Greg, but a little bit of excitement would be nice.'

'What if I really like James and want to see more of him. If you get my drift.'

'Well, isn't that kind of the point?' Clare looks amused.

'Yeah, but… oh I don't know… it's not about sex for me. Not really. At least I don't think it is. It's about wanting someone again. Does that make sense?'

'Yes, but sex is the natural progression then isn't it?'

'Scary pants! I can't imagine getting naked with anyone else – there's only been Paul for so long.'

'I don't recommend your scary pants. A thong or something lacy might be better.'

'Jeez. I suppose in the moment it'll all come together.'

'You should be so lucky,' Clare giggles.

'Well, I'll cross that bridge when, and if, I come to it. Got to meet him first. He might not fancy me.'

'When you've got a where and when, let me know – someone needs to know what you're doing, just in case.'

'I will, but I promise to be careful. We'll meet somewhere public.'

'The first time, anyway! Then it'll be all hotel rooms and "do not disturb" signs.' Clare still has the giggles.

'Oh God! Can't think about that. Too scary. One step at a time.'

We sit in comfortable silence for a few minutes, sipping

our coffees and lost in our own thoughts, until Clare breaks the silence:

'I just had a thought,' she says.

'Steady on there! Thoughts can get you into all sorts of trouble – just look at me.'

'No, seriously, Lucy, what if you found Greg on the site? Or someone else's husband you know?'

'God. Told you thinking was dangerous. And the answer is, I honestly don't know.' This is definitely a curve ball.

'What would you do? Would you tell the wife? Or let the husband know you know?'

I stop to think for a minute. 'Well, I certainly wouldn't rush to a decision - it's one hell of a minefield. If I told the husband, then he'd know I was on the site too – pot, kettle and all that. I can hardly judge him can I? When I'm doing the same thing. What right do I have to wreck a marriage which he may well be trying to save? I think I'd probably keep shtum.'

'I get that, but as a wife I think I'd want to be told.' Clare looks thoughtful.

'Really? Blimey. Well, let's hope I don't find Greg on there then!'

'I really do. I think I'd want the chance to either try and fix things or agree to separate. I deserve better than half a husband.'

'Well don't go after Paul then! Mr Half-a-Job!' I'm trying to lighten things, but Clare's having none of it.

'I'm serious. Think about it – what if it was Paul on there? Wouldn't you want to know? Would you really want to carry on in blissful ignorance?'

'What we don't know can't hurt us, can it? To be perfectly honest, if Paul's physical needs were being met elsewhere, we'd probably tick along much better. That's really the only area of our marriage that's a bit rubbish. It might be the perfect solution.'

'Hmm… Not sure I agree, but I can see what you're saying.' Clare looks unconvinced.

'From most of the chats I've had on there, these men do love their wives and they have no desire to end their marriages – they just need to feel close to a woman again. I don't think it's even all about sex – it's about closeness, tenderness, feeling wanted. I think more than anything men need to feel wanted, desired.'

'I think you're right about that. I s'pose you've kind of seen this from both sides now – the wife who wants to want a man, and the husbands who want to be wanted. Still not convinced though – I'd want to know.'

'Well, Greg adores you, so I don't think it's something you need to worry about. And I promise that if I do stumble across him on there, about the same time as hell freezes over, I'll tell you straight away. Deal?'

'Deal.' Clare looks slightly happier now she has that completely unnecessary assurance. 'And you have to promise to tell me if you see anyone else on there we know!'

'Ooh you little minx. OK, promise. I really don't think I will though, do you?'

'Doubtful I s'pose. You never know, though. It could happen. God, can you imagine? Seeing one of the mum's fellas on there?'

'Please God, no. I think I'd be so shocked I'd probably delete my own profile for fear of being discovered myself.'

'Anyway, back to James – let me know when you're meeting him. And I want to hear every last detail afterwards. I'm so excited for you.' Clare claps her hands together and grins at me, all thoughts of Greg cheating on her gone.

'I will. If I don't bottle it.'

'You won't. Right, I must away. The carpets await.'

'I don't know why you hoover every day. I only do it if we're having visitors nowadays. Paul and Tom never notice anyway.'

'Dunno. Habit probably. Besides, I'm working on a new art installation – writing 'fuck it' with the cordless Dyson along the hall carpet.'

'Ha ha! You're mad. I do love you. I need to walk the hound – he'll think I've forgotten him. See you on pick-up.'

We head back to the car park and set off in convoy; Clare waves in her mirror when we part ways at the junction.

CHAPTER 22

Lovebirds

Half an hour or so later and I've picked up the dog and set off in the car again. I need to log back on to Secret Affair to try and arrange a time to meet James, and the car is the safest place to do so. Alfie whines – he doesn't understand why we've parked but aren't getting out of the car.

'Won't be long, boy,' I tell him as I type my password and wait for my messages to load. It gives me a thrill every time I see an entry from LonelyArms.

Hi Lucy. I'm so looking forward to meeting you. I've checked my diary for next week and can do Tuesday or Thursday. Don't know if either of those works for you – hope so. I don't know how far you want to drive, but am assuming you don't want to meet too close to home?! Look forward to hearing from you. In anticipation… James xxx. I don't know how to describe the feeling I have right now – it's a nervous excitement that starts in the pit of my stomach and travels up to my throat, making it hard to get my breath. It's palpitations and a flush to my face. It's a feeling that's life affirming. And probably addictive.

Alfie whines again, his patience wearing thin.

'Ssh! Just a minute.'

I quickly compose a reply: *Hi James, lovely to get your message. Tuesday works for me. I'll have a think about the best place to meet – happy to drive up to about 30 miles. Just off to walk the dog now... and daydream... Lucy xxx.*

I don't bother logging out of the app. I want to know the second James replies. I put my phone in my pocket, ensuring that the volume is turned up to the max, and try to focus my attention on getting the dog out of the boot. We set off into the park – we're not taking our normal walk on the hills as the phone signal is often non-existent.

We've barely gone a hundred yards and I'm already checking my phone, just in case I haven't heard the beep that signals a new message. 'For God's sake, woman,' I reprimand myself, 'sort yourself out!' I'm behaving like a lovelorn teenager over a man I've never even met. I can't help it though. I'm feeling more alive than in a very long time. And I like it. I like it a lot.

I vow not to check my phone again unless it beeps. It takes every ounce of willpower I can muster. I look around for Alfie, and realise I haven't taken in my surroundings at all. There's a lake to my left with a small island in the middle where I can just about make out a pair of swans. They mate for life, don't they? Unlike me, I think wistfully. I don't seem able to make a lifelong commitment to one man. I'd like to. It makes me sad that I've failed thus far. I shake off the thought and look away from the lovebirds with a sigh.

At the far end of the park a spring feeds the lake and there's a tree which grows out over the water, forming a natural bench. It's an idyllic spot and I can't resist taking a time out to sit down and check my phone. Alfie's paddling in the shallows nearby. I refresh the page and am disappointed that there's nothing new from James. I rationalise that he's probably working – I can tell he's not online and that he hasn't read my message yet.

I'm feeling unreasonably impatient. I lean back against the tree with yet another sigh.

After a few minutes of staring in to space, I snap myself out my reverie, and set off back the way I came, calling the dog as I go. Typically, he waits until he's right beside me to shake his shaggy wet coat.

'Yuck! Thanks, Alfie. I already had a shower today.' But I don't really mind.

We're almost back at the car park when I hear it: the much anticipated ding from my phone heralding the arrival of a new message. My heart rate quickens as I check to see if it's from James. It's not. It's actually from Rob. I'm disappointed and I feel a bit ashamed for not being pleased to hear from him. I read the message as a kind of penance:

Hi Lucy, how are you? Hope all's well. I'm feeling rather disillusioned on here at the moment – I think you may well be the only normal and nice woman on here! So far this week I've been propositioned by four women who are clearly… er… ladies of the night, and another who stated she'd need an allowance for clothes, travel etc. My gob has been well and truly smacked if I'm honest. Hope you're having better luck. Here any time you want to chat. Warm wishes. Rob xxx.

I can't help smiling at Rob's words. He does seem like a genuinely nice man. Am I being horribly shallow to rule him out on looks? I wonder. It's irrelevant anyway as I'm completely convinced that James is the one. No harm in chatting to him though, so when we get back to the car I quickly tap out a response.

Hi Rob and thanks for your message. I did have a little chuckle – sorry! It does sound like a bit of a nightmare for the men on here. At least us women don't have to pay for the privilege. On the whole the men on here seem to be genuine. Genuinely terrifying at times too – I've blushed at the more direct approach some men take. I'll hang in there if you will. Lucy xx.

There's still nothing from James, but I can't put off going home any longer, so I log out reluctantly, start the engine and head for home.

CHAPTER 23

Uncharted territory

Tuesday comes round surprisingly quickly, even though I haven't slept particularly well since arranging the meet up with James. I've spent the last few days forcing myself to go through the required motions of wife and mother, when really my head's been totally elsewhere. I appear to have got away with it though. Nothing to be proud of, Lucy, I tell myself. My inner dialogue, while always pretty busy, has gone into overdrive, and there's a constant tennis match of thoughts going on. I think the score's at deuce right now, but bad Lucy probably has a set point.

It's been surprisingly easy to get around the logistical issues. Tom now (reluctantly) does an after school club on a Tuesday and as Paul finishes work at four o'clock he is able to collect him. I've even managed to persuade Paul that this could be a regular thing and that it would be nice for both of them – after all, Paul misses out on a lot of the school stuff due to working office hours. Tom helps in no small amount by being pretty excited at the prospect. There's no chance of Paul bumping into Clare at the school gates as she will have collected Chloe over an hour earlier. It's all coming together.

During our last chat, Clare had suggested that I tell Paul I'm spending the day with her:

'What are you going to tell Paul about where you're going?'

'Haven't got that far yet. Not really sure. Shopping maybe – Bluewater or Ikea? Any brilliant suggestions?'

'Shopping's good – somewhere far enough away that you can't usually do on a school day. You can say you're going with me if it helps.'

'Really? That would be a big help. Thanks, Clare. As you're the only person who knows what I'm really doing, I guess it makes sense too.'

'No worries. You know I'll do anything I can to help.'

'My partner in crime, eh? Do you want to be Thelma or Louise?'

'Which one gets to sleep with Brad Bitt? I'll be her.'

'Well, I suppose that's only fair, given what you're doing for me.'

'I'm not driving off a cliff with you though. Even I have my limits.'

'Fair enough. I'm really not up for that either.'

And so, my alibi's been sorted just like that. I can't help wondering if it should be this easy. I wonder if I'm missing something crucial, something which will trip me up and get me caught. It's scary. But it's still exciting. I feel more alive than in a very long time.

I mentally run through everything in my head: Tom is sorted for pick up and Paul has promised to take the dog round the block during his lunch break. I can justify dressing a bit smarter than usual, and wearing a little make-up, for my *shopping trip*. I can't think of anything that can go wrong.

So, here I am, checking my appearance in the hall mirror one last time, trying to remember to breathe. Paul has a fresh coffee on his desk, and a sandwich in the fridge for his lunch. The dog knows something's different this morning and is sitting on the rug looking up at me, his big soulful brown eyes boring into me. It's as if he's trying to read my mind and also communicate with me using some sort of doggy telepathy. I don't need even more guilt, and from the dog of all... er... people. You know what I mean.

'Sorry, boy. Dad will take you out at lunchtime though,' hoping he'll understand some of what I'm telling him. I think he does, as he gets up and skulks off into the lounge, jumping up on to the sofa and curling up with a doggy sigh.

'Tom!' I call, pushing the nagging guilt away. 'Time to go. Shoes on.'

And we're off. We shout a goodbye to Paul.

'Bye! Have a great day both of you,' comes his shouted reply down the stairs. This, of course, causes another pang of guilt. Lucy, you're a bad person and will surely go to hell. The tennis match is back to deuce.

And now I'm alone in the car, Tom safely deposited at school. I am beyond nervous and feeling kind of nauseous. I take a chewing gum from the pot in the centre console, hoping the peppermint will help settle my stomach. The radio's on, but is failing to distract me. What the hell am I doing? I force myself to take a few deep breaths and try to calm myself. What am I doing? I'm changing something. Something has to give if I'm to save my marriage, and this is that something. I know I'm trying to justify my decision and I know it's stupid. There really is nothing that can justify what I'm doing, is there? Advantage good Lucy. Bad Lucy tells her to sod off – where's the harm? No-one needs to get hurt. I'm doing this for a good reason. Deuce.

I try to focus on my driving. We've arranged to meet in a village about forty minutes' drive away, somewhere I've probably been through in the past, but don't know anyone who lives there. Hopefully it's not the sort of place anyone I know would have reason to visit. I'd be stupid to think that there's no risk associated with what I'm doing. Is that part of the excitement? I wonder. The risk of being caught, being found out. I'm suddenly struck by a rather disturbing thought: is there actually a part of me that wants to be found out? I'm not prepared to give this any more airtime right now though – that really is deeper than I'm willing to go. I know, however, that the question will remain, lurking somewhere in my subconscious, waiting to jump out when I least want, or expect, it. At some point in the future it will demand my attention, demand an answer.

I need to concentrate on the road, on where I'm going. I haven't put a postcode in the sat. nav. for fear of discovery, and am heading into unfamiliar territory. In more ways than one, I think wryly, causing another jolt in my belly. I know roughly where I'm heading as I had a quick look on AA Routefinder on my phone, but I don't want to take a wrong turn and end up being late. I'm already so anxious just about finding the place and getting parked. My parking's rubbish at the best of times, but under this sort of stress…. I just hope James isn't already parked up when I get there. I'm hoping to arrive a bit early to give myself time to check my face in the mirror and calm down a bit.

As I settle into driving I become aware of the song that's

playing on the radio. Duran Duran's 'Hungry Like a Wolf' is just coming to an end. I often try and recall the artist and song by the intro when I'm driving, before checking my answer on the stereo's display. The next one that comes on is unmistakeable and I can't help but appreciate the irony as I start singing along to Tina Turner's 'What's Love Got To Do With It'. Time will tell, Tina, time will tell, I mutter out loud as the song comes to an end.

The next thirty miles pass quickly and before I know it the village sign is visible on the horizon. A moment of panic has me wondering if I should just keep driving until I've passed this sign and the one that marks leaving the village. But I know I won't. I've made an arrangement to meet James and I will not renege on it, whatever the outcome of this, our first, meeting.

I'm now parked a few spaces down from the café we're planning to go to. I've asked James if we can meet outside as I'm nervous about going in on my own and waiting for a strange man inside. I just imagine everyone looking and knowing, somehow, what I'm up to. No good, that is. All I can do now is wait as it's still twenty minutes until our allotted meeting time.

Just ten minutes later, a sleek pale blue Aston Martin DB9 pulls in to the kerb in front of me. He's here. Mr Tall, Dark and Handsome. And he drives the car of my dreams.

CHAPTER 24

James

As I watch him readying himself to get out of the car, I realise I'm holding my breath. So bad is my nervous anticipation that I'm actually shaking slightly. Come on, Lucy, you've got this. You're a grown up. Start acting like one. But I'm feeling anything but grown-up right now: more like a love-struck teenager. I wonder how James is feeling; if he's nervous. I don't imagine so. Certainly not to this ridiculous extent. He has so far struck me as a confident man who knows what he wants and isn't afraid to go after it.

He's getting out of the car now, so I take a deep breath and open the car door, still muttering to myself. You can do this. Just breathe. Just be yourself. What's the worst that can happen? Damn. Delete that last question. And breathe.

He's putting on a dark grey suit jacket and turning towards me as he does so. I self-consciously tuck my hair behind my ear and busy myself with getting my bag. Another deep breath and I look up and at him. James. And he's everything, and more than, I could have hoped for.

'Lucy, hi, so good to meet you in person.' He's walking the few feet that separate us and smiling a smile that reaches his eyes. He has an air of authority about him, a self-assurance that tells people he's a man who gets what he wants. I feel small.

Small and self-conscious. I force myself to meet his eyes.

'Hello. It's lovely to meet you too. I'm so nervous. Are you nervous? Sorry...' I'm in danger of letting loose with a stream of gibberish. He'll think I'm completely gauche. Not at all like his usual women I'm sure, who are probably sophistication personified.

James is laughing. 'Please don't be nervous. What's the worst that can happen?'

That bloody question again. 'Sorry,' I say again, 'it's just that I haven't done this sort of thing before...'

'What? Had coffee with a friend?' Is he teasing me? I wonder.

'Not a friend like you, anyway,' I mutter.

'Look,' James says matter-of-factly, 'what have you got to lose? The worst that can happen is we have a coffee and a chat and then decide not to take it any further. And the best that can happen is we have a coffee and a chat – maybe even some cake – and decide to embark on a wonderful affair. There's no pressure to do anything you don't want to, Lucy. You're in complete control of the situation.'

I can't help smiling. 'I wish that were true – I'm certainly not in control of my knocking knees right now.'

James laughs. 'Right then, let's get those knocking knees sat down at once. Shall we?' He gestures with his hand for me to lead the way into the café. I'd rather he took the lead, but I go ahead nonetheless and open the part-glazed door, which has a rather frilly lace curtain at it and a rather ancient-looking 'We're open, come on in!' sign hanging at a jaunty angle.

As we enter the café, every head turns towards us, looking to see who's coming in. Nobody smiles and the room goes noticeably quiet. The message is clear: this is a local café for local people. James and I look at each other and, without either of us uttering a word, turn on our heels and walk out, carefully closing the door behind us. The second we're back on the pavement, we burst out laughing and suddenly my nerves are gone.

'I didn't realise we'd arrived in Royston Vasey,' James says, still laughing.

'*League of Gentlemen* fan too eh?' I say as I push the tip of my nose upwards with my finger, in an attempt to look like one of its characters. Even as I'm doing so, I'm thinking how unattractive I must look, and I quickly remove my finger. 'You'll never leave,' I say, echoing the sentiment that appears on the Royston Vasey village sign.

'If it means spending more time with you, I think I can live with that.'

I can feel myself blushing, which makes James laugh again.

'Lucy, you're adorable,' he says. 'Now, where on earth are we going to find a coffee?'

'I passed a pub on the outskirts of the village – we might be able to get one there if they're all day opening.'

'Worth a look. Let's take my car – no point taking both.' He must have seen a shadow of doubt flash across my face. 'Only if you're comfortable with that, of course – silly of me to assume it.'

I push the doubt away. 'No, it's fine. As you say, silly to take both.' Clare's voice pops into my head, telling me not to take any risks, and the anxiety returns. But I can't backtrack now, and anyway I have a good feeling about James and I trust my instincts.

We walk the few paces to James's car and he holds open the passenger door for me. The point of no return, I think, as

I sink into luxurious cream leather. The pleasure at being in such a beautiful machine overtakes any lingering worries and the throaty growl of the engine sends a shiver of excitement down my spine. James spins the car round and we head out of the village.

We're in luck and the pub is open and serving coffee. We're the only customers in there and a friendly, ruddy-faced landlord directs us to a comfy-looking sofa by an open fire at the far end of the bar, saying he'll bring our coffees over. The fire isn't lit, with the weather still being so mild, but it's a pleasant place to sit nonetheless.

'So, how are the knees now?' James asks. 'Knocking a bit less?'

'Yes thanks. Although I'm still feeling a bit nervous. This isn't the sort of thing I usually do on a Tuesday.'

'No, it's not an average Tuesday for me either. But it's infinitely preferable I assure you.'

We both go quiet as the barman appears through a door next to the bar carrying a tray with two steaming cups on. Setting the tray down on the low table in front of us, he disappears again. I'm grateful to have something to do with my hands. I'm feeling shy again under James's gaze and the coffee is a welcome distraction. I wonder what he's thinking as I tear open four sachets of demerara sugar and shake them into my drink. He probably doesn't take sugar and no doubt won't approve of a woman who takes so much. I focus my attention on stirring. When I look up again, James is smiling at me.

'How refreshing to see a woman who's not afraid of a few calories,' he says. 'Most of the women I know are permanently on a diet.'

Wrong there then, Lucy. I should know better than to make

117

assumptions about people. I think it comes from a place of self-criticism. I assume people will think badly of me because I think badly of myself. I'm also now wondering what the catch is with James – he really is too good to be true.

'Actually I would like to give up sugar – for health reasons rather than calorific content. But I have zero will-power, especially where's food's concerned,' I tell him.

'Well, I hope you'll have zero will-power where I'm concerned too, young lady.'

I can feel myself blushing again. He seems to have already made his mind up about me, about us. I also feel a flutter of panic somewhere deep in the pit of my stomach. I actually feel a little scared. There's something in his tone and the way he said 'young lady' which has become a little sinister. Maybe sinister's too strong a word, but I feel unsettled, out of my depth. I want to slow things down, but I don't want to appear naive.

'Time will tell, I suppose. This is a big deal to me – I won't do anything just for the sake of it. It has to be right.' I'm not sure if I'm making sense; I just know it's important to assert myself.

'Absolutely,' James replies, back to his charming considerate self. 'Like I said, you're in complete control, Lucy. There's absolutely no pressure.' Something about the way he says 'complete control' makes me feel that this would be the only time I'd have control. This is a man who takes charge. He's saying all the right things, but I'm still feeling unsettled. There's definitely an undercurrent of something a bit dark and I'm starting to wish I hadn't agreed to coming here in one car. I take a breath and tell myself to calm down.

'Thank you. I appreciate your understanding,' I say. In my head I'm giving myself a good talking to, trying to convince myself that it's all in my imagination, just nerves. 'So, tell me something about you,' I say, trying to keep that control James says I have.

'What would you like to know? You can ask me anything.'

I had been hoping he'd just start talking and telling me about himself, taking the pressure off me. I try to think of something to ask him. My mind is uncooperative, a blackboard with no chalk. I frantically wrack my brain for an interesting or original question. Nothing.

'Oh, I don't know…' I begin before the silence grows any longer, 'Um… tell me about your previous affair.' I don't know where that came from and I wonder if I've overstepped the mark by asking something so personal.

'OK, she was called Faith, we met when she came to do some temping at my firm. I didn't really notice her at first to be honest. I don't normally mix business with pleasure. Anyway, I occasionally take my staff out for lunch and it was at one of these that I really noticed her. There was something fragile about her. She wasn't what you'd call traditionally beautiful, but she was attractive, and I found her rather intriguing. So, I asked her to dinner, she said yes. You can guess the rest.' He sounds very matter of fact about the whole thing and I'm not sure what to think.

'Did she know you were married?' I ask.

'Honestly? I don't know. At first anyway. I didn't volunteer the information, and she didn't ask. I don't wear a wedding ring – never have. I did tell her after the affair started. Turned out she'd not long come out of a bad relationship. I think she was looking for some sort of reassurance – you know, that she was still attractive to men. And I was happy to oblige. I'm no saint.'

'Well, I can hardly judge you, can I? The very fact that I'm sitting here with you makes a call from the Vatican pretty unlikely.' A wry smile escapes my lips and I start to relax again. Maybe I'd got James wrong. Again.

James laughs. 'You're funny. I like that you're funny, Lucy. And I like that you're here and willing to sacrifice sainthood.'

We slip into comfortable conversation and I feel more and more at ease. James is charming and thoughtful. I must have been wrong about the vibes I picked up earlier. I still can't quite believe that he seems to really like me.

'How are you for time?' he asks me, pulling back his cuff to look at an expensive-looking watch.

'What time is it now?'

'Just gone midday.' I can't believe how the time has flown by.

'Is it really? Well, I'm OK for a bit longer then.' I don't want to think about leaving just yet.

'Great. Can I tempt you to lunch? We could see if they serve food? Or go somewhere else if you'd prefer?'

I look around the pub. It's still fairly empty, just a couple of men at the bar who look like regulars.

'Lunch would be lovely. Here's fine if they do food.'

'I'll go and find out.' James heads over to the bar and comes back with two A4 sheets of paper. 'We're in luck,' he says. 'Menu looks reasonable.' He hands me a menu and we spend the next few minutes discussing what looks good. I swallow the urge to say that James does.

'I think I'll have the Hunter's Chicken, please,' I say when I've chosen. I hand the menu back to James and then excuse myself. 'Just nipping to the ladies.' Picking up my bag, I look around for a sign to the loos. It's just occurred to me that Clare is probably worrying and I want to let her know I'm OK. I get out my phone and compose a quick text:

OMG! He's gorgeous. All is well so please don't worry. Xx

Back at the table, James asks if I'd like another coffee or something else to drink. I'm about to ask for a cranberry juice, but stop myself. Last thing I want is him thinking I've got some kind of bladder problem. So I ask for an orange juice and lemonade.

'Can't tempt you to a glass of wine?' James asks.

'No, thank you. I'm really not much of a drinker, and I'm driving.'

'Surely one wouldn't hurt? I'm having one.'

'No, really, I'd rather not.' I'm refusing to let myself give in to any pressure to do something I'm not comfortable with. James seems to accept this and heads off to the bar once more.

We move to a more suitable table for lunch and the food, when it arrives, isn't at all bad. James has ordered a steak and has obviously ordered it rare judging by the amount of pinky-red juice which oozes onto the plate when he cuts into it. There's something kind of primal about watching him eat, a red-blooded male devouring his prey. My spine tingles with a sensation I can't quite put my finger on. I think I'm imagining that I'm his prey, weak and helpless, being stalked and hunted and devoured. I can't help but conclude that resistance would be futile. There's something intrinsically dominant about this man in front of me.

I realise James is studying my face. 'Penny for them,' he says.

I'm caught off guard. I can't possibly tell him what I was thinking.

But I do. Sort of. 'I was just thinking that you're not a man to mess with; that you probably always get what you want. You're not a man who'd take no for an answer.' I'm surprised at how bold I've been.

'I suppose you're right. I do go after something if I want it, and I don't give up easily,' he shrugs.

I feel that tingle again. I'm a deer, he's a hunter. He's going in for the kill and I don't stand a chance. 'How does it make you feel if you don't get what you want?' I'm pushing him and I don't know why.

'Don't know,' comes the reply. 'It's never happened.' His supreme confidence both thrills and alarms me, but something in me, some spark of self-preservation, needs to push back. I can't surrender to this man or I might just be lost forever.

'Well, there's a first time for everything,' I say with a smile I hope hides how vulnerable he's making me feel.

He just smiles. 'We'll see,' he says. 'But there's nothing better than the thrill of the chase.'

I'm feeling decidedly flustered now, so I turn the conversation back to the food. But the sense of how vulnerable he makes me feel stays with me. We finish eating in silence. I can't think of anything to say, and James seems fine with that. He shows no sign that he is finding the silence awkward or uncomfortable. I, on the other hand, am feeling horribly anxious. Something about this supremely confident man has me rattled. At this point I can't tell if I'm incredibly attracted to him, or a little bit scared. My women's intuition is leaning towards the latter.

James finishes eating a little before me, and I can feel him watching me. I can feel my cheeks flushing under the intensity of his gaze: he could pounce any minute and I'd be helpless. I give up on eating – I can no longer swallow comfortably. I force myself to speak:

'That was lovely.' It's inane, but just the act of speaking gives me back some modicum of control.

'Good. The steak wasn't bad either. Can I tempt you to pudding?'

More food is the last thing on my mind right now. 'Not for me, thanks, but don't let me stop you.' As I say those words, I'm thinking that I couldn't stop him doing anything if he'd made up his mind.

'Oh, I won't, Lucy. Trust me.' His words send a chill down my spine. I'm really not imagining the slightly sinister undertones. 'I think I'll just have a coffee though.'

I'm trying desperately not to show how vulnerable I feel. 'Good idea. I'll have a peppermint tea.' The thought of coffee makes my already churning stomach lurch.

James gestures towards the bar, and is soon giving our drinks orders to the barman, who disappears back to the kitchen with our plates. Turning back to me, James reaches over and places his hands over mine. I want to pull mine away at once. It feels like some sort of static charge just went through me.

'Relax, Lucy. I won't bite,' he says.

I realise my fingers have been anxiously pushing at my cuticles. I'm clearly not doing a very good job of hiding my feelings. Although I don't think anyone could hide their emotions from James. He has a way of making you feel that he can see into your very soul. My default setting is to apologise:

'Sorry. Still can't quite shake off the nerves. This is the first time I've done anything like this and I'm still not sure if I'm doing the right thing.'

'No apology needed – you're a good person, I can tell, so

it's only natural that you'd feel nervous. But all you've really done is have lunch with someone. Admittedly someone who would like to do much more than just have lunch with you.' He smiles, almost angelically, but I can still see the devil in his eyes. Do I really want to sell my soul to him? Because I think that's what it would mean if I were to pursue anything further with this man. I would be lost, in the depths of his eyes, and the encompassing of his arms.

I force myself to look away from him and busy myself with checking the time on my phone.

'I really have to go soon. It's been lovely though.' I just want to get back to the safety of my car, away from his penetrating gaze.

'Of course. We'll have our drinks and then I'll run you back to your car.' As he says this, the barman appears with our drinks and I silently curse myself for ordering a herbal tea which will take ages to cool down sufficiently for me to drink. I focus on dunking the teabag up and down. I don't know what to say. I don't know what the rules are for an occasion such as this. Do we have to make a decision about whether we want to see each other again? To be honest, I just want to get away. As if he's reading my mind again, James intervenes:

'No need to decide what happens next. Not right now anyway. Just message me. I think you already know what I want though, don't you? You know I want you. I want you very much, Lucy.' He's reached over and taken my hand again, and his voice oozes seduction. It's a heady moment and I have to remind myself to breathe.

'Thank you,' is all I can utter. I'm not sure what I'm thanking him for – for wanting me, or letting me off making a decision here and now.

I start to sip the tea, knowing that it will probably scald my mouth. It does. James leans back in his chair, coffee cup in hand, watching me intently. My face continues to burn under his gaze and I'm trying desperately to keep my hands from trembling and giving me away. But he knows. He already knows how intimidating I find him. He already knows I'm drinking the too-hot tea so I can escape quicker. He probably already knows I have blisters forming on the roof of my mouth. There is nowhere to hide.

Finally, after what seems like an age, we finish our drinks and I excuse myself, popping to the ladies while James pays the bill. I offered to pay my share, but he wouldn't hear of it. I tried objecting – I don't want to feel in any way in debt to him – but it was wasted breath. I run the cold tap over my wrists for a minute and try to calm my breathing and regain some composure, telling myself I just have to get through a few more minutes. When I get back to the table, James is holding out my jacket and he helps me into it. The close proximity is too much and I'm flustered once more. James seems to find it amusing judging by the smile on his face.

On the surface he's behaving like the perfect gentleman as he holds open, first the door of the pub, and then the car. But always there's an underlying sense of something darker. Even the beautiful machine I'm in can't distract me from it.

A couple of minutes later, James pulls in to the kerb just behind my car. As I reach for the door handle, he reaches for my other hand, preventing me from getting out. My heart is pounding in my chest, but I force myself to look directly at him.

'Lucy,' he says, in a voice of pure silk, 'it's been wonderful.

You're wonderful. I'll be waiting for your message. Don't keep me waiting too long, will you?' The words themselves are innocent enough, but that sinister undertone is there again. The interpretation is that there will be consequences if I do keep him waiting.

'It has been lovely, thank you. And thank you for lunch. I promise not to make you wait to long for my answer.' I'm surprised to hear my own voice, saying the necessary words. I start to pull my hand away, but he doesn't let go immediately. Instead he leans across to me, putting his free hand to my neck and applying a little pressure, and he kisses me on the lips. A surge of panic rises through me and I pull myself away and open the car door in one movement, desperate to get to my car. With a muttered 'thank you, bye' I cover the ground to my car like a thing possessed. Only once I'm behind the wheel, with the doors locked, do I feel safe.

CHAPTER 25

Comfort zone

It's some miles before I start to feel calm and back in control again. All I can think about is getting home. Everything else can wait. I don't want to think about the last few hours – not yet anyway. I just want to be back in my comfort zone, and right now that means being at home with Paul and Tom. Yes, I said with Paul. It's a sudden realisation that he still represents something important in my life. It's confusing, but now's not the time for analysing that either.

Thankfully, the traffic is light and I'm pulling onto the drive about forty minutes later. Checking the time, I see that's it's only three thirty. Paul will still be working. Alfie is waiting behind the door when I open it, so pleased to see me as always. I crouch down and ruffle his ears, telling him what a good boy he is. I'm home. I'm safe.

Putting my shoes on the rack in the hall cupboard, I toss my bag on the table and jog up the stairs. Paul looks up from his monitor, surprised to see me. He's on a conference call, so just gives me a wave and points to his watch as if to say 'you're home early'. I smile and shrug before going into the bedroom. I want to get out of these clothes and back into my jeans. My comfort zone uniform. Heading into the bathroom with my facial wipes, I rub away the make-up and then clean my teeth. I want every trace of my meeting with James wiped away, expunged.

Back downstairs, I find that the breakfast dishes have been cleared away. Paul must have loaded them into the dishwasher in his lunch break. I feel a stab of guilt, and wonder, not for the first time, what I was thinking by going off and meeting up with James. I'm a fool.

It's not long before Paul appears, his familiar cough reaching me before he himself does. For once, I don't grit my teeth on hearing the hack that normally gets my hackles up. My encounter with James has made me realise how much I value the safety and security of my home life.

'You're home early. Good day? What did you buy me?'

My brain freezes. Damn. Shopping. I was meant to be out shopping.

'Sorry! I didn't end up buying anything. Clare was on a mission to find an outfit for Greg's cousin's wedding, and I spent most of the day sitting on stools in changing rooms while she tried on a gazillion different dresses. I got a bit bored in the end, so every time she came out of a changing room to show me yet another one, I was sitting there wearing a different hat.' What the hell am I saying? I ask myself. Talk about over-egging the pudding. Just shut up, Lucy.

Paul's laughing though. He doesn't seem to have noticed anything amiss.

'As I'm back, shall we go and pick Tom up together? He'd love that.'

'Good idea. Maybe we can all go and do something? What about that crazy golf place he loves? They're open 'til the end of the month.'

'Brilliant. Yes, let's do that. Let me quickly grab a change of clothes for Tom.'

When Tom sees both his parents standing at the school gate at four-fifteen, his face lights up. We've really made his day, and my heart swells with love, all thoughts of my encounter with James forgotten. For now, at least.

As we walk back to the car, Tom in the middle holding a hand each side, Paul tells him of the plan.

'So, how do you fancy crazy golf and dinner out then?'

'Yessss!' comes the reply as Tom temporarily withdraws his hand from mine and punches the air. 'We have to try and beat Mummy this time, Dad.'

I laugh. I managed to fluke wins the last few times we'd played and the boys are getting competitive. 'No chance,' I say. 'I'm the champion and you don't have a hope of beating me.'

'We'll see about that, won't we, Tom? Challenge accepted.'

Tom chatters happily during the drive to the miniature golf. Paul's driving and I can see him looking at Tom in the rear view mirror every so often, and smiling. He adores his son. I'm turned towards Tom, offering the occasional word or 'uh ha' to show I'm listening, when really I'm just thinking how much love is in this car right now.

Tom changes his clothes when we park up and soon we're heading for the first hole of the pirate-themed course, with Paul already doing his best pirate voice to make Tom laugh. Apparently, I'm going to be walking the plank soon.

I decided before we got here that I'm going to do my best to do my worst. I want Tom to have a chance of winning. However, in spite of making no effort at all, I keep getting lucky and stay annoyingly in the lead. Paul glares at me, as if to say, let Tom have a chance. I contort my face and shrug my shoulders. There's only one thing for it and I start hitting the ball so wildly that it goes out of play. I'm soon racking up the sort of score you'd see in ten-pin bowling rather than crazy golf. Tom is elated.

'Mum, that was rubbish!' he exclaims delightedly as my ball goes sailing into the air, narrowly missing the man about to putt at the start of the next hole.

'Oops! Sorry!' I call out, as I make my way over to retrieve my ball. Losing shouldn't be this hard. 'I'm so sorry,' I repeat to the man, who has now picked up my ball and is holding it out to me, with an expression that says 'bloody women golfers'. I feel the need to explain my unusually bad play. 'I'm not normally this bad – honest. I'm trying to lose on purpose to give my son a chance,' I tell him with a smile that I hope melts his steely heart.

He looks slightly mollified, and I reach out to take the ball. 'Well, maybe you could just wait until I've played my turn before you take yours? I don't particularly want to end up in hospital with a concussion.'

'Yes, of course, no problem, and sorry. Again.' I'm backing away as I speak and I manage to control my facial expression until I turn back to the previous hole where Paul and Tom are waiting, matching expressions of resigned amusement on their faces.

'Oops,' I say again. 'He's not a happy bunny.'

'I'm not surprised,' Paul says. 'You could've ruined his game.'

'Jeez, it's only crazy golf, not the British Open,' I return. 'Anyway, it's not like I did it on purpose.' Although I kind of did, I suppose, in my attempts to lose.

An hour or so later and a delighted Tom is victorious. It's been worth all the lost balls and crawling around on my hands and knees in the foliage to see him so happy. Paul managed to lose without going to such extremes and is looking smug.

'Right, winner chooses dinner!' Paul announces.

Predictably Tom selects his current favourite restaurant, his choice being based solely on the quality of the play area rather than the quality of the food. For once, Paul doesn't try and talk him into something a bit more civilised, which normally results in Tom getting upset and me getting quietly cross with Paul. Thankfully, today Paul seems to have got the memo that tonight is about making our little boy happy and keeping the peace. I'm grateful to him as I really don't want anything to shake my equilibrium again today. I simply want to enjoy us as a family. I still shudder when I think what could have happened earlier in the day.

CHAPTER 26

Winner, winner, chicken dinner

We've arrived at the family-friendly restaurant and Tom has chosen chicken goujons from the Children's Menu before dashing off to the play area. Paul is still mulling over the menu, with a look of dissatisfaction on his face. He would really rather be at a better class of eatery.

'Cheer up,' I tell him. 'It could've been a lot worse – he could've chosen McDonalds.' Paul hates McDonalds. With a passion. He groans.

'Over my dead body! Mind you, if they had a play area, he would've done, wouldn't he?'

'Yep. But it wouldn't kill you to have Maccy D's occasionally.'

'You sure about that?' Paul's only half joking.

'Pretty sure. Maybe just a mild case of food poisoning.'

'I'm not actually sure it's physically possible to get sick from their food – there are so many preservatives and rubbish in everything.'

'That's probably true – I remember someone who kept a burger happy meal for weeks and it never went mouldy.'

'Yuck. Food should rot, shouldn't it?' Paul shudders.

'Well, I'm really looking forward to my Angus steak burger now. Mm. Not.'

Paul finally selects something vaguely acceptable from the

menu and pushes his chair back, ready to head to the bar to place our order.

'Can you check on Tom on the way?' I ask him. Just as Paul turns away, I hear a beep from my handbag. It's a text message from Clare. Damn, I should've told her I was back safely.

Hi, hope you're OK. Let me know so I can stop worrying that you're dead in a ditch somewhere. Seriously, hope you had fun. Xx

I feel terrible and quickly compose a reply.

So so sorry. I'm fine. With Paul and Tom at The Duke's for dinner. Fill you in tomorrow. Sorry again for worrying you. Xx

No probs. Just glad you're OK. Can't wait for the gossip. See you in the morning. Xx

As I send a quick smiley face and a couple of kisses, James' face flashes into my head. That handsome, confident face. That charming, unsettling man. I shudder involuntarily at the memory of him and mentally tell him to sod off.

Paul's soon back with our drinks. 'Tom's fine. Seems to have palled up with a boy about the same age. I told him he can play until food comes.'

'Great. Glad he's having fun.' Suddenly I'm feeling a little uncomfortable sitting here with Paul, without the distraction of Tom. I've been going to great lengths to avoid being in intimate situations for the last few days, and now there's nowhere to hide. I realise I'm fidgeting with my nails again.

Paul takes a big glug from his pint. 'Keep meaning to talk to you about France,' he says. 'We don't seem to have had a minute on our own since I got back.' He's noticed too.

'I know. That's family life, I guess. Par for the course.' I'm trying to keep things light and impersonal.

'Speaking of which, what was your final score today?'

'Dunno. I rather lost count after my ball ended up in the road for the third time. Who knew crazy golf could be so high adrenaline. Barely escaped with my life.'

Paul laughs. 'Well, your efforts didn't go unappreciated – you made a small boy very happy.'

'Unlike the man in front of us, and the unsuspecting seagull. I never thought losing could be so ruddy hard. And embarrassing.'

'Never mind, we'll let you get back to your winning ways next time. So, about France… They want me out there for two or three days a month from now on. There's no way I can get out of it – sorry.'

I let his words sink in for a few seconds before answering. 'That's OK, if you have to you have to. Tom and I will be fine.' I'm remembering how much happier I'd been while Paul was away recently. I'm actually excited at the prospect. The admission makes me feel bad. And sad.

'I know you will, but I still hate leaving you both.'

'Who knows, might do us good? The whole absence/fonder thing.' I know it's wishful thinking on my part.

Paul reaches across the table and covers my hands with his. 'I couldn't BE any fonder of you, Lucy, you know that.'

I just smile. It feels like a sad smile. I hope Paul doesn't notice. I'm saved from having to answer as Tom appears from around the corner. He's red in the face from his exertions.

'I need a drink,' he puffs as he reaches us. He picks up the glass of apple juice and has downed it before I've had a chance to say 'save some for your dinner'. 'Gotta go,' he says, 'Josh is waiting for me.' And he's off again. Paul and I just look at each other and laugh.

'I suppose I'd better get him a refill then?' Paul says and he sets off for the bar once more.

Alone at the table, I realise how tense I've become. My shoulders and neck are tense and my jaw clenched. It takes a conscious effort to relax them. I'm noticing that this is happening more and more when Paul and I are alone. I'm too afraid to think about why, because deep down I already know the answer, and it's not a satisfactory one.

Seeing Paul heading back, I fix my crayon smile back on. Thankfully, just as he sits back down, the waitress appears with our food.

'I'll go and get Tom,' I say, only too happy for the distraction.

The rest of the meal passes easily with Tom, as ever, being the perfect camouflage. By the time his chocolate sundae appears, I can see that he's flagging though, and it's a very tired boy Paul carries from the car when we get home.

CHAPTER 27

The debrief

I catch up with Clare the following morning at school. I can tell by the look on her face that she can't wait to hear all about my meeting with James.

'Hope you haven't got to dash off,' she says. 'I want details.'

We walk back to where the cars are parked and both get into mine.

'Well?' Clare says as she pulls the door closed.

'Well… I think I was in way over my head…' I begin. 'Honestly, Clare, I've never seen such a good looking man in all my life, but he scared the pants off me.'

Clare grins.

'Not literally! I promise I kept all my clothes on. It's hard to describe him – on the surface he was charm personified; perfect good looks, lovely manners, AMAZING car… but there was some scary kind of undercurrent. He kept reassuring me that I was in control, but I've never felt less so. I felt like a rabbit in the headlights most of the time.'

'Sounds a bit creepy,' Clare looks concerned.

I pause to consider her words. 'Not creepy exactly… more like commanding, authoritative. Someone you wouldn't mess with. Maybe it was my imagination, you know, with it being illicit and everything, and feeling guilty, but I don't think so.

He was intimidating. Even when he was saying all the right things, I still felt kind of uneasy.'

'Hmm… sounds dodgy. How did you leave it?'

'Like a rat up a drainpipe!' I can't help laughing.

'Very funny. Seriously, though, what happened?'

'I just sort of muttered thanks, I think, and said I'd be in touch as I was getting out of his car.'

'You what? Why were you in his car, Lucy?'

'I know, I know, it was stupid – it just sort of happened. The café was no good, so we drove to a pub down the road. He said let's go in one car and I found myself going along with it. It was hard to say no to him. It would have seemed childish.'

Clare looks a bit cross with me. 'Better to look a bit childish than end up kidnapped and raped!' she says. 'God, Lucy, you can't take chances like that. Jesus.'

'I know. It was stupid. I was stupid. I'm sorry.'

'I'm sorry too. I don't want to scare you, but you can't be too careful if you're going to do this.'

'I don't know if I am going to do this now. Not after my encounter with James. It was such a relief to get home to Paul and Tom.'

'I bet. But be honest, what's going to change with you and Paul?'

I sigh and rub my fingers across my eyes as anxiety stabs at them. 'Oh, I don't know, Clare. It's all such a sodding mess. I want to want Paul. I want to work things out, but…' I leave the sentence hanging uncomfortably.

'But…?' Clare's not giving up.

'But… I spend all my time worrying about the physical side of our marriage. Or lack thereof. I'm constantly anxious about the fact that I don't want to have sex with him, constantly looking for excuses to avoid it. It's a permanent state of dread. And I don't understand it – we used to have an amazing sex life. Now I get so tense that it's impossible on the rare occasions that we do try.'

'What does Paul say about it?'

'He's sweet, and tries to be understanding, but I know he doesn't understand and he feels rejected. I think he feels emasculated, and I hate myself for being the cause.' The stabbing pains behind my eyes are getting worse.

'Don't be so hard on yourself – you can't help the way you feel.' Clare gives me a sympathetic smile.

'He deserves better. He deserves someone who wants him the way he wants them. I don't know how to be that someone anymore.'

'Then you have two choices, Lucy. You either set Paul free, or you get back on Secret Affair and have another go. Don't let one failed meeting put you off. It would have been a miracle if the first guy you met off there was the one. Just be more sensible next time. You have been a lot happier since you joined the site.'

'Maybe... I know I can't leave Paul, so...'

'All internet dating is a numbers game, Luce. You might have to kiss a few frogs before you find a prince.'

'Mm... I suppose I was really enjoying chatting on there. Maybe that's enough?'

'Maybe. Doubt it, personally, but no harm in trying.' Clare checks the time on her phone. 'Have to love you and leave you.'

'Got the DTs from hoovering?' I joke. 'I think there's a support group for that. VA –vacuumers anonymous.'

Clare chuckles. 'I'd have to have the damn thing surgically

removed first.'

'Well, whatever floats your boat. Have a good day and I'll see you on pick-up.'

'Yep, see you later. Have fun.'

I wave Clare off, but don't start the car engine. I need a few minutes to think. I haven't logged on to Secret Affair since my meeting with James and I'm curious to see if he's messaged me. Also, I'm starting to realise I need to close the door on him once and for all. My mind isn't going to rest until I have closure.

I log in and scan the list of new and unread messages, looking for James's username. When I spot it, dated yesterday, my heart pounds and the sharp pain I've been experiencing in my temples returns. Even a message from him has a profound effect on me. Taking a deep breath, I click on the message:

Hi, Lucy. So lovely to meet you today – you're everything I hoped for, and more. Much more. I don't think you realise how lovely you are. Message me soon and put me out of my misery. Yours, James xxx.

They're lovely words. Confusing words. Words that are designed to make me feel that I'm in control. But I'm not, I know that. They are just the bait on the hook and if I take the bait, I'll be yanked out of the water to lie gulping for air on the river bank. I cannot, will not, be seduced by them. I know I need to reply to James, but I have no idea what to say. In spite of the way he makes me feel, I still don't want to offend him. I decide there's only one thing for it: lie.

Hi, James, and thanks for your lovely message. It was great to meet you too. So far, so easy. What to say next? *Apologies for not messaging you yesterday – I needed to sleep on it. I was so terribly nervous yesterday that I'm really having second thoughts about the whole thing. I'm not sure I'm cut out for this after all. I suppose you don't know until you try. I'm sorry if I've wasted your time, but I'm sure you'll have no trouble finding someone amazing. Take care, Lucy x.* I press send and heave a sigh of relief. I just hope that James will accept what I've said. I suppose it was a bit cowardly to generalise my anxiety, when really it was directed squarely at him, but hopefully the end result will be the same: he'll leave me alone.

Feeling a little lighter, I return to my inbox. I thought I'd spotted Rob's name amongst the senders. I was right.

Hello Lucy. How are things? Hope you're ok. I've missed chatting with you. I'm about ready to give up on here – I don't think I'm going to renew at the end of the month. I'd really like to keep in touch with you though – if you'd like to, of course. Warmest wishes, Rob xx. He's also included his email address.

He does seem to be a genuinely nice man, but I now know that it's impossible to tell what someone's really like from an online chat. I almost feel that James had been grooming me from the start. I want to believe that Rob's not like that. Anyway, I do really enjoy chatting with him. I decide to tell him about my meet up.

Hello again, I write, *I've missed chatting with you too. Confession time – I met up with someone from here and he scared the living daylights out of me! I wasn't sure about coming back on if I'm honest, but here I am! I would like us to keep in touch though. Lucy xx.* I add my secret email address and press send.

I'm smiling for real again as I start the engine and head home.

CHAPTER 28

Sticky situation

My phone announces the arrival of a text message as I'm driving home. I resist looking at it until I pull onto the drive. It's a group text to us mums from Charlie.

Help! Anyone free after school – play and dine at PJs? Xx

I reply straight away: *Count me and Tom in – hope you're OK. Xx*. Then I message Clare to see if she and Chloe can make it. I'm delighted when she says yes.

I expect Charlie needs to vent about the ongoing wedding saga, and I'm more than happy to have someone else's problems to focus on. Somehow they're always so much simpler to resolve than one's own. It's much easier to give advice than to take it. It's also an excuse to be out of the house.

I keep myself busy for the rest of the day and even escape having lunch with Paul who has to work through on a conference call. I sneak in with ham and tomato rolls and then take myself off to the summerhouse to stick some more sea glass on frames. And fingers. Today would be a good day to commit a crime as my fingerprints are once more unrecognisable. The thought of committing a crime brings my meeting with James into my head again, but I shake the thought away. I hadn't really done anything wrong, had I? I don't want to think too deeply about this, but the thought process persists. I've lied, and

I've met up with a man who's somebody else's husband. That's wrong, Lucy, I tell myself. Another tennis match threatens and I'm really not in the mood. I get up and switch the radio on and force my attention onto the music. Toto's 'Africa' hooks me and takes me away, thankfully.

I engross myself in the task at hand, and am surprised when I sit up and stretch to find it's almost time to collect Tom. I switch off the radio, close up the summerhouse and head back indoors. Realising I haven't told Paul that I'm taking Tom out after school, and that I haven't thought about his dinner, I quickly check the freezer for a solution, before taking the stairs to the office.

'Forgot to say – going to PJs after school – Charlie's having another wedding crisis I think. There's a meat feast pizza in the freezer. Probably some salad stuff in the fridge. Actually, make that possibly. Not. Sorry.'

Paul laughs. He's used to me being less than perfect. 'No worries. Go and have fun. I'll be fine. Probably going to have to work late anyway. And pizza's fine, with or without salad.'

God, why does he have to be so reasonable and understanding? I think. This whole situation would be so much easier if he was a git. If only he'd have an affair so I could leave him without the guilt. I don't know where this thought has come from, and it's like a slap round the face. I can feel colour on my cheeks almost as if the slap had been real.

'OK… great. See you later then,' I say, hoping my voice sounds steadier than I feel.

I'm still thinking about it as I drive to school on autopilot. Would I really not care if Paul had an affair? Wouldn't I be devastated? More thought ping pong, and still no answer.

Thankfully, Clare's on hand to take my mind off it.

'Look, I perfected it,' she says, holding out her phone to me. There's a photo of her hall carpet and I can just make out the words 'FUCK IT' on it.

'Oh my God, I thought you were joking,' I say through my laughter. 'That's hilarious!'

'I never joke about hoovering,' Clare replies with a look of mock seriousness on her face. 'You have to have quite a deep pile though for the writing thing to work.'

'Brilliant. Have you left it like that?'

'No, just in case Chloe sees it. That would be all I need, her telling Grandma that mummy wrote 'fuck it' on the carpet.'

'Hmm… good point. So, what's your next project?'

'Well, inspiration struck last night actually. The lawn needs mowing…' Clare grins. I'm not entirely sure she's joking and we're still laughing as we arrive at the school gates. The kids are thrilled to hear we're heading to the play centre and run happily ahead to the cars. Clare takes the opportunity to ask if I've thought any more about Secret Affair.

'I messaged James back. Said I was having second thoughts about the whole thing. Bit chicken, I know, but even at a distance he intimidates me. I did have another message from Rob though, and he gave me his email address – says he'd like to keep in touch.'

'And…?' Clare asks.

'And, I gave him my email address too. I do really like chatting with him. Maybe we'll be like pen pals? It's nice to chat to a man who understands how I'm feeling and doesn't think badly of me because of it.'

'Will you stay on the site too?'

'I don't know. I probably shouldn't, but it is kind of addictive – you do get a buzz from the attention and the messages. It's a real ego boost.'

'Keeps your options open, anyway. Right, see you up there.' We've arrived at the cars and I can see an excited Tom hanging off the door handle, eager to get going.

It's only a short drive to the play centre and Tom is in chatty mode.

'Mummy, is Lewis coming today?' Lewis is Charlie's son from a previous relationship.

'Yes, Lewis is coming. Why's that?'

'He said that his mum and Rich had a big fight last night. They were both shouting and saying bad things. He was a bit sad.'

'Oh dear, poor Lewis. I'm sure everything's OK though. Sometimes grownups have arguments and say things they don't really mean. But then they say sorry and are best friends again.'

'You and Dad don't.'

I pause. It's true. Paul and I don't argue. I've never been one for confrontation – I just bottle everything up.

'No, we don't, do we? That's good isn't it?'

'Yes. I wouldn't like it if you shouted. You never shout.'

I just smile at Tom in the rear view mirror, making a mental promise to myself never to shout around him.

CHAPTER 29

Wedding? What wedding?

We're settled at our favourite table: me, Clare, Charlie, Zoe and Sarah. The kids are off having fun and all our attention is focused on Charlie, who looks as though she hasn't slept, and has obviously been crying. I've already rummaged in my bag and have a packet of Handy Andies at the ready.

Even before she speaks, we can all see the tears welling in her eyes. 'It's all off. The wedding's off.'

All at once, four hands reach out for hers, wanting to offer comfort and maybe take away some of the pain by some kind of osmosis. Charlie's trying desperately to keep it together, but the tears are rolling silently down her unusually pale cheeks. I immediately pass her a tissue.

'I'm so sorry, Charlie.' I'm the first one to speak, although I know we're all thinking the same thing. 'What happened?'

Charlie wipes away the tears and takes a deep breath. 'Nothing really. Well, not any one thing. I just couldn't take any more of Rich's mum. I just wanted Rich to stand up to her and put me first. But he couldn't. It's supposed to be our day, the happiest of our lives, but I'd started to dread it. How can I marry someone who doesn't put me first?' Charlie's fighting sobs now, and I can see I'm not the only one whose eyes are also filling up.

'Oh, Charlie, you poor love.' Sarah this time. 'You've done the right thing, though, if that's how it's making you feel.'

'I just wanted him to stand up for me, for us.' I pass Charlie the packet of tissues. 'Thanks, Lucy. Thanks you guys. I'm sorry to lay this on you.'

We all chime in, all wanting to reassure her.

'Don't you dare say sorry…'

'You have nothing to be sorry for…'

'That's what we're for…'

Charlie manages a smile. 'Thank you. I don't know what I'd do without you all.'

'Well, you never have to find out,' Zoe says, squeezing Charlie's hand, 'because we'll always be here for you.'

'What are you going to do now? You're not going to break up with Rich are you?' Clare asks.

'I don't know. I don't want to. I do love him, but…' Another of those hanging sentences we're afraid to finish.

'But… he's got to man up, hasn't he?' I finish for her.

Charlie pauses to reflect. 'Yes, he bloody well has. He's got to stand up to the old witch, otherwise…'

'Otherwise… he loses the best thing he's ever had.' My turn to squeeze Charlie's hand.

Charlie's bottom lip is trembling. 'I'm really scared he won't be able to. He's been under her thumb his whole life, just like his dad. What if he can't…?'

The answers to all Charlie's questions are too scary for her to verbalise. It's time to change tack.

'Rich is crazy about you, Charlie. He'll do the right thing. I'm sure of it,' I tell her. Inside, though, I'm really worried that his love for Charlie won't be enough to make him confront his formidable parent.

'Lucy's right,' Zoe says. 'Anyone can see how much Rich loves you. Mothers and sons can be tricky though – my ex was ridiculously close to his mum. I don't think he ever really cut the apron strings. You just need to make Rich understand what's at risk here. He won't want to lose you.'

'What if that's not enough…?' Charlie sounds hopeless.

'It will be. It will,' I say, trying to sound more optimistic than I feel. 'And whatever happens, you've always got us.' I pull a mad face to try and snap Charlie out of the doldrums.

Clare takes the hint. 'Here, this'll make you laugh, Charlie. This is what us old married women get up to when hubby's at work.' She's opening her phone as she speaks, and soon everyone has seen her carpet art work.

'You mad cow,' Zoe says. 'Love it!' Even Charlie is laughing.

The mood is lightened for now, and Charlie is more composed by the time we call the kids for dinner. When the sausages, chips, beans and fish fingers have either been consumed or consigned to the floor, and the kids have gone off to play again, the conversation naturally turns back to relationships. The consensus of opinion is that relationships with men, whether married or not, are bloody hard work.

Zoe is regaling us with stories of her husband's uselessness around the house.

'I asked him to bring the hoover upstairs for me the other day – my back's been playing up. He didn't even know where we keep the fecking thing. And you all know about the time I asked him to put the oven on – I had to leave him a diagram of the knobs and written instructions. Not forgetting the one and only time I asked him to do a load of washing – that apparently was a step too far. And I've given up asking him to stack the dishwasher – I only have to redo it anyway. For an intelligent man he's a bit useless.'

We all nod sympathetically.

'Tell me about it,' Sarah sighs. 'Gary does sod all around the house and completely takes it for granted that the house will be clean and tidy and dinner on the table every night.'

'That's really not fair when you're both working,' Clare says.

'I agree – Gary should do his share. Maybe you should go on strike?' I suggest.

'I'm really not sure that would do any good. He'd probably just go out for a curry every night.'

'You shouldn't let him get away with it, Sarah. He's being totally selfish,' Clare says.

'Yeah, I know, but it's all about keeping the peace isn't it? Good little wifey keeping the home harmonious.'

'Maybe their mums are to blame a bit?' I'm thinking out loud. 'You know, doing everything for their precious sons, rather than training them up to be good husbands.'

'Hmm…maybe,' Sarah says. 'We should make sure our boys grow up to be respectful and considerate towards women – break the cycle.'

Charlie has been quiet, but pipes up now.

'Rich is amazing at home. Apart from never emptying his rugby bag, he's brilliant. I suppose the old bat must have done something right, after all.'

'He was probably too scared to be anything except perfect. You mustn't let her ruin what you have, Charlie. You and Rich are made for each other.'

'That's what I thought, but there are three of us in the

148

relationship and one of us has to go.' Charlie looks desperately sad.

'Don't let it be you. Fight for what you have! Wedding or no wedding, you can't let her win.'

'I'm scared, though. What if I lose?'

'You won't. You just have to be strong and show Rich what's at stake. And, if there's anything we can do to help, you only have to ask.'

We all nod in agreement and Charlie smiles a small smile of thanks.

When we leave a short while later, exchanging hugs of support with Charlie, I'm wondering what will happen between her and Rich and if there's something more we can do to help. But I have no answers. About her relationship or my own.

CHAPTER 30

The space between us

Later that night, with Tom asleep in bed, Paul and I are sharing a rare bottle of wine together. We're sitting on opposite ends of the sofa to take advantage of the recliner seats. Alfie has happily bagsied the space between us. I'm acutely aware of the space between us, physical and emotional. I've been filling him in on events at the play centre earlier. It's safe talking about other people.

'I really don't know what to do to help Charlie. There must be something.'

'Sounds to me as though you're already doing everything you can by being there for her and listening. You can't interfere.' Paul, pragmatic as ever.

'I know, but you haven't met Rich's mum. She's an absolute witch. Charlie's going to need all the allies she can get.'

'And she has them in you and the rest of the coven,' Paul looks at me and laughs.

'Cheeky sod! Watch it or I'll turn you into a toad.'

'Seriously, Luce, I don't see what more you can do. You can't come between Charlie and Rich.'

'I don't want to come between them – I want to make sure they stay together.'

'You care too much, that's your trouble. You can't fix

everything and everybody. Shit happens, relationships end. All you can do is be there to help pick up the pieces.'

Paul talking about relationships ending makes me feel uncomfortable. How can he be so matter of fact about it? Would he feel like that if it was our relationship? I wonder. I force my thoughts back to Charlie's situation.

'I know you don't know the other dads very well, but I was wondering if maybe you could all go out for a drink – invite Rich along and have a bit of a man to man chat…' I ignore the sceptical look on Paul's face and continue. 'Let him know what he stands to lose if he doesn't stand up to the wicked witch of the west.'

Paul doesn't even take a second to consider my suggestion. 'No, Lucy, that's a terrible idea. It's none of my business. No.'

I can tell from the look on Paul's face that there's no point pursuing this right now, so I drop the subject and reach for the TV remote. Safer to watch television than to talk about relationships anymore.

'What do you want to watch?' I ask as I start flicking through the channels.

'Actually, if you don't mind, I'm going to play on the Xbox.'

'Of course I don't mind,' I tell him. 'Just don't have the volume up too loud.' The playroom is directly under Tom's bedroom, although I don't for a minute think anything would wake Tom after two hours at the soft play centre.

Soon I can hear the sound of shooting coming from the playroom. It is a bit too loud, so I get up and shut the lounge door. I'm relieved to be on my own. *DIY SOS* is on the television, but I'm not really focussed on it. Fetching my laptop from the dining room, I'm soon logged in to my emails. Seeing a message from Rob puts a real smile on my face.

Hi Lucy, thank you so much for trusting me with your email address – I'm really delighted that you want to stay in touch. I'm sorry to hear you had such a bad experience from your meet up. Are you OK? I hope it hasn't put you off completely. We're not all bad, I promise. I can only imagine how daunting this whole thing is for you. It must be pretty scary to meet up with a man you really know nothing about. It's all too easy to say the right things online, isn't it? Anyway, I just wanted to say hi and hope you're OK. I look forward to hearing from you soon, and thanks again. Warmest wishes, Rob xxx.

I want to reply straight away. I refuse to let what happened with James put me off. I have a good feeling about Rob. Of course, I could be completely wrong, and he could be a seventy-year-old train-spotter with a penchant for wearing ladies' underwear, but I have to trust my instincts.

Hi Rob and thanks for your email. I'm OK thanks. Trying not to let one bad experience put me off. Just promise me you're not an axe murderer?! It is all a bit scary I must admit. I think that I'm a bit more savvy now, though, so maybe Mr. Intimidating did me a favour? I will definitely go into any future meetings with my eyes wide open. I think it's impossible to tell from an online chat what someone will be like in real life, isn't it? You can get on brilliantly in this crazy virtual world, but that doesn't mean the same will be true in the real world. And, as a dear friend said to me, you might have to kiss a lot of frogs…! Lucy xx.

I hit send.

I log into Secret Affair next. I can't resist. At the top of my list of new messages is one from the admin team.

Hi Toe Dipper! it reads. *Congratulations, you have unlocked*

152

The Message Board. This is where you can read or post messages about the men you've talked to or met. Here you can share your experiences, good and bad, of potential suitors. It might just help you make up your mind whether he's Mr. Right-for-you or not. We're all about keeping you safe so don't forget to check out our dos and don'ts page. Have fun and stay safe!

I'm intrigued by The Message Board idea and click straight through on the link provided. I'm already wondering if anyone has posted about James, or indeed Rob. A quick search under Rob's username produces no results and I'm relieved. When I type in James's username, however, I'm rewarded with a post.

Steer clear of this guy unless you're into pain and humiliation! it reads. *Don't fall for the charm and good looks, he's a sadistic pig. Please, please, please, let my experience stop anyone else suffering at his hands.*

I realise I'm shaking. I really have had a lucky escape by the sound of it. My instincts about James have been proved right and I shudder as I remember getting into his car. It was stupid and not a mistake I will be repeating. I catch myself: repeating. I'm clearly still thinking about going ahead with another meeting.

Looking back at the message board, I want to see if I can reply to the lady who's posted about James. I feel I need to show solidarity.

So sorry to hear about your awful experience at the hands of this man. Thank you for warning the rest of us. I hope that you find someone wonderful to restore your faith in men. Take care. It's not much, but I want her to know she's not alone. For some reason I don't want to share the fact that I too met with James, but got away relatively unscathed. Physically at least. Some sort of survivor's guilt I think. Besides, her warning is enough without my adding anything. I will definitely be checking The Message Board before I arrange any future meetings.

Flicking back to the tab with my email account, I find a reply from Rob.

Ribbit! he starts, and I laugh out loud. *Lucy, so glad you're OK. You must please promise me that you'll take great care on the site. Don't take any chances, will you? I won't lie, I would dearly love to meet you. I will, however, go entirely at your pace and maybe one day you'll feel comfortable enough to say yes to meeting up. I promise you nothing but my respect, whatever happens. I'm just happy that we're chatting. Rob xxx.*

He seems like a genuinely lovely and sincere man. Bizarrely, it doesn't seem odd that he cares so much about my wellbeing when he doesn't really know me. The shared secret of being on the site brings with it a strange sort of camaraderie. Having Rob in my life, even in this virtual world makes me feel better than I have in ages.

Thank you, Rob. For understanding, and for caring. My instincts tell me you're one of the good guys! I reply. I tell him about The Message Board too, and the post about James. *Don't worry though, no one had posted about you. I'm sure it would only be nice things if they had,* I add.

His reply comes only a minute or two later.

I'm intrigued about this message board. I've never seen anything similar for us men. Maybe they think we don't do sharing?! I could put a cautionary tale or two on there! I suppose it's good that they are doing everything they can to keep you safe. I wonder why they don't block the men who get such damning reviews?

Good question. I suppose one post could just be sour grapes?

And some women might be into the whole 'Fifty Shades' thing. Personally I can't think of anything worse, but it takes all sorts.

Maybe you should put something up about him too, Lucy? They can't ignore two women saying the same thing. And while you're there, you can tell everyone how wonderful I am?! Only joking. I don't think I'll be going back on there now. I'm quite content chatting with you.

Maybe you're right and I should post something. Although, for me it was only a feeling. He didn't actually do anything to hurt me, thank God. I'll give it some thought.

Rob and I chat until I start to feel tired. We say our good-nights and promise to chat again soon, and I log off and put my laptop away. Popping my head into the playroom, I find Paul still engrossed in assassinating people, so I take myself off happily to bed alone.

CHAPTER 31

SADder and badder

As September wears on, the air temperature starts to drop and the onset of autumn announces itself. That awkward time of year when it's getting too cold for flip flops, but it's not yet cold enough to dust off your boots. The reverse happens in the spring, of course. The dilemma of what shoes to wear in that awkward in-between-seasons season.

The inevitable end of summer always makes me a little sad. It means that another long, grey winter is drawing ever closer and must be endured. Somehow. Everything is just that little bit easier when the sun's shining. Bad things don't seem so bad. Winter makes the bad things seem badder. Yes, I know badder's not a word, but that's what winter does. It messes things up. Even more than usual.

I'm driving home from yet another Monday morning school drop-off, and Heart 80s is failing to cheer me up. They're playing The Bangles' 'Eternal Flame' and it's dreary and depressing. The windows are closed for the first time this month and I'm seriously considering putting the heated seat on. I don't want to go home and my entire body feels like one big sigh waiting to happen: I'd be like a deflated balloon if the sigh ever escaped my lips.

I come up to a junction in the road: one direction takes me

home, to Paul. The other takes me to the park. And possibility. I don't choose home and in a couple of minutes I'm in the car park. I don't get out or switch off the engine. The radio is playing 'Hold Me Now' by The Thompson Twins and I'm transported backwards in time to my bedroom in 1983. It's a song so full of memories, of teenage angst and tears, and I can feel every ounce of that emotion again now. Hands are squeezing my heart, my throat, and the inevitable tears trickle down my face. I let them flow, not bothering to wipe them away. I'm kind of hoping for some sort of cathartic release from them, I think.

Release doesn't come, just sadness. I feel just as lost and hopeless as I did at fifteen when unrequited teenage love felt like the end of the world. I have love now. I know Paul loves me. The unrequitement is on my side this time. I wish it wasn't. I wish Paul didn't love me. It's a painful admission. The silent tears continue unabated, but I brush at them now with the back of my hand. I'm tired of crying. I'm tired of lying. Of living a lie, at least. Sadness starts to turn. To resentment. I grab onto it with both hands. 'God damn it!' The expletive escapes my lips and I realise I've been gripping the steering wheel so hard my fingers hurt. I let go and take a deep breath. I refuse to feel like this anymore.

I ferret in my jeans pocket for a tissue, hoping to find a clean one with which to wipe my face and blow my nose. Assessing the damage in the rear view mirror, I'm not too distressed by what I see. My eyes are a little red, but I have escaped the puffiness that real sobbing brings. The radio DJ has obliged with a song that always lifts me: 'My World' by Secret Affair and I can't help but chuckle as I log into my emails. I'm taking it as a sign: an omen. It seems to me as good a reason as any to do what I'm about to do.

I email Rob. *Let's meet. Soon. X.*

Nothing more. And then I wait.

I feel calm now that I've made a decision. It might prove to be a terrible decision, but it doesn't really matter.

I don't have to wait long for a reply and my heart quickens with anticipation as I click on it.

Lucy, I would love that. If you're sure? Xxx

Yes, I'm very sure. For the first time in ages. When are you free? X

I can clear my diary any day that works for you. Xxx Rob includes his mobile number. It's escalating. It's getting close. Real.

Tuesdays are best for me. During school time. Xx. I start typing my mobile number and then hear Clare's warning voice in my head. I ignore it. I'm feeling a little reckless right now. I recognise it's dangerous, but I simply don't care. I enter the rest of the eleven numbers and press send. I'm acutely aware of the blood pumping through my veins right now, making me feel vital, really alive.

My phone soon alerts me to a text message.

Tomorrow? Or is that too soon? I will admit I'm impatient to meet you. You have no idea of the enormous smile I have on my face right now. Xxx.

Yes, tomorrow. I don't want to wait any longer. I guess we just need a where and when. Any ideas? Xx.

I'll have a think. Is it ok to text you any time? I can email if not. Xxx.

Might be better to email for now if that's OK? Just in case. Xx.

OK, I'll come up with a plan and email you later. Thank you,

Lucy. You've made an old man very happy! Xxxx

Good. I hope you still feel like that after we meet. Catch you later. Xx.

Rob's comment about making an old man happy gives me a moment's pause as I remember his online profile and picture, and how much older he'd looked than the stated forty-six years. Then I think about James, with his devastating good looks, and the entry on The Message Board about him being a sadist. I know better than to judge a person on their looks now and resolve to keep an open mind about Rob. I just know I have to meet him. And find out one way or the other.

I can face going home now. I have something to look forward to; a secret that will sustain me through the day and enable me to keep up the act for a while longer. I turn out of the car park and once more head for home.

Once home I make coffee for Paul and head upstairs to the office, hoping he won't notice I've been crying. He's not the most observant of men so I'm not too worried. He looks up from his computer as I walk in.

'There you are. Thought I was going to have to make my own coffee there for a minute.' I know he's only joking, but I still feel a small pang of guilt.

'Sorry, got chatting to Clare at school – you know what we're like.' The lie comes too easily.

'Do I ever,' Paul says. 'I don't know what you find to talk about when you see each other every day.'

'Oh, you know, just how demanding our husbands are… expecting coffee every five minutes.'

'Watch it, you! You don't know how lucky you are to be married to a god like me.' Paul winks at me and I can't help laughing.

'Yeah, yeah! And your body is a temple that should be worshipped at daily,' I throw back automatically. I regret the words as soon as they're out of my mouth.

'Well, now you come to mention it…' Paul grins at me.

'Calm down, Buddha. Think of your blood pressure. Anyway, you will have to make your own coffee tomorrow – I've promised to go shopping with Clare again. She's still looking for a wedding outfit. Tom's late finish, so you can pick him up if I'm not back in time.'

'Who's the demanding one now then? I'm just the poor downtrodden husband.'

'Yeah, yeah, pass the violin.'

The banter between us is real, but it hides both lies and undesirable truths. I need to end it.

'Right, slave, back to work. The washing machine demands my attention.' I leave the room, pulling the door to behind me.

CHAPTER 32

Tuesday yawning

It feels like I've only just fallen asleep when the alarm goes off at six thirty the next morning. In truth I probably had as I was too excited and nervous to sleep. My mind had been spinning with the endless possibilities of Tuesday. And meeting Rob for the first time.

I know I must manage my expectations of our first encounter. There may simply be no chemistry between us. After all, I wasn't blown away by his photograph. Whatever happens, though, I hope to have a very special new friend in my life. And maybe that will be enough; something and someone who's just for me. Oh, and his wife of course. But you know what I mean… something that's nothing to do with the rest of my life. My real life.

Paul is already downstairs making tea, so I head for the bathroom. Standing in the shower sudsing up my hair a few minutes later I let my mind drift to my last email exchange with Rob. I'd managed to find some time yesterday evening while Paul was playing with Tom to find out the arrangements for today.

Hi Lucy. Right… I have a plan in mind for tomorrow. It's only a suggestion and I'm more than happy to go along with whatever you want. The most important thing here is that you feel comfortable. There's a rather lovely country house and gardens about forty-five minutes from you, and they are still open until the end of October. I've been there many times and they have a stunning café in the old Orangery. How does that sound? I can be there from ten o'clock onwards. It's easy to find and to park and hopefully far enough from home for you to feel anonymous! Let me know. I can't wait. Rob xxxx.

I knew the house Rob meant: Claremont House. It had once been home to an eminent Romantic poet and locally had become known as Lovelorn House due to the owner's unrequited love which had subsequently led to his tragic death. I'd never actually visited the place, but knew the sad story associated with it. It was either the perfect choice for our encounter or the absolute worst: I wasn't sure which and decided to reserve judgment.

I was more than happy with Rob's plan and was touched at the thought that had obviously gone into it.

Hi Rob. That all sounds perfect – thank you for thinking of everything. I should be able to get there for ten o'clock too, traffic permitting. I hope it's not too much further for you to come? I've always wanted to visit Claremont. You do know they say the grounds are haunted, I suppose? I can't wait either, I'm so looking forward to meeting you. Lucy xxx.

That's great, glad you approve. The weather forecast is favourable too so we might be able to have a wander round the gardens if you'd like? Assuming you haven't been scared off on sight?! Tomorrow morning can't come soon enough.

I'm sure we'll get on like a house on fire. We'll know very soon. Until tomorrow.

I won't lie, Lucy, I'm hoping for sparks. But rest assured, I will behave like the perfect gentleman I am. Unless, or until, you tell me otherwise… Goodnight, lovely lady.

Smiling here. Goodnight, Rob.

And now the day is here. I take a little more care over drying my hair today, and pluck out a couple of greys that dare to sparkle in the sunshine of the bedroom mirror. And I take a little more time over my face too; a pale purple shadow under my eyes from my sleepless night requires a few dabs of concealer. I want to look fresh and natural, rather than made-up, and I'm pretty happy with the end result. When I go in to wake Tom up at seven fifteen he tells me I look pretty. And that he loves me. I bundle him into my arms.

'I love you too, Tom. More than anything in the whole wide world. And I always will,' I tell him.

We stay like that for a minute and I breathe in the scent of his hair, absorbing the warmth of his little body and feeling the beating of his little heart against me. I experience a moment of discomfort as I remember what I'm doing today and make a silent vow that whatever happens, it will not impact this little boy, this piece of me that matters more than my own life.

I squeeze Tom a little tighter before we separate and I pass him his dinosaur dressing gown from the hook on his bedroom door.

'Let's go and get breakfast,' I say, and we walk downstairs hand in hand. The balls of dust have once more gathered in the treads but I choose to ignore them today, with more pressing matters on my mind.

The morning routine takes over for the next forty-five minutes. Paul is at his desk by eight, having hugged his son goodbye and told his wife to enjoy shopping.

163

'I've got a call first thing, so don't shout goodbye when you leave,' he tells us.

'OK. Don't forget you're picking Tom up at four fifteen if I'm not back,' I remind him as he heads for the stairs. 'I'll text you either way. Have a good day.'

His answer is lost as he turns onto the landing.

Tom and I finish getting ready for our respective days, and I have to acknowledge the butterflies in my tummy as they begin to flutter in earnest. I'm feeling more than a little anxious after my encounter with James, but am trusting my instincts that Rob is one of the good guys. Anyway, we're meeting in a public place and I will be careful. No more getting into a strange man's car for me. That reminds me, I need to let Clare know what's happening.

I catch up with Clare at school.

'Looking forward to our shopping trip today?' I ask her.

She looks confused. Then the penny drops.

'Oh my God! You're meeting someone. Spill,' she says nudging my arm.

'It's Rob. You know, Surrey solicitor who looks older than forty-six?'

'Ooh! Yay! He sounded nice. Where are you meeting?'

I give Clare the details.

'That's one of my favourite places – Greg and I used to go there a lot when we were first together. It's really romantic.'

'Oh lordy, is it? I thought it might be a bit depressing given its history.'

'No, quite the opposite. It's idyllic.' Clare looks wistful. 'I'm excited for you, Lucy, but please be careful. And DO NOT get into his bloody car. I don't care if he drives a Ferrari!'

I laugh. 'I won't, I promise. Cross my heart.'

'You'd better not. I will not be happy with you.'

'I'll be careful, truly.' I'm touched by how much she cares. 'Please don't worry about me.'

'Hmm. Easier said than done. Text me when you can to let me know you're OK.'

'I will.' I hug Clare as we say our goodbyes.

'Have a wonderful time. I really hope Rob's as nice as he sounds.'

'Thanks, Clare. Have a good day and I'll catch you later.'

And I'm back behind the wheel, taking a deep breath and setting off into the unknown.

It's a ten-minute drive to the motorway and then a straight road almost all the way to Claremont. Once again I'm grateful to Rob for being so considerate in his planning. He seemed to know instinctively that logistical things like parking caused me stress.

As usual Heart 80s accompanies me on my journey: my musical comfort zone and apparently with a song to suit every occasion. With his unfailing link to my psyche, the DJ's playing 'Something About You' by Level 42. I can't resist singing along. There really is something about Rob and I hope it is something so right.

CHAPTER 33

Rob

I've arrived. I'm early, as usual, and the car park is empty of other cars. Not surprising really as Claremont House doesn't open its doors until ten a.m. So much for the safety of meeting in a public place. I've already checked my reflection a dozen times; there's nothing I can do except wait.

I don't have to wait long though. Just five minutes later, a sleek black Mercedes Coupe slinks into the car park. I know instinctively it's Rob before I even catch sight of the driver. My heart is drumming in my chest – in my head it's loud enough to drown out the purr of the car's engine as it draws nearer and pulls into the space next to me. I take a deep breath and turn to look at Rob. He's looking at me. He's smiling. I smile back, an unsteady breath escaping my lips. His smile grows wider, reassuring me. He knows I'm nervous.

I feel unsure about what to do next. We can't gain access to the house for another fifteen minutes and we can't possibly sit in separate cars until then. Rob gets out of his car and I roll down my window. In the couple of seconds it's taken him to get out and step over to my car, I've taken in his full height, his slim frame, long legs encased in light blue denim, rolled up shirt sleeves revealing tanned forearms. He moves effortlessly, with the ease of a man happy in his own skin, confident of his place in the world. My eyes reach his face just as he crouches down to window-height. It's a rather lovely face: tanned and slightly rugged, with the crinkly laughter lines of someone who loves life and the outdoors. He's still smiling broadly, and that smile reaches his deep brown eyes.

'Lucy, hi, it's so good to meet you. How are you feeling? Are you still OK with this?'

His voice is quite deep, but soft and cultured. The combination of this and his smiling eyes is a heady one.

'Hi. I'm OK thanks. Nervous, but OK. It is really lovely to meet you too.' I'm relieved to have got the words out successfully. I don't know what to do next, whether to suggest Rob gets in my car. I needn't worry. Rob is reading my mind.

'As we're both here early, why don't we find a bench to sit on and wait? They know me here so I'm sure it won't be a problem. I once did some work for the owner – saved him a small fortune.'

I'm grateful to Rob for taking control of the situation, and he steps aside as I get out of my car, all too aware that he must be assessing me as I had him. I find myself fervently hoping that he likes what he sees. I too have kept my clothes casual: cropped white jeans, a cornflower blue shirt which ties at the waist and wedge-heeled sandals. I'm thankful that the predicted good weather has prevailed. I grab my bag and cardigan and then Rob and I are facing each other, neither speaking, just standing. And smiling.

'This way.' Rob, taking control once more as he gestures towards the gates.

As we walk side by side I'm powerfully aware of his maleness. But it's somehow reassuring rather than threatening. Unlike with James, I'm not hearing warning bells.

We don't speak again until we're seated on an ornate bench just through a small side gate which apparently the staff use to gain admission. Looking around I can see a couple of gardeners in the distance but we are otherwise quite alone. Should I be alarmed, I wonder? I hear Clare's cautionary words again, but I feel no fear. Nothing about the man sitting beside me feels frightening. Quite the opposite in fact. I feel strangely calm and very much at ease.

Rob speaks first again: 'Thank you for this, Lucy, for agreeing to meet me. I know it can't have been an easy decision after your last encounter.'

'Thank you for making me want to do this again. Once bitten and all that.'

'I want you to know that there's absolutely no pressure today. Let's just enjoy each other's company and see how we both feel. Sound good?'

'Sounds very good. You certainly picked a beautiful spot to meet.' The bench looks out over manicured lawns and lushly planted borders to acres of rolling green parkland as far as the eye can see. Clare was right, it's idyllic.

'I love it here – come whenever I can get away. It's my thinking place.'

'I can understand that. It's somewhere I've always wanted to visit, but somehow never got round to. I'm very glad to be here now.'

'I knew you'd like it. I sense you have the soul of a poet, Lucy. And no one with a good heart can fail to be moved by Claremont.'

'I thought it might feel sad here – you know, given its history and the Lovelorn nickname.'

'I've never found it to be so. And I've never encountered the ghost of William Clare either.'

I'd been gazing at the stunning vista laid out before us, and when I turn back to Rob he's looking at me intently.

'You really are very beautiful, Lucy.'

I can feel my cheeks flush as I stammer out a thank you.

'You are. And I'm very honoured that you agreed to meet me. I hope you're not disappointed now you've met me?'

'Goodness, no! Quite the opposite in fact.' My shyness is dissipating and I'm relaxing into Rob's presence. 'I had a good feeling about you and I'm glad I trusted my instincts.'

'I'm so glad you did too.' As Rob says this, he's looking at his watch. I follow his eyes to an understated watch with a brown leather strap. It suits him. There's nothing flashy about Rob. It makes me like him even more. 'Right, let's head to the orangery and get a coffee. They do amazing homemade cakes too if I can tempt you? The carrot cake is particularly good.'

I'm thinking that this man could probably tempt me to pretty much anything.

'Ooh, carrot cake is my absolute favourite. You can definitely tempt me to that.' The other thoughts remain unspoken. For now, at least.

'Splendid,' Rob says as he stands up. He reaches out for my hand, the perfect gentleman as promised, just taking it while I get up, with no expectation of us holding hands as we walk.

Rob leads the way along a path which takes us around the far side of the magnificent manor house to the orangery which houses the café. I'm aware of a synchronicity in our strides; we somehow match. It's hard to explain, but I just know that if we walked holding hands it would feel right; we would fit.

The orangery takes my breath away as we round the corner and it appears in all its glassy beauty. Rob holds open the door for me to enter and I step into a little piece of paradise. It's full of lush shrubs and foliage, citrus trees and orchids. The fragrance is intoxicating. Chairs and tables are placed at discreet intervals amongst the plants – it really is the perfect setting for a romantic tryst. Rob guides me past an ornate fountain to a cast iron table and two chairs hidden amongst jasmine and citrus.

'This is my favourite table. Is it OK for you?'

'It's absolutely perfect. Thank you,' I say as Rob pulls a chair out for me. I want to tell him that it couldn't be more perfect and that he couldn't be more perfect. We've only been in each other's company for about fifteen minutes, but it already feels as though something wonderful might be happening between us.

Rob hands me a menu and I study it for a few seconds, but I already know what I want. He's not on the menu though. I smile to myself, and when I look up Rob is looking at me quizzically. I just laugh and shake my head.

'I'd like a filter coffee, please. With milk. And an enormous slice of carrot cake.'

'Coming right up,' Rob says and he pushes back his chair and heads over to the counter which is situated at the far end of the orangery, not too far from our table. I can just about make out the brief conversation as Rob places our order. There's a slightly plump middle-aged lady serving.

'Good morning Mr. Clare, how lovely to see you again. What can I get for you today?' she asks.

Did I hear that right? I wonder. Did she just call Rob Mr. Clare? I shake the thought away. I must have misheard her. It's a strange realisation though, that I don't know Rob's last name. Nor he mine for that matter. It brings home the bizarre nature of the dating site. Does it make any difference? I ask myself. The question remains unanswered as Rob arrives back at our table. I don't mention the surname thing; I figure if he wants me to know, he'll tell me.

'It's a good thing we got here early,' Rob is saying. 'Apparently they've got some coach parties booked in later.'

'I'm glad we beat the rush then. Still, it's good for the business.'

'Indeed. So, Lucy, how are you feeling now? More relaxed, I hope?'

'I'm feeling surprisingly relaxed actually. How about you? I can't imagine you ever suffering from nerves.'

Rob laughs. 'You'd be surprised how nervous I was about meeting you today. I guess I've learned how to hide my nerves over the years. Nature of the job somewhat too.'

'Yes, of course. Do you enjoy your job?'

'On the whole. I'm not sure I'd choose the law if I could go back and do it all again though.'

'What would you have done instead?'

'Something outdoorsy – landscape gardening perhaps. How about you? What would your dream job be?'

'Oh, I don't know… watching you landscape garden maybe.' The words are out of my mouth before the filters kick in and I feel suddenly shy again. I needn't have worried though as Rob is grinning broadly.

'I'd have to take lots of breaks then to come and keep you company,' he says.

'You'd never get the jobs done,' I say with a smile.

'Be worth it to spend more time with you.'

'When do we start?' My confidence is returning once more and I can't resist flirting with Rob.

'Twenty years ago,' comes the reply.

I'm a little taken aback and don't know what to say. This is all happening so crazily fast. But it doesn't feel wrong. Instead of speaking, I reach over and put my hand on Rob's. I lift my eyes to his and we just sit like that, our gazes locked, neither speaking. Rob turns his hand under mine and locks our fingers together with a squeeze. I feel the pressure travel to my throat, my chest. It's as though a circuit just completed and the power began to flow. Before either of us can acknowledge what's happening, the lady arrives with our coffees. I pull my hand away, hoping she hasn't spotted us holding hands. She might know that Rob's married. And not to me.

I turn my focus to putting milk and sugar in my coffee. As I stir, I'm thinking about the fact that Rob is married. And that I am too. I should be feeling guilty. But I'm not. As I analyse all the things I'm feeling right now, guilt is not one of them. Excitement, anticipation – I'm feeling both of them. But more than that. I'm feeling pure, unadulterated joy. I know that's an ironic choice of word, but it's how I feel. And I haven't felt like this for a really long time.

'Penny for them?' As Rob speaks, he's placing his hand on mine. I'm still holding the teaspoon, stirring absentmindedly. 'I think the sugar's probably all dissolved now!' He's smiling at me again. It's like he's inside my head, reading my thoughts.

'Oh! Sorry. Miles away there for a minute.'

'Well, wherever you were, I hope I was there too.'

'You know what? I think you probably were. Am I imagining what's happening here, between us?'

'Well, if you're imagining it, then I am too, so I guess that makes it real. And rather amazing.'

CHAPTER 34

Pinch me

We sit in companionable silence for a while. There's no awkwardness about the silence, no feeling the need to say something to fill the void. Apart from appreciative noises over the wonderful cake, no words pass between us until coffee is drunk and cake finished.

'That was delicious,' I say as I lay my pastry fork on the plate and sit back in my chair with a contented smile.

Rob laughs. 'You're delicious, Lucy.'

I think we're both blushing.

'Sorry,' Rob continues, 'that was so corny! But you are, delicious and delightful. And probably dangerous to my sanity.'

His words puzzle me. 'Why dangerous?' I ask.

'Because I'm quite sure that I will fall in love with you.' Rob shrugs his shoulders and smiles a slightly melancholic smile that goes straight to my heart. I reach out for both his hands. I don't have any adequate words.

The moment passes as Rob quickly regains his composure.

'Right, how about I show you around the gardens?'

As we get up to leave, we both call out a thank you to the lady who served us. Rob knows her by name, and my curiosity is piqued once more. I shake the thought away: he told me he's a regular visitor here. Rob once more holds open the door for me and we head out into the garden.

Rob picks a path leading further away from the orangery and the main house. There are still no other visitors in sight, but I feel no anxiety at our aloneness.

'You must come back in the spring, Lucy. There's a forty-foot long pergola which is absolutely smothered in wisteria. In fact, you should come back several times over the course of the year: the seasonal changes are stunning.' Rob's voice and face are full of animation. He clearly adores it here and his passion for the place is obvious. It's yet another aspect of the man that I find incredibly attractive. I find myself thinking that I want him to feel as passionately about me as he obviously does about Claremont. It's madness. We've just met.

As we continue to walk side by side, I slip my hand into Rob's. He acknowledges with a small squeeze, but neither of us speaks. It feels right, as I knew it would. We have that synchronicity I instinctively knew we would. We simply have to be connected, to be touching. I don't stop to analyse what's happening, although I'm sure I will later. This is all about doing what feels right; obeying our instincts. And mine are screaming that this man, whose hand I'm holding, is meant to be with me.

We soon reach the end of the formal gardens and we stop and look back the way we've just walked. I hadn't realised how far we'd walked; I've been so lost in Rob's voice and presence.

'It's stunning,' I say, turning to look at Rob. He's not looking at the view though, but at me. My heart does that little skippy thing again. He has such an effect on me – quite unlike anything I've ever experienced before. It should be unnerving, unsettling, but it's simply wonderful.

'Let me show you the folly – you'll love it; it's not much further on. If you'd like that, of course.'

'I'd like that very much. I'm very happy to let you be my guide.' I squeeze his hand again and Rob returns the pressure. It makes me smile. He makes me smile.

We set off across the park and it's not long before a small circular building comes into view. It's a stone confection of columns rising out of a floor and up to a ceiling, but with no walls. Just a perfect bit of nonsense which I love immediately.

'I do love a folly,' I tell Rob. 'I love the idea of building something with absolutely no purpose, but just because you want to, because it took your fancy.'

As I say these last words I know exactly what Rob's thinking and I look up at his face and laugh.

'Reading my mind, eh, Lucy? I'm resisting the urge to state the obvious, but you really do take my fancy,' he says with a laugh.

I'm feeling braver with every minute spent in Rob's company and I don't hesitate in my reply.

'Good, because I would hate to think this was one-sided.'

Rob smiles at me, the crinkles around his eyes deepening, his eyes sparkling. He looks kind of emotional for a split second, but then pulls his hand out of mine and sets off at a slow run.

'Last one to the folly buys lunch!' he calls out.

I laugh and set off in pursuit. It's quite obvious that Rob has no intention of letting me lose and I arrive at the funny little building a couple of seconds before him, slightly out of breath, but smiling from the exertion. It felt so good to be free and childish and silly. Rob jumps up onto the old stone floor to join me. And then I'm in his arms. And we're kissing. And

I never want this moment to end.

There is no awkwardness in our first kiss: it feels like the most natural thing in the world and it awakens senses in me long-forgotten or disused. I feel tendrils of desire curling through every part of me, like the jasmine in the orangery, and I feel heady the way its scent made me feel. Rob's hands are cradling my face as he kisses me, on and on, deeply and passionately, his eyes tightly shut when I briefly open mine. There is a hunger, almost a desperation in his kisses, like a starving man given food after so long a time without. I return his kisses with equal appetite and press my body against his, desperate to close any gaps that dare to come between us. I can feel his hardness against me and I know that he wants me as much as I want him.

We don't pull apart when the kiss ends, but cling to each other. It's as though our lives depend on it, each the other's life raft on a stormy sea. I never want to let go of him. I can feel his heart pounding and racing in his chest and I place my hand there, feeling the power of him travel through me. I have to catch my breath as emotion threatens to overcome me. I lift my head and our eyes lock, communication with words is redundant in this moment; our eyes say everything we're thinking and feeling.

Rob places his hands each side of my face again and leans down to kiss me once more, tenderly this time, without the hunger, but the intensity is the same. The response in my body is the same. I am in awe of the way this man makes me feel. I can't tell you how amazing it feels to want someone again.

I realise that I'm feeling a bit shaky from the pure rush of emotion. 'Can we sit down for a minute?' I ask. 'I'm feeling a bit wobbly.'

Rob's face immediately registers concern. 'Oh, yes, of course. Are you OK?'

'I'm more than OK,' I reassure him. 'I'm absolutely amazing. That was amazing. You're amazing. Just wow. Sorry, I'm not being very eloquent right now. I think I'm in some sort of wonderful shock.'

'It was amazing. You're amazing. We're amazing. I guess I'm in the same state of shock as you,' Rob says with a smile as he leads me to the edge of the folly to sit down.

'Do you think there's any cure for it? This state of shock,' I ask. 'I'm not convinced hot sweet tea will do the trick.'

'Now there's a question. I guess all we can do is keep kissing and see what happens. I think maybe we'll have to persevere for quite some time though to find out.'

'I think you're right. Amazing.'

'Yes. It is. It's amazing.'

CHAPTER 35

Pinch me harder

I don't know how long we sat like that, not talking, just being. Being at one. Being at peace. With ourselves, with each other. With the world. Nothing can intrude, nothing can come between us. We exist in a beautiful little bubble world, impenetrable to all else. It's not real, I know, but right now this fantasy, this man, this feeling is all encompassing and I refuse to let the real world burst the bubble, with its piercing judgments and its harshness.

I realise eventually that my back has started to ache: I hadn't wanted to acknowledge it I think, and disturb our peace. I arch it and stretch out the muscles.

'You too, eh?' Rob says. 'My back's killing me, but I didn't want to say anything when this feels so good.'

'We're a right pair,' I laugh as Rob stands up and reaches out his hands to pull me up.

'We certainly are,' he agrees. 'Let's go and find somewhere a bit more comfortable to sit.'

Taking his hand feels like the most natural thing in the world as we walk back in the direction of the house. It's hard to explain this connection that we have. If I believed in such things I would say that our souls have met before, in some previous life, and have simply been biding their time, safe in the knowledge that they would find one another again, some-time, somewhere. There is an inevitability about our meeting. A rightness. I know, I know, how can this be right, when we're both married, but it's how it feels.

I'm more than content to follow where Rob leads. Any resid-ual anxiety or fear has long since evaporated, and I feel only a deep sense of joy and peace in his presence. I already trust him implicitly. The path we re-join takes us further on from the orangery to some rather wonderful old greenhouses. Rob leads the way to an old wooden bench tucked away between two of the glasshouses. It's a relief to sit down and lean back. We sit close, our thighs touching; I can feel his body heat through double denim, his jeans and mine. We're holding hands – it's impossible not to.

Rob's holding my left hand and I feel him twist the band of gold on my ring finger. When I glance up at him, he's looking sad, and maybe wistful. I don't want to be reminded of the fact that I'm married. I don't want that thought in our bubble. It belongs outside. I put my free hand over his to stop him.

'I know.' It's all I can say. All I need to say.

'This is crazy, Lucy. We only just met, but I feel like I've known you my whole life. Or been waiting for you. Something… I don't know. How can it feel so right?' I can hear the confusion in his voice.

'I don't have an answer to that. I only know that I feel the same. I feel like I've been holding my breath for such a long time, and only now can I breathe.'

'Yes! It's the same for me. It's the difference between existing and living. I feel alive with you. And it feels sublime.'

'Let's just enjoy whatever it is that's happening between us, be in the moment, and not think about the bigger picture, the future.' I sound more sensible than I feel.

'You're right, of course. Sorry, Lucy, I didn't mean to bring the mood down... Just the sight of your ring... you know...'

'Yes, I do. But this is something separate, something apart from our other lives. It's the only way I can get my head around what we're doing.'

'I understand. And the last thing I want is to be the cause of any upset. I hope you know I would never to anything to hurt you, or to jeopardise things for you. But I can't help wishing things were different or that we'd met a lifetime ago.'

'I think we probably did,' I say with a wistful smile.

Rob doesn't say anything, just raises my hand to his lips and kisses it.

'So, what happens next?' I ask.

'What happens next is that I treat you to a wonderful lunch somewhere. After all, I lost the race to the folly.'

I laugh. 'You completely threw the race to the folly, you mean?'

'Maybe just a little bit. But let me spoil you. Nothing would give me greater pleasure.'

'Well, if you insist then I accept gracefully.'

'Good. I have been a bit cheeky and booked somewhere – just in case things went well between us. I hope you're not offended?'

'Not at all. I appreciate the thought you've taken over today. It's been simply perfect.'

'Right, well the restaurant's only a short drive from here. Are you happy to come in my car? I'd completely understand if you wanted to drive there in yours.'

Clare pops into my head right on cue, but I take no notice.

'I'm happy to go in one car. Will mine be alright in the car park here?'

'Yes, absolutely fine. You'll have to forgive my taste in music though. I'm a closet 80s fan – only get to listen to it in the car.'

I pull a face of mock horror before admitting to him that my car stereo is always tuned in to Heart80s.

'Really? God, you really are the perfect woman!' Rob looks genuinely delighted. 'My wife insists on Classic FM at all times.' The words are out of his mouth before he can stop them and he looks distraught when he sees the effect on me.

'Damn, Lucy, sorry. I'm so sorry.'

I shake my head. 'Please, don't apologise. We both know the score. It's stupid of me to think we can pretend our real lives don't exist.' I want to make him feel better. But the truth is that the mention of his wife has shaken me a little. Her presence in the bubble is unwelcome. She's a reminder that what we're doing is wrong. And would hurt her if she found out. It's the first pang of guilt I've felt today, and it's naturally made me think of Paul too. The sadness is obviously showing on my face.

'I've really messed up, haven't I?' Rob looks sad too.

'We'll get past it. Please don't feel bad. This is all new to me and it's going to take some getting used to. I think maybe we have to make the rules up as we go along? Maybe we *should* talk about our real lives? Trying to pretend they don't exist might actually be a bad idea. If we can't be open and honest with each other, then what sort of relationship will it be?'

'You might be right. I just don't want to do anything to hurt you.'

'And I know you wouldn't intentionally hurt me, I really do.

I think we should be as open and honest as possible. About everything. Otherwise we'll be constantly worried about saying the wrong thing. What do you think?'

'I think you're a very wise and wonderful woman, and that I am a very lucky man.'

'Well, before you realise what an utter crazy woman I am, let's go and get that lunch you promised.'

We set off for the car park, hand in hand.

CHAPTER 36

The Mulberry Tree

It's the next day now and I'm still in the bubble. I'm function-ing on some kind of autopilot and have managed to deliver Tom safely to school, whilst really having little idea of how we got here. Clare comes running the second she sees me and practically pushes Chloe into the playground, so eager is she to catch up on my news. I can't help laughing as Chloe looks back indignantly at her mum.

Clare relents and blows her a kiss: 'Have a lovely day, sweet-heart,' she says with a wave, before turning straight back to me. 'Well?'

'Well, your daughter just gave you a filthy look,' I say with a chuckle.

'Oh, she'll get over it. She's been a right little madam this morning. Her teacher's welcome to her.'

'You do realise she's probably angelic for Mrs Price?'

Clare sighs. 'No doubt. Anyway, now that she's out of my hair, we have more important things to talk about. I want to know everything.'

'Oh, Clare, it was amazing. We had the best day.'

Clare claps her hands together in prayer position and raises them to her lips. Withdrawing her hands from her face, she then grasps mine. 'Oh my God, Lucy! Really? I'm so excited for you. I was really worried about you yesterday – thank you for texting me to let me know you got home safely.'

'I'm sorry you were worried. I hate the idea that what I'm doing to find happiness causes you worry. It's the last thing I want.'

'Don't give it another thought. It's a small price to pay to see you smiling again. Have you got time to talk now?'

'I have, but could we meet in the park in about half an hour? I feel after my absence yesterday that I ought to pop home, make Paul a drink and grab the hound.'

'Yes, of course. I can't wait to hear all about Rob.'

Thirty or so minutes later and we're reunited on a picnic bench outside the café in the park. We can't take Alfie inside, so Clare has been in and fetched coffees. Alfie has been here before and has flopped down under the table, resigned to the fact that we won't be walking anywhere anytime soon.

Clare is now looking at me expectantly.

'I don't know where to start, really…' my voice tapers off as I am transported back to Claremont and to thoughts of Rob.

'At the beginning will be just fine. Although judging by the soppy look on your face, I think I know everything I need to,' Clare says with a grin.

'Yep. You might need a sick bag,' I joke back.

'I'll risk it. If it gets too sickening, I'll just leave.'

I laugh. 'You would too, wouldn't you? That's just one of the many things I love about you – you're true to yourself and don't give a stuff what other people think.'

'Hmm… I suppose that's true to a degree… anyway, don't change the subject. Start talking or the dog gets it.'

'OK, OK… well, he doesn't drive a Ferrari… and I think I might just have found my soulmate.'

'Blimey O'Reilly.' Clare looks a little stunned.

'Honestly though, Clare, it was perfect from the moment we set eyes on each other. He's much better looking in real life for starters – yes, he does have lines on his face and is kind of… I dunno… weathered looking, but it just makes him even more attractive.'

Clare says nothing, just indicates that I should carry on.

'He has these soulful eyes and a voice that sends shivers up and down my spine. Long legs and strong, tanned arms…' I'm picturing Rob in my mind's eye as I speak, and I close my eyes to feel closer to him, drifting into a sort of reverie.

'Earth to Lucy,' Clare's words break through and I open my eyes to see her grinning at me. 'Bloody Nora, you have got it bad. You only just met him though, Lucy.'

'I know. It doesn't make sense to me either, but there's such a powerful attraction between us. And I don't just mean physically. I hate to sound cheesy, but it was kind of spiritual. It's as if we already knew each other, or were meant to meet. Something. I don't know. I can't explain it. I can only tell you how right it felt to be with him.' I look at Clare, wondering if she understands what I'm saying and if it makes any sense at all.

'Wow.' Clare looks stunned.

'I know. Wow pretty much sums it up.'

'I don't want to burst your bubble, just playing devil's avocado here, but you don't think you're just seeing and feeling what you want – you know, because of how unhappy you are with Paul? I just don't want to see you get hurt.'

I feel no resentment at Clare's words. I know that she only has the best of intentions. 'I know what you're saying and I understand, but I genuinely believe there is something special about Rob, about him and me. I probably will get hurt though. I think we both will and I think he knows that already too.'

Clare looks at me questioningly.

'We'll fall in love. I think we already did. A bit.' I smile a wistful smile and shrug my shoulders. 'It can only end in heartbreak, can't it? After all, we're married.' I'm surprised by how calm I feel about how inevitable the pain is.

'Oh my God, Lucy. Why would you put yourself through that? If you know you're going to get hurt already?'

'Why? Because I feel alive and because I'm so sure that the pleasure will be worth the pain. I want to experience the highs, even if it means terrible lows too. I know it's crazy,' I say with another shrug.

'It is crazy. You're crazy. But we knew that already. So, madness aside, tell me all about yesterday.'

I start at the beginning and relive every second of the day for Clare.

'So, what happened when you got back to the car park? Did you go in one car? You bloody did, didn't you?!'

'Er... yep. I know, I know, I promised I wouldn't, but I didn't have any of the doubts I had with James. I trust Rob, I really do.'

'You're a bloody nightmare, woman. What am I going to do with you?' Clare looks a little exasperated.

'Trust me to do the right thing? I'll be fine, Clare, I promise,' I try to reassure.

Clare sighs resignedly. 'Go on then, where did he take you for lunch?'

'The Mulberry Tree. Do you know it? It's in the middle of nowhere.'

'God! First you get in his car, and then he drives you out to the middle of nowhere. Great!' Clare winks at me to let me know she's only joking. Sort of.

'Well, anyway, it looks rather like someone's house from the front, but then you go inside and it's all wooden floors and contemporary tables and chairs and really tastefully decorated. Turned out Rob had booked a table in the garden.'

'Lucky the weather was good then.'

'Yep. Anyway, the table in the garden turned out to be a wooden gazebo with a tiled roof – it was really pretty, and the seats were all covered with crimson and purple cushions. It was kind of Moroccan I suppose – really pretty and ever so romantic.'

'Sounds gorgeous.'

'It was. Honestly, he couldn't have picked a better location. I was really touched at how much thought he put into everything.'

'Careful, I might be needing that sick bag. He sounds too good to be true.'

'Well, he is married, so I guess that's a fairly fatal flaw.'

'Good point,' Clare said, picking up her cup and having a glug of coffee. I realise I haven't touched mine. 'So, what was the food like?'

'Lovely. I think. To be honest, I couldn't really concentrate on what I was eating. I think I remember Rob telling me the restaurant's got a Michelin star. Or two. Or it could have been two AA Rosettes. I think I was a little bit away with the fairies.'

'You're not kidding. This guy really has bowled you over, hasn't he?'

'Yes. Completely and utterly. I can't wait to see him again.'

'Have you arranged your next meeting? What did you do after lunch? How did you leave it at the end of the day?'

'Ooh, so many questions. Well, we left his car in the restaurant car park and went for a walk down the lane – it's a beautiful part of the country. Very rural. Didn't see a single car as we walked.'

'Oh great. Get in his car, drive to the middle of nowhere and then walk away from civilisation. I can see I'm going to have to put a tracker in your phone,' Clare says, raising her eyebrows at me in an attempt to look disapproving.

'Well, I think you can be pretty confident he's not a serial killer or something.'

'Or he's just lulling you into a false sense of security. Check his car for duct tape and a bottle of chloroform next time.' Clare is somehow managing to keep a straight face.

'You've been watching too much CSI,' I tell her, laughing. 'You need to get out more.'

'Ain't that the truth. Maybe I should join Secret Affair too. We could double date.' Clare's laughing too now.

'God, can you imagine?'

'Er… no.'

'No. Me neither. As much as I love you, I'm not ready to share Rob. I'm so excited about our next meeting – hopefully next Tuesday if he can move a couple of meetings. I'm going to have to come up with a different excuse though; I can't keep saying we're going shopping.'

'Well, you can use me as your alibi whenever you need to – just make sure I know in advance so I can keep a low profile. It would be so much easier if we were double dating…'

'Stop it, you muppet. I know you'd never join the site.'

'Wouldn't I, though? I have more of a relationship with the hoover than with Greg these days,' Clare says with a sigh.

'Aw! But you still love him though, don't you? Greg, that is, not the Dyson.'

'Yes I do. Even if he can be a bit of a knob at times. I'm still a little bit jealous of what you're doing though.'

'Well, you can have an affair vicariously through me. Although there are limits to how much I'll share with you.'

'Spoilsport!' Clare sticks her tongue out at me.

'I will tell you that we're going to a hotel next time. Eek!'

'Oh my God! Really? You minx!'

'It sounds a bit seedy saying it out loud. We talked about it and it's more about being somewhere we can relax and talk in comfort, rather than about sex.'

'Yeah, yeah,' Clare says with a wink.

'Honestly, it is. We just want to be able to shut out the world – be on our own,' I protest.

'And shag each other senseless,' Clare grins.

'No! Well, maybe! Who knows? I guess time will tell. I'm a bit nervous thinking about that. There's only been Paul for so long.'

'Don't overthink it, Luce. If it feels right, just do it. I'm sure you'll be fine.'

'I suppose so. I do feel a bit anxious about my scars though. What if he's turned off by them?'

'If he's even half the man you think he is, he'll love them – they're part of you. He probably won't even notice them. I'm sure they're not as bad as you think anyway.'

'I hope you're right. Anyway, I'm not going to think about that yet. I'm just looking forward to getting to know him better.'

'Intimately, you could say.'

'Sod off. Stop winding me up, you ratbag!'

Clare laughs. 'Sorry! I am actually genuinely happy for you. Just enjoy it, but take care. And for God's sake, don't get caught. I'm not sure I could convince Greg to let you move into our spare room.'

'I will be careful, I promise. The last thing I want is to hurt anyone.'

'Hmm. Except yourself by the sound of it. I hope he's worth it.'

'I really think he is, Clare. I'm not under any illusions about the nature of our relationship. I'm just going to enjoy it for as long as possible.'

'What if he's crap in bed?' Typical Clare. Straight to the point.

'And right there's another reason I love you: you just cut to the chase, don't you?' I'm laughing. 'I can't imagine for a minute that he is. He's too... um...' – I pause, looking for the right word... 'sensual. You know what I mean – you can just tell with a man. There's something vital and powerfully masculine about him. Just the touch of his hand told me how he could make me feel. I suppose I'll just have to wait and see when – or if – it happens.'

'Indeed. He does sound very sexy...' Clare appears to drift off at this point.

'Earth to Clare,' I say with a grin, reaching over and nudging her arm.

'Sorry, I was just picturing Greg naked. It wasn't pretty.' Clare sighs. 'I am horribly horribly jealous of you right at this moment. Still happy for you, of course, but oh my...'

'Oh my indeed. I can't believe my luck really.'

'How did you leave things at the end of the day?'

'He drove me back to my car at Claremont. I hated leaving him – neither of us wanted the day to end. To be honest, I felt really sad saying goodbye. We sat in his car for quite a while longer, just holding hands and talking about next time. Eventually, he leaned over and kissed me and we sort of clung onto each other. I had to drag myself away in the end. Honestly, Clare, if it wasn't for Tom I don't think I could've left him.'

'Oh, Lucy, you do realise it's only going to get harder? And no, for once, I'm not being smutty.' Clare looks concerned.

'I know. I'm just hoping that having a *next time* to look forward to will make it bearable.'

'Maybe. I don't know. I don't envy you the goodbyes. Maybe old Willy Shakespeare was onto something with his sweet sorrow malarkey though.'

'I hope so. Rob and I are no Romeo and Juliet, but we certainly have some pretty insurmountable obstacles in our way!'

'Well, whatever happens next, I'm here for you OK?'

'Thank you, Clare. I really would be lost without you. Thank you for understanding – I'm not sure many people would.'

'No worries. I just want you to be happy. But now I have a hot date with a hoover – we can't bear to be parted for too long.'

'Nutter. I'd better give Alfie a quick walk too. Thanks again, Clare.'

'No problemo. I'll see you on pick up.'

CHAPTER 37

Thoughts of you

Clare and I wave our goodbyes as we set off in opposite directions: she to the car park and Alfie and I further into the park for a walk. As usual my thoughts wander with us.

Thoughts of Rob are all encompassing and I want time alone with them, so Alfie and I take a less popular route through the back of the park and up onto the wooded hills beyond. I barely notice the increasing incline, just keep putting one foot in front of the other. In my mind I'm back at Claremont with Rob by my side; I can feel his presence, the touch of his hand on mine and the skin tingles with a trace of memory. I acknowledge the rapidness of my heartbeat, putting a hand to my chest and stopping on the path for a moment to catch my breath. It's the steepness of the path, of course, but it's something else too. It's the vivid recall of my response to Rob. Some kind of physiological echo. It's alarming. And wonderful. And terrifying. And probably addictive.

How am I going to get through the next week? I wonder. How am I going to function normally, not give anything away? It's surely not possible. But I must. I cannot ruin this before it has even begun. And I cannot risk hurting anyone. I have to find a way of compartmentalizing my real life with Paul and Tom, and my secret life with Rob; but it won't be easy when thoughts of Rob are constantly pushing themselves to the fore. I must find some self-discipline from somewhere. An inner strength I'm not sure I possess. But I will do it. Somehow. For Tom. For Paul. And for myself. I'm under no illusion that I'm doing this primarily for myself, but still I cannot risk hurting my child or his father.

I carry on up the path, checking that Alfie is still in sight. Thinking about Paul has dampened my mood a little. And rightly so, I suppose. After all, what I'm doing is cheating on him, isn't it? There's no point pretending otherwise. No point wrapping it up in pretty sentiments and excuses. He doesn't deserve it; I'm not under any illusion about what I'm doing. It's wrong. However right it feels with Rob, ultimately it's wrong. I just no longer know what the alternative is. Now that I've met Rob, there is only one way this can go. I cannot give him up. I don't want to.

Finally, I reach the top of the hill, and the woods clear to reveal a panorama of green hills sweeping down to the valley below. I have a favourite spot to sit and rest before turning back and I'm surprised to see someone has beaten me to it.

'Charlie?' I call out, sure that the blonde head belongs to her.

The blonde head turns. 'Lucy. Oh! Hi.'

'You found my spot. You ok?'

'Not really. Hiding if the truth be told. Didn't think anyone would find me up here.'

'Sorry! I can bugger off if you want?'

'No, stay. Please. It's nice to see you. I'm just not very good company at the moment.'

'That makes two of us then. We can be miserable together.' I'm now sitting on the grass next to her, and Alfie has flopped down next to me. I bump my left shoulder against Charlie's right in a gesture I hope conveys solidarity. 'Anything I can do to help?'

'I don't know. Probably not. Unless you can make Rich's mum emigrate with immediate effect?'

'Would if I could, Charlie. I hate seeing you like this. Have you tried talking things through with Rich again?'

'Not really. I don't know where to start. I think I'm too afraid of where it might lead.'

'Totally understand that. I'm the queen of avoiding difficult conversations. I like to keep my cans of worms firmly shut. Not very healthy though I don't think. For me or the worms!'

'I'm worried that any conversation with Rich would lead to me giving him an ultimatum. And I'm terrified that she'll win if that happens.' Charlie looks and sounds utterly bereft.

'I do understand, but you can't go on like this indefinitely.' So much easier to give advice than to follow it, I think wryly. 'Do you believe that Rich is *the one*? That you absolutely one hundred percent want to spend the rest of your life with him?'

Charlie doesn't hesitate. 'Yes, completely and utterly. I love him so much, Lucy.'

'Then you need to fight for him. For what you have.' Easier said than done, I think. 'You're one of the strongest people I know. You've got this. You've just got to believe – have a little faith. In yourself, and in Rich.'

'I'm so scared though. I couldn't bear to lose Rich. I know I can't ignore the problem, but the alternative terrifies me.' Silent tears are rolling down Charlie's cheeks. I dig into my pocket for the ever-present tissue and pass it to her.

'I wish I could do more to help. I'm always here to listen

though. Even if you need to scream and shout – anything I can do. Ultimately, though, my lovely, only you can make the decision.'

'Thanks, Lucy, I really appreciate that. You and the other mums have been amazing.'

'That's what we're for. We all just want you to be happy.' I give Charlie's hand a squeeze. 'Right, speaking of screaming, up you get.'

'What? Why?' Charlie looks confused.

I stand up and reach down to pull Charlie up by her hands. 'Come on. Up.'

Charlie obeys and I lead her to the edge of the hill. 'Right, now scream. Or shout. Swear. Whatever you're feeling, just let it out.'

Charlie looks at me as if I've lost the plot. Years ago, I think to myself.

'Just try it. You might just like it. I'll do it too. On three. One, two, three…'

Two voices scream out simultaneously. Alfie jumps like a scalded cat. Charlie and I look at each other and laugh.

'Sorry, boy,' I make an apology to the dog and ruffle his head.

'Oh my God, that really did feel good.' Charlie grins at me.

'Told you. You'd be surprised how many times I've done that. Better out than in, and it's much easier than getting angry at someone directly.'

'I do feel a bit relieved. I've been so tense for weeks – it felt good to let some of that tension out. Thanks, Lucy.'

'Any time. It's much better than bottling up the feelings.' I so need to listen to my own advice. 'Right, I need to wend my weary way.' Alfie looks up as he always does when I say 'right'

– he knows it means something's about to happen.

'Yep, me too. Can't hide up here forever, however tempting that is. I'm really glad you found me today. I was more than a little lost.'

You and me both, I muse. 'I'm glad too.'

We head back to the path through the woods, with Alfie running ahead. Neither of us speaks. I think we're lost in our own thoughts. I wonder to myself what Charlie would think if she knew what was in my head.

Charlie and I hug each other goodbye in the car park, with her vowing to try and find the strength to speak honestly with Rich about their future. I wish her luck and wave as she heads off. I start the car's engine and open the windows, but don't leave straight away. I want to check my emails before I go home, back to my real life. The car's stereo comes on and I laugh out loud when I realise what song is playing: 'Secret Lovers' by Atlantic Starr.

I feel a flutter of anticipation as my emails load, and am thrilled to see not one, but three messages from Rob. I click on the first one, my heart in my throat:

My dearest Lucy, I read, *there are no words that can adequately express the joy meeting you has brought me, but I will try. The moment I set eyes on you sitting in your car, looking so nervous, and so utterly beautiful, I knew that I was lost. Lost in those sparkling green eyes which seemed to penetrate to my very soul. I've never believed in love at first sight. Until now. I am under your spell and I wouldn't have it any other way. For as long as you want me, Lucy, I am yours. Completely. Rob xxx.*

I'm more than a little stunned by Rob's words. I can't believe that he feels the same way I do. I wanted to believe that he did, but a small part of me was afraid to hope. My whole body seems to exhale with relief and I click eagerly on the next message:

My Lucy, I hope my last email didn't scare you away. I couldn't help myself. You've awoken something in me I thought was gone forever and I'm truly thankful to have found you. I dare to hope that you feel the same. I can't wait to see you again, to take you in my arms once more. Please know that we can take things as slowly as you want to; I just want to spend time with you. As much as I already long for you, I know you are worth the wait. Your Rob xxx.

I have the biggest smile on my face as I select Rob's third email:

I've cleared my diary for next Tuesday. Let me know if it's still OK for you. It can't come soon enough. Rxxx.

It can't come soon enough for me either as I hit Reply and start typing a response to Rob.

Dearest Rob, thank you for your lovely emails. I think I'm probably the happiest woman alive right now. I feel the same and I can't wait to see you again. Yes, to Tuesday – I'm already impatient for it to arrive. It's going to be a long week! I feel like I've been living in darkness for so long and suddenly sunlight has burst through the dark cloud hanging over me. I'm already so grateful to have met you, whatever happens next, and however long we have together. I am yours. Lucy xxx.

I hit send and lean back in my seat. I can't believe what's happening. I've met this man just once and he already feels like my whole world. I know it's madness, but I'm not imagining it. I'm sure I'm not. He feels the same as me and it feels amazing.

I can't wait to tell Clare about Rob's emails, so I text her.

Oh my God! Rob says he didn't believe in love at first sight until now. I can't believe it. Definitely seeing him again Tuesday. Soooo excited!! Xx.

Clare, as always, texts back promptly.

Holy cow! So excited for you! Xx.

Bumped into Charlie on my walk. She's really struggling poor thing. Tried to help, but I'm probably not the best person to give marriage advice! Xx.

Ha! Well, if you can't be a good example, be a dire warning! Clare added a crazy face emoji.

Lol. I'm that alright. Although no-one except you knows how bad things are between me and Paul.

I know. You hide it well. I hope Rob is the answer you're looking for.

Thank you. I know he's probably not the right answer, but he's a very welcome distraction.

Just be careful won't you?

I will, promise. Have a good day. See you later.

You too. Laters.

Before heading home, I check my emails once more, but there is no reply from Rob. I reassure myself that he's probably working, and make my way to the exit.

CHAPTER 38

Blurred lines

Driving back, I will admit to feeling a bit anxious about how things are going to be at home. I'm really not sure that I'll be able to keep the soppy grin from my face whenever Rob's on my mind. Especially as this is likely to be pretty much all the time.

You'll just have to keep busy, Lucy, I tell myself. That will help the time pass quicker too, hopefully. I catch myself on that thought, like a hem on barbed wire. I'm already wishing my week away to spend time with this man I've only just met. That's not right, is it? That implies that my time with family doesn't matter, isn't precious. I feel a pang of confusion. This is all so new though; maybe I don't need all the answers right now. I just need to roll with things for a while. But I mustn't wish my days away or pin all my happiness on my meetings with Rob.

So, keep busy, but don't neglect others. That seems to be the way forward for now, I decide, as I pull onto the drive.

'Let's get you a drink, boy,' I say to Alfie as he jumps out of the car. 'And then one for your master.' But not mine, I add silently.

Five minutes later and I'm heading upstairs to Paul's office. I don't announce my arrival in case he's in a meeting. Paul looks up as I go in, and smiles.

'Perfect timing,' he says. 'Just got off the phone. How was your walk?'

'Good, thanks. Made it up to the top of the hill behind the park.'

'Blimey! Well done. That's a steep path.'

'I wasn't the only one who made it up there this morning – Charlie was there.'

'Really? What on earth was she doing up there? They don't have a dog, do they?'

'No. No dog. She said she was hiding. Poor thing. She's having such a hard time of it right now.'

'Well, she can't hide forever can she? She needs to sort things out.' Paul, pragmatic as ever.

'No, of course not, and she knows that. Doesn't make it any easier though. She's terrified of losing Rich.'

Paul grunts. 'She needs to man up, if you ask me.'

I have to bite my tongue at his remark: everything is so black and white to Paul.

'Rich is the one who needs to man up,' I retort, unable to completely hold back what I'm thinking. 'He needs to stand up to his bloody mother.'

Before Paul can say anything else, and before we fall out, I turn to leave the room. 'Anyway, must get on – a woman's work and all that.'

I down a quick cup of coffee before heading into the garden. Operation *Keep Busy* is to commence with mowing the lawn, a job which I actually quite enjoy and find strangely therapeutic. It's also fairly mindless, and will allow me to focus my thoughts on Rob. Not that they need focusing: he's already there at the forefront of my mind all the time it seems.

As I walk up and down the long lengths of the garden, leaving stripes as I go, I'm reminded of Clare's carpet art. I wonder idly if anyone would actually notice if I mowed a giant 'R' into the grass. Probably not, but I'd better not risk it. Thoughts of my next meeting with Rob are vying for attention with memories of our first, jostling for pole position. I'm nervous about being alone with him in a hotel room, although I don't think for a second he'll pressure me into doing anything I don't want to. I try to analyse why I'm feeling so nervous.

Is it my scars? I wonder. I am so very conscious of the seams sewn into my body. I know rationally that they don't change me as a person, but still… men are so visual aren't they? Should I talk to Rob about them? Tell him about my surgeries? At least then it wouldn't be a shock. Or should I say nothing? Not risk putting the grisly images in his head? Perhaps I am doing Rob a disservice by thinking he might be bothered by my scars. He's not a shallow man, that much I'm sure of. Maybe this is only a problem in my head, my own lack of confidence. I realise I'm furrowing my brow and I can feel tension in my shoulders. I force myself to relax – the lines between my brows are already far too established. My forehead art installation, I think with a grimace.

Running parallel to my nervousness, like the contrasting lines on the lawn, is great excitement. The anticipation of what lies ahead is as thrilling as it is daunting. I already know from Rob's touch and our first kisses, that he has a powerful effect on me. Everything about him is a delightful assault on my senses. I can feel him, smell him, taste him, even now amidst the sound of the mower and the sweet smell of freshly cut grass. He has the power to overshadow everything. No, not overshadow. Maybe eclipse? But no, because Rob brings light – he doesn't obscure it. My thoughts are drifting and I suddenly realise my line is too; I now have a decidedly wonky stripe in the lawn.

I go back over the errant stripe with the mower and tell myself that I'll have to be more mindful of my thought train, which is otherwise going to run away from me, calling at *Awkward Conversation* and *Adultery* and terminating at *Divorce*.

Emptying the final load of grass cuttings on the compost heap at the end of the garden, I pull my mobile out of my back pocket and flop down onto one of the garden chairs on the deck. I can't resist checking my emails. The deck is pretty much hidden from sight of the house, but I will still see Paul should he decide to come looking for me. I am rewarded with an email from Rob.

My Lucy, sorry I'm ridiculously busy today, rushing between meetings, but I just wanted to say how much I look forward to seeing you again on Tuesday. It really can't come soon enough and I will be wishing my life away 'til then. Your Rob xxx.

You too, eh? I think to myself with a smile. I wonder whether I should reply or not? I don't want to be a nuisance when he's busy. But I can't resist.

My dear Rob, no apology needed – I totally understand that you're busy and that there'll be times when you can't email. Please don't worry about those times. To know that I'm in your thoughts, as you are in mine, is enough. Wishing my life away 'til Tuesday too. Lucy xxx.

Logging out of my email account, I return my phone to my pocket and set about coiling the mower cable and wheeling the machine back to the shed.

CHAPTER 39

Forever autumn

An autumnal chill hangs in the air as the days pass. Summer sandals are consigned to under-bed storage, and jumpers retrieved from the depths of the airing cupboard where they've languished these past months. Normally undertaking such chores would get me down, but nothing can dampen my mood this week. I hug the secret of Rob to myself and barely notice the lowering temperatures and the drawing in of the evenings. Thoughts of Rob are a constant source of warmth and light. For once it's actually Paul who first broaches the subject of turning on the central heating in the evenings.

We're all sitting in the playroom watching *Over the Hedge*, Tom in the middle and Alfie at my feet as ever.

'Anyone else a bit chilly?' Paul asks, giving a little shiver as he speaks.

His words reach my brain through the heat haze of my thoughts and I stop to analyse how I'm feeling. I put my hands to my face and realise with surprise that they are a little cold. I'd been completely unaware of this fact, when normally I'd be the first in the house to feel the cold.

'I am a bit, now you come to mention it,' I say. 'Time to put the heating on I s'pose. I'll do it.' I get to my feet, grateful for something to do. I don't want Paul to have a chance to express surprise at the turn of events. Tom hasn't spoken, engrossed as he is in the movie. I touch his little arm as I get up, and am relieved to find it is warm. It prevents yet another pang of guilt assaulting me. I realise that I haven't been fully present at home since I met Rob. I chide myself silently for this and vow yet again to do better.

Disturbed by my getting up from the sofa, Alfie trots after me to the utility room.

'Want to go out, boy?' It's a rhetorical question of course, but I open the back door in case he does, and the chill of the evening air hits me. I shiver involuntarily – a purely autonomic response - and step over to the boiler, quickly checking the timer and clicking the heating on. Summer is officially over, but for once I don't really mind. I have something wonderful to sustain me through the dark and colder months. I hug my arms around me as I stand by the door waiting for the dog to return from his sniff around the garden. I'm smiling. I'm thinking about Rob, of course, and the beaming smile on my face could probably light Alfie's way back. I can't remember the last time I felt this happy.

Returning to the playroom, I take up my place on the sofa once more and let my thoughts drift where they will. I just hope that Tom won't want to talk about the film when it finishes as I haven't actually taken any of it in. Hearing a light snore, it becomes apparent that Paul won't either.

The film finishes. Paul sleeps on, so I put a finger to my lips, gesturing to Tom that we should keep quiet. We tiptoe out of the room and go to the kitchen before we speak. I'm keen to distract Tom from any discussion about the film.

'How would you like a hot chocolate before bed? With cream

and marshmallows?' I ask him.

'Yesss! Just white marshmallows though. Pink ones are for girls.'

I laugh. 'OK, no pink ones. They're all mine now! You go up and start getting ready for bed and I'll be up soon.'

Tom sets off upstairs obediently and I set about making his drink, popping each of the little pink mallows into my mouth as I remove them from the small heap I've poured out. I let them melt on my tongue, acutely aware of their cat's tongue exterior dissolving into a sugary gooey rush; probably not what either of us needs before bed, but I seem to be constantly trying to make amends for my lapses in concentration; my unintended absences from my young son's life. He's probably going to get pretty spoiled while Rob is in my life, I think with a wry smile.

Mug in hand, I head upstairs to Tom's bedroom. As I pass the playroom I'm relieved to hear gentle snoring still. Reaching his bedroom, I see that Tom has made no attempt to get into his pyjamas and is busy battling Transformers. I stand in the doorway for a few seconds, just watching him play. As always, the surge of love I feel at watching my son rushes through me, and once again I make the silent promise never to hurt him.

'Time to get ready for bed,' I say, breaking the silence and bringing Tom out of his little fantasy world. 'I've got your hot chocolate – white marshmallows only, as requested.'

'Thanks, Mummy. You're the best!' Tom says, putting his action figures to one side.

'No, you're the best!' I tell him with a laugh. I feel a little guilty that I haven't been the best of late, but am relieved that it doesn't seem to have affected Tom's opinion of me. Maybe I've been better at hiding things than I thought. Or maybe

I've just been over-compensating for my mental absences, and spoiling Tom with treats.

Soon Tom's tucked up in bed with his hot chocolate, and I'm squeezed onto the bed next to him, book in hands. He doesn't always want a bedtime story, but tonight he seems happy for me to read to him. I'm trying to initiate him into the delights of Enid Blyton, but I'm not sure it's working. Maybe the books of my childhood simply don't translate into my son's generation. Bless him though, he tolerates my attempts and waits patiently for me to finish reading.

'Can we have Power Rangers tomorrow instead?' he says as I close the book.

'Yes, of course we can.' I tell him, a wistful smile on my face. I guess some things don't stand the test of time, do they? As with my favourite childhood stories, so with my marriage. I feel a little wave of sadness wash over me, and am reluctant to let go of Tom as we share one last goodnight hug. Eventually though, he wriggles out of my arms and I kiss him on the forehead as he snuggles down under his duvet.

'Night night,' I say, brushing his hair with my hand.

'Night night, Mummy,' he says, as he turns on his side, taking his head away from my hand.

As I leave his room, I realise a tear is trickling down my face. It's a tear composed of pure love, the love of a mother for her child and, as I wipe it away I know that this love is probably the only love that will last a lifetime for me.

CHAPTER 40

Suction

The next few days are uneventful, just the usual routine of family, school and work; going through the motions, killing time. I'm doing my best to be fully present for my husband and son, but, if I'm honest, I'm constantly catching myself drifting in a reverie of Rob.

Autumn continues to make its presence felt with October almost upon us. Tom now wears a sweatshirt over his school polo shirt, Paul has a jumper draped over the back of his office chair and I now wear a fleece on my morning walks. Just life, going on, seemingly as normal. Warm clothes on the surface, but under it, a seething mass of emotions and longing warm my blood.

All I can think about is seeing Rob again, being alone with him. Being alive again. Being honest again. I know that makes no sense, but my feelings for Rob are honest, however messed up that seems. Clare, as my confidante, has to put up with a lot, and our meetings on the school runs are little pockets of relief in my days.

'Morning, Lucy,' she says. It's Friday. The end of a long week as I count down to Tuesday. 'How are you holding up?'

'I'm not. In fact, the only things holding up are my socks.'

'Well, small mercies and all that,' Clare laughs. 'It'll be

Tuesday before you know it. I'm so excited for you.'

'I can't wait, Clare. That's if I don't go completely to pot before then. I've never known time go this slowly,' I groan.

'Enjoy it – the anticipation, the build-up...'

'Don't you dare say climax,' I laugh, wagging a finger at Clare in mock crossness.

Clare's laughing too. 'As if!' she says, trying to look like the injured party. 'Anyway, climaxes are the last thing that would be on my mind. The lack thereof maybe. I mean, I enjoy hoovering, but...'

'Oh dear. Do I sense a little dissatisfaction there?'

'Yup. My sex life is about as exciting as an episode of *Songs of Praise*. With Cliff Michelmore, not Aled Jones. Always quite fancied Aled.' Clare drifts off for a second, clearly absorbed in inappropriate thoughts of Mr. Jones.

'You never said anything.' I'm surprised at Clare's revelation. 'I always thought things in that department were pretty good between you and Greg.'

'Nope. Not for a while now. They used to be amazing. Not so much now.'

'Oh bum. Sorry, Clare. Why didn't you say anything?'

'I don't think I really let myself acknowledge it before – it's only really since you joined Secret Affair that I've admitted the truth to myself.'

I feel a familiar pang of guilt. I pull a sad face: 'Sorry.'

Clare squeezes my arm. 'Don't be daft, you've got nothing to be sorry for. I'm genuinely happy for you, Lucy. It's not your fault the most exciting thing happening in my bedroom is new curtains.'

'That sucks.' I don't know what to say.

'Nah, that's the Dyson!' Clare retorts, with a nudge of her elbow, never one to be down for long.

I laugh. 'Well, maybe you should take a leaf out of the Dyson's book?' I say, nudging her back and giving an exaggerated wink.

We're both laughing loudly at this point and starting to get funny looks from the other parents waiting for the school gates to open. Even Tom and Chloe have moved further away from us, obviously trying to distance themselves from their embarrassing mothers. Of course this just makes us laugh all the more.

'Maybe I will. When the novelty of the new curtains wears off.'

'Seriously though, Clare, I hope you can turn things around – at least you still want Greg. Can't you initiate things?'

'Yeah, I suppose so. We've just let things drift for a while now and both of us have stopped making the effort.'

'I know! Remember when it didn't used to be an effort? When you couldn't keep your hands off each other?'

'Yep. Good times. Seems like forever ago.'

'Me too. I don't understand why it changes, do you?'

'Nope. But it does, doesn't it? I think the rot set in after we had Chloe if I'm honest.'

'Yep. Everything changes after you have a child.'

'I wouldn't give up Chloe for the world, but I do wish it hadn't changed things between me and Greg so much.'

'You can get it back if you really want to though. I'm sure you can,' I tell my now slightly melancholy friend.

Before Clare can reply, the gates open and we usher our two offspring onto school property before heading back up the road to our cars. We walk in contemplative silence, each lost in thoughts of our love lives. Only when we reach the cars do I break the silence.

'Oy, missus, get off Aled and talk to me.'

'How very dare you? I'm a happily married woman I'll have you know. And anyway, it was Brad.' She's back. I laugh.

'Ha! Well, you need to give Brad his marching orders, draw those new curtains of yours and make things happen with Greg again.'

'Alright, bossy boots. I'll try. But I'm keeping Brad on the substitutes bench.'

'Fair enough. Right, I'll see you on pick up. Have a good day.'

'You too. See you later.'

CHAPTER 41

Counting down

I feel as though Tuesday will never arrive, and the weekend looms large. Weekdays are easier somehow, with Tom at work and Paul closeted in his office. I am so impatient to see Rob again and am becoming aware of a feeling of resentment towards anything that stands between me and time with him. It's becoming harder to conceal my emotions and I have to make a conscious effort to keep on top of them.

In an effort to keep us all busy, I've filled the weekend with diversions and distractions: a trip to a garden centre on Saturday to buy spring-flowering bulbs to plant, with cinema in the evening, and a boot fair early on Sunday, followed by lunch with Paul's parents and a woodland walk with the dog. Neither Paul nor Tom looks thrilled at the prospect of the first part of my plan.

'It'll be fun,' I tell Tom, after he's pulled a face upon being told where we're going. 'It's not just plants - they have animals too, rabbits and guinea pigs and lots of others.' Tom looks slightly appeased. Paul still looks unconvinced. 'And they have a really nice café which does an amazing cream tea.' Paul looks slightly less mutinous, and we set off. I'm hoping we can while away the morning at the garden centre and much of the afternoon planting the spring bulbs I plan to buy. I'm picturing swathes of daffodils come the spring. I'm still not sure how I'm going to sell bulb planting to my mutinous crew, however.

Thankfully, chinchillas and scones do the trick, and Saturday's plan pays off. We make bulb planting into a competition when we get home and it's a tired Tom who falls asleep in the car on the way back from the cinema. Paul carries him upstairs to bed and once he's settled I take myself off for a soak in the bath while Paul heads for the Xbox.

As I lie back in the scented water, I heave a sigh of relief that Tuesday's another day closer. I just have to get through two more days, which I have to say feel like an eternity. I close my eyes and bring a picture of Rob to my mind, wondering what he's doing right now, and if he's thinking about me. I suppose he's with his wife… I'm shocked by how much that thought hurts me and I immediately force it from my head, pushing it out with memories of our time together at Claremont House. Wanting to feel closer to Rob, I reach out for the towel I have next to the bath, dry my hands and pick up my mobile. I haven't had a chance to check my emails all day. I'm rewarded with a message.

My dear Lucy. I think I'm going to lose my mind waiting for Tuesday to arrive! I have never known time go so slowly. All I can think about is shutting the world out and wrapping you in my arms again. I already know it will feel like coming home. I'm growing impatient with everyone around me just because they're not you. It's a wonderful kind of madness though, and I know it will all be worthwhile when Tuesday finally rolls around. I want to know everything about you, Lucy. I want to share everything with you. I want to be one with you. Counting the hours. Rob xxxx.

Rob's words bring a surge of pure joy to me and a sense of

relief that he's feeling just the same as I am. I hit reply and compose a message:

Dear Rob, I'm feeling exactly the same! I'm trying so hard to keep busy and fill my days, but every day that's not Tuesday is driving me crazy! I feel so impatient. You're all I can think of, all the time. I keep replaying our time together – it was so magical, so perfect. I want more. I want you. It will be wonderful to shut the world out, won't it? I don't want to share you with anyone. Your Lucy xxxx. I hit send and try to picture Rob reading the email. It makes me smile.

Sunday's plans go without a hitch. We arrive at the boot fair at eight a.m. and for once I let Tom and Paul buy whatever rubbish they want. We soon have bags full of toys and Xbox games, and a couple of plants I can't resist. Tom has sugar all round his mouth from the three doughnuts he's eaten, and Paul has happily consumed the most enormous bacon baguette. Time is passing, everyone's happy. Operation Keep Busy is working.

We call in and collect Alfie before heading to Paul's parents for lunch, and spend a perfectly pleasant couple of hours over roast lamb and apple crumble. I offer to make tea and clear up afterwards, happy to be alone with my thoughts for a while. Paul heads to the conservatory with his parents and Tom disappears off to watch TV. When I check on him, he's hanging upside down from the sofa watching Power Rangers. I take my time over the dishes, using the time not only to think about Rob, but to compose myself for the rest of the afternoon.

I finish clearing up, check on Tom and pop my head into the conservatory.

'Anyone want another cuppa?' I ask. But even as I'm speaking

I realise all three occupants have dozed off. Paul has his hands clasped over his belly and is snoring quietly. His mum is still clutching her mug, so I gently remove it and tiptoe from the room. I'm in no hurry to wake them as any time alone with my thoughts is precious. I retrieve my mobile from my handbag and head back to the dining room. I'm hoping, of course, for an email from Rob. I'm not disappointed.

My Lucy, it begins. *Your email made me chuckle – we're a right pair, both wishing our lives away. I've been making plans for Tuesday – I hope that's OK. I don't want to take over; I just want everything to be perfect. I've booked the Langley Hotel and arranged for early check-in. It's not far from Claremont. And I promise there is no pressure to do anything more than just be together. Except hug. I will need to hug you. A lot. Your, Rob xxxx.*

I hug my phone to my chest. I can't describe the emotions tumbling through me, but they're amazing. I don't think I realised just how empty I've been feeling; how much of a toll was being taking by the weight of my crayon smile, and the pretence of happiness. There is more to my life now. There is Rob. I start to compose a reply:

My dearest Rob. Thank you for your message – you have no idea how happy it made me. But then again, maybe you do – we seem to think and feel alike about so much. Thank you for organising the hotel. Knowing where we will meet makes it all the more real and all the more exciting. I'm trying so hard to keep busy, but all I can think about is being with you again. And yes, to hugs. Please. As many as you can muster! I may never want you to let go. Yours, in anticipation, Lucy xxxx.

I sit quietly for a few minutes, breathing deeply and centring myself to face the rest of the day. If we're going to walk Alfie in the woods, we need to set off soon. I'm determined to wear everyone out again, to bring bedtime about as early as possible and bring Tuesday that bit closer.

Taking one last deep breath, I go to the lounge to give Tom his five-minute warning; thankfully this will coincide with the end of his programme. I cheat a little bit with waking Paul. Alfie has also succumbed to the drowsy warmth of the conservatory, but I call him quietly to me now.

'Alfie! Where's Dad? Find him. Go find Dad.' He trots off obediently once more, and I know full well he will stick his wet nose into his sleeping master's hand. That should do the trick, and I won't be the bad guy for waking him up.

'Ugh! Get off dog! Yuck.'

I chuckle to myself. Thanks, Alfie.

Soon we're waving goodbye to Paul's parents and heading the short distance to the woods for our afternoon constitutional. AKA operation Wear-out-Tom. And Paul, if I'm being totally honest.

The rest of the afternoon actually proves to be pretty good, although Alfie ruins our game of hide and seek by constantly giving away hiding places. We switch to hunt the fungi instead and Tom enjoys being the first to spot a new one. To the outside world we would look like a happy little family. I suppose we are in some ways. But there is a gaping, aching void in me which Paul can no longer fill.

CHAPTER 42

Tuesday's girl

It's here. Finally. My heart is racing. My hands are shaking. It's all I can do to get through the morning routine without giving myself away. Monday, yesterday, seemed to last forever, but it passed, eventually. I struggled to sleep last night, like an overexcited child on the eve of Christmas. Except today is better than Christmas. Today is all my Christmases come at once. Today I will be back in Rob's arms.

I'm thankful, for once, that Paul's not the most observant of men, and he's blissfully unaware of the state I'm in. I've told him Clare and I are shopping for wedding accessories today. As ever I hate lying to him, but I do it nonetheless. Whatever qualms I have about my illicit behaviour pale into insignificance next to my fervent desire to be with Rob. I couldn't change the direction of things now, even if I wanted to.

Paul doesn't notice the extra care I take over my appearance this Tuesday morning. Or the choice of pretty matching underwear. The flush on my cheeks which owes nothing to blusher. He doesn't notice how often I have to catch my breath as the butterflies threaten to overwhelm me.

As usual Clare is parked up before me when I take Tom to school. She sees me pull up in her rear view mirror, and waves frantically, leaping out of the car, clearly impatient to find out how I'm feeling. I can't help laughing. I think she's enjoying this as much as me.

'Well?' she says, the second I'm out of the car. 'How are you feeling?'

'Fine, thank you. How's you?' I put my finger to my lips and nod in Tom's direction. Little pitchers and all that.

Clare takes the hint. 'Looking forward to our shopping trip? I can't wait!' She gives me a very exaggerated wink.

I shake my head at my funny friend. 'I am. I can't wait either. Been looking forward to it for days.'

'It's gonna be great, I just know it.' Clare has a huge grin on her face.

'I think you're right. I hope so.'

We set off to walk the short distance to school, and Clare keeps looking sideways at me and grinning. I know that's she's absolutely bursting with things she can't say in front of the kids, and it's not until they're safely through the school gates that she can speak her mind.

'Oh my God, Lucy. How are you feeling, really? Promise you'll let me know you're OK when you can?'

'I'm just super excited. A bit nervous still, but I absolutely can't wait to see Rob again.'

'I bet! I hope he's every bit as amazing as you remember and that everything fits, if you get my drift.'

I laugh. 'Yes, I get your drift, you nutter. But it might not even come to that today. We're just going to play it by ear. We might just talk. And maybe have a cuddle.' I can feel my face flushing.

Clare repeats the word cuddle while making speech marks in the air with her fingers.

'Muppet.'

'Sorry! I'm just so happy for you. You will be careful won't you?'

'Of course. And please don't worry about me, Clare. Even if I get carried away and forget to text you, I don't want you to worry. I'll be fine. I trust Rob completely. I just know he won't do anything I don't want.'

'No, but hopefully he'll do lots of things you DO want.'

We're back at the cars now and Clare gives me a big squeeze of a hug before letting me go. 'Let me know how you get on. Have a wonderful time.'

And I'm back in my car, taking a deep breath as I put my seatbelt on and set off to the accompaniment of Foreigner's 'Waiting for a Girl Like You'. I wonder if Rob's already in his car and listening to the lyrics too.

As the miles go by and my destination gets ever closer, the nerves increase. I find myself forgetting to breathe and start to experience a tightness in my chest. I can't remember the last time I felt like this. Did I ever feel like this in the early days of me and Paul? I suppose I must've done, but it seems a lifetime ago. Tom's lifetime in fact. The build up to my second meeting with Rob has been so intense, so longed for. Can it really live up to my expectations, I wonder? I'm not having doubts; I'm just playing devil's advocate with myself, I think.

I'm nervous about checking into the hotel too. It's surely going to be blatantly obvious to the staff why we're there; checking in early without luggage and not staying the night. I feel embarrassed at the prospect of being judged, of them knowing what we're up to. It's an uncomfortable feeling. I've asked Rob to meet me in the car park – I don't think I'd be brave enough, or brazen enough, to walk in to reception on my own. I try to rationalise to myself that the staff will be used to it and won't bat an eyelid, but I'm not completely reassured.

By the time I pull into the hotel car park, my breaths are getting stuck in my throat, I'm so nervous. What if something's different this time? What if we saw what we wanted to last time because we were so desperate for it to be right? I want this to work. I want it to be perfect, like it was the first time. I'm so afraid that one, or both, of us will be disappointed.

Rob has already arrived and has reversed his car into a space facing the entrance so that I can see him immediately upon arrival. I pull my car into the space next to his and turn to look at him; he has the biggest smile on his face. All my fears and worries drop instantly away to nothing and I smile back at him.

Rob is the first to move, and gets out of his car, unfolding his long legs from the confines of the Coupe. He's not wearing jeans this time, but smart corn-coloured chinos with a blue shirt rolled up to the elbows, revealing his strong tanned arms. I experience a brief shudder of pleasure as I remember what those arms felt like around me. He comes over and opens my door, stepping aside to allow me room to get out.

'Hello, you,' he says, before stepping forward once more and enfolding me in his arms.

'Hello.' I'm breathing in his scent and I can feel him doing the same to me. I can feel how fast his heart is beating. Being in his arms is like coming home. I don't want this moment, this feeling, ever to end.

'I can't tell you how good it is to see you again. To hold you, Lucy. I have spent so much of the last week dreaming about this moment. I can't believe it's finally here. That you're really here.'

'I know. I feel the same.' My words seem inadequate, but I'm so enthralled by Rob, drawn in to the warm maleness of him, the woody, citrusy smell of him, that it's hard to focus my thoughts and speech. I don't want to think about anything anyway, I just want to be lost in the moment, back in our untouchable, perfect bubble.

Eventually, of course, we have to pull apart. As we do so, Rob takes my face in his hands and just gazes at it, drinking in everything he finds there. It's as though he can see into my very soul, his eyes penetrating mine, reading my innermost thoughts and not finding them wanting. He has such a powerful effect on me that I feel literally weak at the knees. He notices, and withdraws his hands.

'Come on, let's get you inside and get you a coffee or something. I just have to grab something from my car.'

I busy myself with getting my handbag and locking up my car. When I turn back to Rob he has an overnight and laptop bag in his left hand. He reaches out for me with his free hand and I clasp my fingers between his, gratefully accepting the reassuring squeeze he gives.

'I thought you might be feeling a bit awkward about checking in to a hotel without any luggage, so....' He lifts the bags a little to finish the sentence.

'I was. I am. You're a mind reader. Thank you so much for thinking of it.' It's my turn to squeeze his hand.

'I will do anything and everything to make you happy, Lucy, to make this easier for you. I hope you know that.'

'Thank you. I think I do know. And I'm incredibly grateful.'

We've just reached the automatic front doors to the hotel, and Rob keeps hold of my hand as we pass through and approach the front desk where two uniformed receptionists sit. I hope that I don't look as embarrassed as I feel when they look up.

'Good morning. Reservation for Clare.' Rob's deep voice commands the attention of the nearest receptionist and she smiles.

'Certainly, Mr. Clare,' she says brightly as she taps some keys on her computer. 'You have early check-in, I see. Your room will be ready in about thirty minutes. If you would like to go and wait in the lounge, I will have some refreshments brought over to you. I just need your signature here,' she says, handing Rob a piece of paper. 'Will you be wanting a morning news-paper, sir?' she asks. I can feel myself blush, knowing full well we won't still be here in the morning.

'No, thank you,' Rob replies. I just smile. I'm hoping she didn't see me cringe when she mentioned early check-in and a morning paper.

I'm relieved to get to the lounge and sit down away from prying eyes. I feel that everyone around us must know exactly what we're doing. Rob doesn't seem to be at all nervous, and I start to wonder if it's just my own guilty conscience playing tricks on me. Another staff member appears and takes our order for coffee. Once it arrives I begin to relax a little, and I take a big breath and then exhale slowly.

Rob laughs. 'That bad, eh? Don't worry, it didn't show. All anyone probably thought was what a lucky man I am, to have a woman like you by my side.'

'I thought they'd hear my knees knocking, I was so nervous. And when she asked about a morning paper, I wanted the ground to swallow me up. I'm so NOT worldly-wise,' I say with a groan.

'That's no bad thing in this situation, Lucy. It says a lot about you as a person – and all good I can assure you. It tells me you don't do this lightly.'

'I don't think my nerves could take being a serial offender,' I reply with a wry smile.

Rob looks a little saddened at my choice of words.

'Sorry, that was a stupid thing to say. I don't have a moment's regret about being here with you. I just meant that you're right about not doing this lightly.'

'I know. I guess it just reminded me that you're someone else's. You're not really mine. I wish that wasn't the case.'

'I'm yours now, though, and for however long we have.'

'Then that will have to be enough. I still can't help wishing we'd met years ago though, Lucy. Before…you know… before…' Rob's voice tails off.

'Before we met and married other people?' I finish the sentence for him.

'Yes, before that… Sorry, Lucy, forgive me for being maudlin. We're here together now, and I couldn't be happier.'

Before long, the receptionist appears with our room key which she hands to Rob.

'Enjoy your stay at the Langley, Mr. and Mrs Clare, and don't hesitate to call should you need anything. Anything at all.'

'A time machine springs to mind.' The words are out of my mouth before I can stop them.

Rob laughs. The receptionist looks confused.

'Sorry!' I say through my embarrassment, 'private joke.'

CHAPTER 43

A room with a view

It's only as we're walking to the lift and on to our room that I realise what the receptionist actually said: she called us Mr. and Mrs Clare. And Rob used that name when we checked in. I must have been too preoccupied to register the fact at the time. So, I wasn't mistaken at Claremont House. I wonder if it's just a coincidence. Before I have a chance to think any more about it, or ask Rob, we reach our room. I notice that it doesn't have a number on the door; it just has a brass plaque which reads The Langley Suite.

Rob inserts the key card and opens the door, holding it for me to go in first. As I step over the threshold, it feels like the point of no return. No going back now, Lucy, I think. I don't want to go back anyway and, as Rob closes the door behind us, I can feel my whole body exhale with relief. I don't walk far into the room. I'm not sure what to do next. I have no idea what the etiquette is in this situation. I needn't worry, though, as Rob, reading my mind and body language as ever, drops the bags just inside the door, steps forward and takes me in his arms.

We just stand there like that, wrapped in an embrace, not kissing or speaking, just clinging to one another. He is the citrus. I am the jasmine. And we intertwine, each holding the other up. Eventually, Rob pulls away, taking my hands in his as he steps back a little:

'Let me look at you.'

I feel a little shy under his gaze. I desperately don't want him to be disappointed with what he sees. I can feel him drinking me in, from the tips of my pink-painted toe nails peeping out of my blue wedge sandals, up the fabric of my knee-length navy and white polka dot dress to the crown of glossy brown hair atop my head. His eyes then return to mine and I smile shyly.

'God, you are so beautiful, Lucy.'

I resist the usual urge to make some self-deprecating remark upon receiving a compliment. 'Thank you,' I say instead, lowering my eyes briefly, unused to accepting a compliment graciously.

'You really are. I can't believe how lucky I am to have met you.'

'I'm the lucky one,' I tell him in return. I still feel a little shy, but I want Rob to know how he makes me feel. 'I can't believe you chose me. You could have anyone...'

'But I don't want anyone. I want you.'

'And I want you.'

I'm not sure how it happens, or who moves to whom, but suddenly we're kissing. We're really kissing. As though our lives depend on it. Rob's hands are on my face, then in my hair, kissing me with an urgency that I have never experienced. I can feel desire rippling through me, it's tendrils curling like flames, burning, searing a path across my skin. Rob groans softly. Or maybe it's me. I can't tell us apart anymore; where he ends and I begin.

Rob suddenly stops, pressing his forehead against mine.

'I want you so badly, Lucy, but it has to be what you want too. It has to be right. I don't want to ruin things by going too fast.' His voice is breathy, with none of its usual calm control. I sense that if we don't stop soon, he won't be able to. Will I be able to? Do I even want to?

'It is right. I want you too. I don't want to wait.' I feel strangely calm as I speak the words. All the fear and anxiety has left me. I know what I want. I want Rob. Now.

I put my hand under his chin and tip his face up. Only when our eyes are locked do I repeat the words: 'I want you now.'

And we're kissing once more with an ever increasing urgency, and backing towards the bed, our lips never parting, the kiss never stopping. Rob gently lowers me onto the blue and gold bedspread and the fabric feels cool against my seared skin. I want to feel Rob's skin on mine and I pull at his shirt, tugging it free from his waistband, letting my hands explore under the cotton to the skin beneath. His back is warm and smooth and muscular and the caress of my hands causes Rob to groan. He shifts his weight onto one elbow and starts an exploration of his own, tracing the contours of my body though my dress. I can't bear the layers of fabric between us and suddenly we're tugging at each other's clothes, I'm undoing his belt, his button, his zip; unbuttoning his shirt and pulling at it, desperate to get to the warm skin beneath.

And then we're laughing and tugging at our own clothes, removing shoes and undoing shirt sleeve buttons; I'm pulling my dress over my head, all shyness gone, replaced with sheer desire for this man. I'm standing there in front of him in just my underwear, unashamedly offering him all that I am. And he's standing there in front of me in tight-fitting black boxer briefs, his eyes dark with desire.

He steps towards me and his hands are in my hair, we're kissing, the planes of our bodies touching, melding, absorbing. It is one being that falls back onto the bed again, and four hands that hungrily explore. Rob caresses the contours of my body once more, his hand sweeping down the curve of my waist to my hip, to my thigh. I'm trembling at his touch.

'You are exquisite, Lucy. And your skin... it's so soft, it's like silk...' his words trail off and his lips take the place of his hands, sending shivers of wonder everywhere they touch. I arch my body towards him, telling him I want more. He listens and his hands continue their exploration, travelling to my inner thighs, making me gasp. His fingers tease around the edges of my lacy knickers and I can barely contain myself, but he's not done with exploring me yet, and his hands move to my breasts, caressing them through the fabric of my bra, before pulling the fabric away and kissing the pale fullness he finds there. Then he's lifting me slightly and reaching round to my back, releasing my bra with one hand. He slides the straps from my shoulders and tosses the garment to one side.

For a split second, I think about the scars from my breast reduction, but before I even have time to wonder what Rob will think, he's tracing them with his fingers and then his lips, clearly not repulsed by them. I let myself get lost in the sensations once more, completely in the thrall of this man. I reach behind me to grasp the brass bed frame, gripping on tightly as Rob's kisses travel down my body; the feel of his lips on my skin is almost too much to bear, so sensitized to his every touch have I become. I'm trying not to cry out as his journey down my body continues, but I can hear soft moans which I think are coming from me. It's no good, I can't wait another second. I reach down and put my hands on either side of Rob's head, pulling him back up the bed until our eyes meet again:

'I want you inside me. Now. Please.' I can hear the desperation in my voice, but I need to be as close to Rob as possible.

'Are you sure, Lucy?'

'Yes. I'm sure.'

CHAPTER 44

The naked truth

We're lying naked on the bed now, entwined limbs glistening with a sheen of sweat. Rob's thumb is tracing lazy circles on my outstretched arm, which is lying across his torso. I'm so relaxed I feel almost on the edge of consciousness, drifting in a hazy post-love making glow.

'You OK, beautiful?' Rob's voice breaks through to me.

'Mm,' is all I can manage by way of a reply. Speaking might burst this lovely fuzzy feeling which I never want to end. It's as if I've been drugged. It's amazing and I'm not ready to come down yet.

Rob laughs. 'Are you falling asleep?'

'Mm... no... just incredibly relaxed.' I force myself to come to a bit.

'I'm glad. I only ever want to make you happy, Lucy.'

'Oh, you do! I think I'm probably the happiest woman alive right now. That was amazing. You're amazing.'

'We're amazing. I knew it would be like this with you. The very first moment I saw you. We were made for one another.'

'We were, weren't we? Nothing has ever felt quite this... right.'

'Would now be a good time to ring down to reception to order that time machine?' Rob tries to sound jokey, but I pick up on the sadness in his voice. I know exactly what he's thinking.

'I know,' I say, clinging onto him tighter than ever. 'I know.'

We lie there in silence for a while, each lost in our own thoughts. Probably very similar thoughts, of what might have been had we met years earlier. I can feel an oppressive sadness threatening our blissful bubble.

'Let's not spoil what we've got with what ifs.' I push myself up on my elbow as I speak, and lean over to kiss Rob. 'I don't want to waste a moment of our precious time together feeling sad.'

Rob smiles a wistful smile. 'You're right, of course. Beautiful and wise, eh?'

'You'd better believe it! Now, I'm starving. Feed me!'

Rob laughs. 'So demanding. What would your ladyship like for her lunch?'

'You!' I say as I push Rob back onto the bed and straddle him, pinning his arms to the bed.

'I'm all yours,' Rob replies with a grin.

And then it's my turn to kiss every inch of him, pausing for a few seconds to remark: 'Impressive powers of recovery', before satisfying my hunger, and his, once more.

'Wow.' We express the syllable simultaneously as we flop back on the bed side by side, panting from the exertion. The muscles in my legs are still trembling, and my heart is pounding. I reach over and grab Rob's hand, placing it on my chest.

'Feel my heart. You did that,' I tell him.

'I think you had something to do with it too. I rather liked you taking control like that.'

'Good. I don't like to be completely submissive.' I'd enjoyed the feeling of power asserting myself over Rob had brought about. Right at this moment I feel like a powerful, passionate woman, and I love it. He's brought out aspects of the woman I thought was lost forever and for the first time in so very long, I feel truly happy. And absolutely starving!

Rob, as ever in tune to my thoughts, gets up from the bed and pads over to the desk. I roll onto my side to watch him, taking in every inch of his lean but muscular physique. Just looking at him arouses me.

'God, what have you done to me?' I groan. 'You've created a monster.'

Rob laughs as he picks up the room service menu and turns back to the bed.

'A very lovely monster, with a monstrous appetite by now I should think. Here, see if there's anything on there you fancy,' Rob says handing me the menu. Before I can even open my mouth to speak, Rob jumps back in: 'And no, I'm not on there.'

I laugh. 'You read my mind.' I tug the pillows up and sit up on the bed. 'I don't think I could go again quite yet though. Give me five minutes.'

'God, woman, you're insatiable,' Rob says.

'It's entirely your fault,' I tell him. 'For being so utterly irresistible.'

'Beautiful, wise and in need of a visit to Specsavers,' Rob says with a chuckle.

'Don't pretend you don't know how gorgeous and sexy you are, Mister.' I love how we've slipped so easily into this exchange of playful remarks. It's hard to believe this is only our second meeting.

'I won't if you don't.'

'Deal. I do feel gorgeous and sexy with you. It's a very long time since I felt this way. If I ever did…'

'I know what you mean. What we have really is very special, Lucy. Maybe even once in a lifetime special.'

I give Rob's hand a squeeze, telling him I understand, but don't have the words. It's all too easy to slip into sadness and wishful thinking again. 'Right, food. What do you fancy? And no, I'm not on the menu.'

Rob laughs. 'Touché! Hand me the menu, wench!'

Soon, we're both in fluffy white robes sitting at the small table in the bay window looking out over the well-maintained gardens, and tucking into poached salmon, new potatoes, sprouting broccoli and baby corn with hollandaise sauce, followed by Eton Mess. I'm not at all surprised when we select the same things from the menu. We seem to be in sync in every way.

Scraping the last bit of pudding from the glass, I see Rob looking at me and smiling.

'Someone WAS hungry.'

'Yep. Worked up quite an appetite. That was delicious. Thank you.'

'You're welcome, Lucy. And you don't have to thank me. Giving you pleasure gives me pleasure.' Rob reaches over and places his hand on mine. Just the touch of his hand is enough to send shivers through me.

'Today has been so wonderful. I wish it didn't have to end.'

'Me too. But there will be other days, Lucy. I promise you.'

'I'm going to miss you like mad in between times though.'

'And I you. At least we'll have something to look forward to though – help us get through those times.' It's Rob's turn to try and keep the mood from dropping.

'Yes, we will. I suppose no one ever said this was going to be easy – we knew what we were getting into when we signed up.'

'Did we, though? I'm not sure I expected to find someone as wonderful as you on that site. And I really didn't think I'd find someone who made me wish I could have my time all over again, and do things differently.'

I roll my hand over so that I can hold Rob's. 'This is going to be hard, isn't it? Are we crazy? We're going to get hurt aren't we?' I can no longer turn the conversation back to the light.

'Yes, I'm very much afraid that we are. But I don't want to stop. Do you?'

'God! No! I don't think I could even if I wanted to. Stopping now might be the sensible option – before we fall any deeper – but I don't feel at all sensible where you're concerned.'

'Good. To be honest, sense went out the car window the moment I set eyes on you in the car park at Claremont.'

'It probably collided with mine as it flew out too,' I tell Rob with a smile. 'I think our fates were sealed in that moment, weren't they?'

'Yes, I think they probably were.'

The mention of Claremont House reminds me that I meant to ask about Rob's surname.

'I keep meaning to ask about your last name…' I begin.

'Ah! Yes, I wondered if you'd picked up on that. It is Clare and the current incumbent of Claremont is my cousin.'

'So, that's why you love it so much there? And why the lady in the café seemed to know you.'

'Yes, I know all the staff by name. My cousin's rather… er… standoffish with them, so I try to be the friendly face of the family.'

'The peacekeeper, eh? That's kind of the role I have in my

family too. The glue that binds them all together.'

'I just believe in simple human kindness – in treating people how you'd like to be treated.'

'You really are my perfect man, Robert Clare.'

'Well then, come and give this perfect man a hug.'

CHAPTER 45

Sweet sorrow

We stand there, framed by the bay window, for a long time, just wrapped in an embrace we both wish could go on forever. Thoughts are unspoken, words unnecessary. I know what's in Rob's mind, just as he knows what's in mine. That this day has to end. And we have to go our separate ways. Neither of us wants to be the one to break the silence, to bring us back to reality.

I don't know how much time passes like that. I only know that when Rob tilts my face up to meet his, a tear is trickling a lonely path down my cheek. I am trying so hard to keep my emotions in check, but I cannot stop this solitary tear from escaping.

'Oh, Lucy. My Lucy. Please don't cry,' Rob says as he brushes the drop of emotion away with his thumb just as it reaches the corner of my mouth.

'I'm sorry. I'm trying so hard not to.'

'I know, my love, I know. I feel the same.'

'I can't bear the thought of saying goodbye to you.'

'We'll see each other again soon, I promise. Hang on to that thought.'

'I'll try. I didn't think it would hurt this much. To feel so ecstatic one minute and that my heart is breaking the next.'

'I know. Me too. If we're going to do this, I suppose we have to find a way of coping with the rollercoaster of emotions.'

'I hate rollercoasters!' I say, pouting a little in an attempt to shake off the blue mood.

'So do I. Let's never go on a real rollercoaster. I always preferred the Waltzer anyway.'

'Oh! Me too! That was always my favourite ride at the fair.'

'Don't think I could go on it now though. Just the thought of it makes me dizzy.'

'The thought of you makes me dizzy. And as for the reality…' As I speak, I let my hand wander into the folds of Rob's bathrobe.

'Madam, you are incorrigible,' he says in mock outrage, before scooping me up and throwing me onto the bed again. We're both laughing again and Rob is tickling my ribs until I scream submission.

It's only when Rob gets up to go to the bathroom that I realise I haven't let Clare know I'm OK. I grab my mobile from my bag.

I'm fine. Don't worry. AMAZING! Xx.

I can hear the shower running now and Rob pops his head round the door:

'Care to join me?' he asks with a wicked grin on his face.

'Absolutely. How else are you going to scrub your back?' I smile sweetly back at him and head to the bathroom to join him, shedding my robe as I go.

'I can't remember the last time I did this with anyone,' I remark. 'Or shared a bath. Not with anyone other than my son, at least.'

'Nope. Me neither. It's rather lovely, isn't it?'

'Mm… I could certainly get used to it.'

'Maybe next time we could have a bubbly bath together? If you'd like to, of course? No pressure.'

'I'd love to. And please stop worrying about pressuring me – I know you wouldn't force me to do anything I wasn't comfortable with. And if I'm not sure, I'll tell you, I promise.'

'OK. Good. Maybe we should have a safe word?' Rob's laughing.

'If you go all *Fifty Shades* on me, you'll be the one needing a safe word! And an ambulance. I don't do pain.' We're both laughing now, and soaping each other's bodies with a cocoa butter-scented bar. I deliberately drop the soap as I'm sudsing Rob's back.

'Oops!' I say, pulling an angelic face at Rob. 'Dropped the soap.' I crouch down to pick up the soap, caressing Rob's body as I go, and get way laid on the way back up…

A few minutes later and we're wrapped in brilliant white bath sheets, both pink from the heat of the shower. And what we got up to in the shower.

'Lucy, you are one hell of a woman. That was amazing.'

'Why, thank you, kind sir. We aim to please.'

'Oh you please alright. You please very much indeed.' Rob kisses me on the cheek.

Reluctantly, we retrieve our clothes from the twisted heap we threw to one side earlier and get dressed in silence. Neither of us wants to acknowledge that our time together is coming to an end. For today at least.

'I hate this.' I'm the first to break the silence.

'Me too. But it's not for long. And we can email every day.'

'I guess. I'm going to miss you though. Today has been more

amazing than I ever could have dreamt.'

'Same for me. I don't want to go back to real life. To pretend that everything's OK.'

'It's not going to be easy. I suppose we just have to keep busy.'

'I'm going to be thinking of you every minute of every day, Lucy. And dreaming of you every night.'

'Then I'll come and find you in your dreams.' I step towards Rob and we embrace one last time before taking a final look around the room and picking up our bags.

'Do we have to go out the way we came in?' I ask Rob. I'm already feeling self-conscious about leaving the room after a few short hours. As usual though, Rob has thought of everything.

'No, there's a side door leading to the car park. I've left the key in the room, so there's no need to go out through Reception.'

'Oh, thank you. You really do think of everything.' I heave a sigh of relief and follow Rob to the exit.

We walk slowly across the gravel to where our cars are parked side by side. I have been dreading this moment and am trying really hard not to give in to the tears that are threatening. I don't want such a perfect day to end on a sad note, but leaving Rob is almost more than I can bear. I can see that Rob is trying to stay strong for me.

'I'll see you really soon, OK? No tears. Be happy that we found each other.'

'I am, I couldn't be any happier, really. It's just…'

'I know. Get that radio on and I'm sure Heart80s will play something to cheer you up. That reminds me, they played one of my favourites on the way here: Foreigner 'Waiting for a Girl Like you'. Did you hear it? Love that song. And you're that girl, Lucy. You really are.'

Rob's words are more than I can bear and the tears break through my defences. 'Sorry, I'm OK. Really. I did hear it and it's my favourite song. When they played it this morning, I wondered if you'd hear it too.'

'I suppose we have our song now then.'

'Yes, I suppose we do. I wonder what they'll play on the way home? I swear the DJ has a direct link to my psyche.'

Rob laughs. 'I often think that too. A song for every feeling and occasion.'

'I'm going to miss you so much,' I say, putting my hands on either side of Rob's waist and leaning my head down into his chest.

'I'm going to miss you too.' As he says the words, Rob tilts my head up so that I'm facing him again. 'Be strong, my love. And know that I'm right with you, every day and night, here,' he places a hand on my chest, 'and here.' Rob touches my temple. And he smiles. And I am lost. I am his love and he is mine.

'I'll try,' I tell him. 'I promise.'

'Good. I'll see you very soon.'

I don't know how to say goodbye, or if I can, so instead I just echo his words and turn to unlock the car. Rob opens my door and I reluctantly get in. As he's closing the door, I start the engine so I can wind down the window. I can't bear the glass to come between us. Rob stoops down and leans in to kiss me just once more. Then I'm pulling away and I'm watching him in the rear view mirror as I head to the exit. He's just standing there watching me drive away. Then, just as I reach the gates, he lifts his hand to wave, his hand hanging in the air as I turn the corner.

CHAPTER 46

Fish and chips with a side order of guilt

The image of Rob standing there in the car park is imprinted on my brain. It was such a wrench to leave him and I honestly don't know how I'm going to survive until I can see him again. Or how I'm going to keep up the pretence that everything's OK at home. Home. I haven't thought about home today. Being with Rob felt like home. But now I have to face the fact that Rob's not real life. He's real, oh so very real, and what we feel for each other feels real. But it can't be can it? Because he's someone else's. And so am I.

My head is swimming with conflicting thoughts and feelings. I'm utterly confused about what's happening in my life. My logical side knows that what I'm doing is wrong, but how can it be when it feels so damn right? I hear myself let out a huge sigh, and reach over to switch the radio on. I'm hoping for a distraction I think. The adverts are just coming to an end. I do my usual thing of trying to name the song from the intro-duction as the next track starts up. I have no trouble with this one as the familiar piano intro of Peter Cetera's 'Glory of Love' starts up. I smile, knowing full well that Rob will be listening too, and smiling.

I hug the thought to myself and turn the radio up, singing along with the love anthem from one of the *Karate Kid* films I remember so well, and am overwhelmed by a feeling of euphoria. The feeling stays with me through much of the drive home as I relive every moment of the day with Rob. I can do this, I tell myself: I can cope with real life as long as I have time with Rob to look forward to. I'm already acting my way through my days – it's just now there's one more player on the stage.

The digital clock tells me that it's four thirty-five when I pull onto the drive. I'm checking my face for tell-tale signs of my day when the front door opens. I quickly flip the visor back up and wave at Tom who's standing in the doorway with Paul. I smile my biggest smile. Jumping out of the car I hurry over to Tom and wrap him up in the biggest hug.

'Hello! Have you had a good day? I can't wait to hear all about it,' I tell him as I release him. I stand up and look at Paul. 'Hey. How was your day?'

Paul smiles at me. 'Not bad thanks. How was shopping?'

By now we're all back indoors, and Alfie has joined the welcoming committee, bouncing around and showing me how much he missed me.

'It was fun, thanks. Clare managed to get the right handbag this time.'

'Excellent. Did you treat yourself to anything?'

'No, but I was there to help Clare really. Anyway, I don't need anything. Right, cup of tea?' I'm keen to change the subject to one where I don't have to lie.

'I'll make it,' Paul says. 'You've been on your feet all day. Go and sit down in the playroom with Tom.'

'OK, thanks.' Why does he have to be so kind now? Now, when I don't deserve it. Rather than on my feet, I've just spent most of the day horizontal, in bed with another man. He doesn't

241

deserve this. But I can't help the way I feel, or rather don't feel about Paul. I don't love him, and it's pretending that has led me into Rob's arms. I can't undo what's done now anyway, even if I wanted to. I have no choice but to keep lying, to protect not only my secret, but the feelings of the man I married.

Thankfully, Tom is young enough still to be oblivious to the subtleties of others' emotional states, and he immediately starts to chatter to me about his day. All I need to do in return is smile and interject occasionally. Before Paul comes back in with the tea I quickly text Clare:

Home safe. Speak soon. Nice handbag!! Xx.

She texts back almost immediately. *?? Handbag? Glad you're ok. Can't wait to hear ALL about it! Xx.*

I'm smiling at the phone when Paul comes in with the tea. I feel a wave of anxiety when he sees me on my mobile.

'Clare,' I say, lifting my phone. 'Just saying thank you for today.'

'I swear you two were separated at birth. You can't go five minutes without texting,' Paul says as he hands me a mug of tea. I notice with a pang that I assume to be guilt, that he's used the 'World's Best Mum' mug he and Tom got for me last Mother's Day.

'What can I say? She's my best friend and I'd be lost without her. Not jealous are you?' I'm teasing Paul, trying to keep things light. I know he's not in the least bit jealous; he's not the insecure type.

'Ha! Yeah, right! I'm not jealous, I'm outraged! Had to make my own lunch again today. Shocking.' Paul tries to keep a straight face as he shakes his head.

I put my hands to my face and try to match his outrage.

'That's terrible. You poor thing. You must be shattered.'

'I am. I could do with a lie down actually.' Paul winks at me. I feel a moment of panic and my heart thumps in my chest. I hope my face isn't giving away how much I hate the thought of going to bed with him. I'm grateful that Tom is a ready-made excuse.

'Poor poppet!' I say, sticking my bottom lip out.

'I'll give you *poor poppet*,' Paul says, hands heading for my ribs in threat of tickling.

'My tea!' I cry out, holding my mug aloft before his hands reach their target.

'I'll get you later,' comes Paul's response.

No, you won't, I think to myself as I breathe an internal sigh of relief. I've escaped. For now. But how long can I keep up the game of cat and mouse? Just the thought of it distresses me.

I turn my attention to Tom, keen to change the focus of the conversation and ease the pressure building in my head and chest. We snuggle up on the sofa to watch television. I couldn't tell you what's on though, as I can't focus on anything but the inner turmoil I'm experiencing.

I don't know how much time passes like that, but Paul's voice eventually breaks through.

'Shall I get fish and chips?' he's saying.

'Ooh, yes please. Sorry, feeling a bit pooped this evening.'

'Hard work, all that shopping, eh?'

I feel my face flush and I get up from the sofa as I reply, trying to hide my discomfort: 'Damn right. But what's a girl to do? When her best friend needs her...? Right, I'll warm some plates.' Subject safely reverted back to dinner.

With Paul out of the house, plates warming, cutlery selected and condiments at the ready, I quickly retrieve my phone and log into my email account. It's probably too soon to expect anything from Rob, but I can't resist checking. I feel the usual thrill of anticipation as I watch to see if I have a new message, and my heart leaps when his name appears in bold. Clicking on it, I see that it's a link to something on YouTube. I select it and wait for it to load. It's Peter Cetera and soon the strains of 'Glory of Love' ring out. It's a bittersweet smile that meets with a single tear. How can it be that I feel for this man with such an intensity? And how can I survive the time that we're apart? I wipe the salty streak from my face and return to the email, desperate to see whatever words accompanied the song.

I guess we have a second song. See you in my dreams, beautiful girl. Xxxx.

Just as I'm thinking of how to reply, Alfie alerts me to the fact that Paul is home. There's no time. But I need to say something.

Meet you in them xxxx, I type quickly and press send just as I hear the front door open. Shoving my phone back into my pocket I wipe my hands across my face and take a deep breath to steady myself. This subterfuge is stressful and I can feel my heart thumping in my ears.

I let domesticity reclaim me for the rest of the evening. It takes a conscious effort. I do wonder if this will get any easier. The pretending. Though that is surely a bad thing, isn't it? It would mean I've become a better liar. A better cheat. Cheat. The word pricks me like a thistle on a bare leg. An ugly word. A word I never thought I would be applying to me. I mentally stamp on it, as I would the offending weed. It has no place in my bubble.

CHAPTER 47

Double entendre central

I know the next morning that Clare will be waiting for me, chomping at the bit to hear all about my day with Rob. As I pull up behind her car I can almost feel her impatience and it makes me smile. As usual, she spots me and is out of the car and grinning at me and mouthing something which I take to be 'hurry up!' I grin at her and then, quite deliberately, take my time readying myself and Tom to get out. When I look at Clare, she's literally jumping up and down on the spot.

'What is taking you so long?' she asks as I finally open my door, exasperation in her voice.

'What? I don't know what you mean,' I reply, all innocence.

'Don't give me that butter-wouldn't-melt look, Mrs! Will you get a ruddy move on?'

I laugh at how cross she's getting. I know she just wants to get rid of the kids as fast as possible, so she can grill me about yesterday.

'The gates won't open any faster, you know. No point in rushing.' I can't help pushing her a little bit further.

Clare makes a sort of strangled noise and clenches her fists, and I finally relent with a laugh.

'Sorry, look, we're ready,' I tell her, getting Tom out of the car and ushering him onto the pavement.

'Finally. Let's go!' Clare grabs Chloe's hand and steers her towards Tom. 'You walk with Tom. Mummy needs to speak to Lucy. About shopping,' she adds as an afterthought. Chloe glares at her mother and Clare just wrinkles her nose at her. I can't help chuckling at the dynamic between them.

Clare grabs my arm and makes us hang back a bit, waiting until Tom and Chloe are out of earshot. 'Well?' she asks. 'I know today's Wednesday, but was Tuesday hump day?' Clare gives me an exaggerated nudge, nudge, wink, wink.

'Oh. My. God. Really? How long have you been working on that one? Shocking. Not sure I want to tell you now,' I reply in mock outrage.

'What can I say? Comedy gold. My mind wanders when I'm hoovering.' Clare shrugs.

'I see… thinking of incorporating a bit of stand-up in your art installations are you?'

'Ha! Don't suppose you did much standing up yesterday?'

I groan. 'Don't give up the day job just yet.'

'Speaking of jobs…'

'You had to go there, didn't you?' We're both laughing now.

'Yep. Question is, did you?' Clare turns and looks directly at me and my flushed face tells her everything she needs to know. 'Oh my God, you did! And? I want details.'

'Well, you're not getting them. You'll have to content yourself with an overview.'

'Is that what you get when you're on top?' Clare cackles.

'God, woman, you're like a dog with a bone. You'll be bringing out the thumbscrews next,' I say, shaking my head. One look at Clare's face tells me I shouldn't have used the words *bone* and *screw*. 'Don't!' I warn her.

'Oh, but I want to,' Clare is relentless. 'Is that what you said to Rob?'

'Mm hmm, amongst other things.' I relent a little as I know Clare won't give up until I give her something. 'God, Clare, it was amazing. He's amazing. We're really good together.'

Clare's face softens. 'Oh, Lucy, I'm so happy for you. And totally jealous, of course.'

'Thank you, Clare. It means a lot having you on my side – not judging me.'

We've reached the school now, so we press pause on our conversation, both waiting impatiently for the gates to open. As soon as the kids are safely inside, we press play once more. Clare links her arm through mine.

'Seriously, Lucy, I am genuinely happy for you. You deserve some happiness.'

'Thanks, Clare. I'm not sure how I'm going to cope with this double life though. Rob's all I can think about. I just want to be back with him.'

'Well, it was never going to be easy, was it? You knew the risks. Only you can decide if they're worth it.'

'I s'pose so. I think I hadn't really considered how hard it would be if I really fell for someone though.'

Clare can't resist. 'And how hard was it?' She's giggling like a twelve-year-old who just doodled a knob on the blackboard.

'Well, put it this way, I have no complaints. Quite the opposite in fact.'

Clare pounces on my words again.

'God, are there no safe words? You're incorrigible.'

'Ooh, you have a safe word? I thought you weren't into all that?'

'Shut up, woman. Although we did joke about having a safe word. I think it'd probably be *ambulance*.' It's my turn to laugh now as Clare looks confused.

'I'm not even going to ask. Pervert,' she says in mock disgust.

'God, Clare, what am I going to do?'

'Rob. As often as possible by the sound of it.'

'Seriously, I think I might love him. That's mental, isn't it? We've only seen each other twice.'

'It can happen like that, I think. You just know. Or maybe you're in love with the idea of it – you know, because you've been unhappy for so long.'

'Maybe. It feels so real though.'

'I guess time will tell. I do worry you're going to get hurt.'

'Me too. It feels kind of inevitable, if I'm honest. We can't have a happy ending, can we?' The words are out of my mouth before I have time to think. Clare pounces on them at once, and now we're both giggling like schoolgirls because she just added a few extra strokes to the picture on the blackboard.

CHAPTER 48

Time stands still

September plods along, seemingly in no hurry to meet October. The days are apparently in no rush either, as I wait impatiently for my next meeting with Rob. Don't they know how I long to be back with him? It's as though they're conspiring against me, taking Paul's side; punishing me for my thoughts and deeds. I wait impatiently each day for bedtime to arrive. Hours spent in sleep are the only peace I know right now, and I welcome them gratefully each night, fast forwarding me to Rob that little bit more. I go through the motions each day, doing what's required, expected. I try to fight the resentment I feel towards everything that stands between me and him.

Everything except Tom, that is. For him I feel nothing but love and protectiveness. I hadn't thought it possible to love him more than before, but he is in danger of being hugged to death. I tell him constantly how much I love him, how he means the world to me. I renew my vows to him daily: to never let anything bad happen to him. Protecting my child gives me the resolve to keep going, to keep my secret and take no risks. I cannot, will not, get caught.

Paul appears not to have noticed anything different about me. Certainly he hasn't said anything. I guess I've become a proficient actress over the years. I'm constantly amazed that the strain I feel under doesn't show on my face. Every time I look in the mirror I expect the face looking back at me to be more like Edvard Munch's *The Scream* than my own. When I think about living like this for the rest of my life though…

I push the thought to the back of my mind, but I'm aware of it festering there, giving off its noxious fumes, threatening to overcome me.

To the casual observer we must look like a happy little family. Only Clare knows the truth and I'm conscious of the burden I've placed on her shoulders. I find myself apologising to her time and again, and thanking her for being my rock. I've just been doing it again at the school gates. She has her fingers in her ears:

'La la la la la! Can't hear you.' She pauses. 'Have you stopped yet?'

I nod and she takes her fingers out. 'I really am sorry though, Clare,' I'm laughing now.

'Grrr! Will you shut up and stop apologising.'

'Sorry!'

We're both laughing now, as we wave goodbye to the kids and head back to the cars.

'So, when are you seeing Rob next?'

'I don't know. Not soon enough. He's busy with work at the moment, and I'm struggling to come up with an excuse to be away for the day. Can't keep saying we're going shopping.'

'Hmm. Tricky. Isn't Paul away again soon? Maybe you could do something then?'

'Yes, he's back in France at the beginning of October, but I'd have to be back to pick Tom up from school each day.'

'What about his grandparents? I'm sure they'd love a chance to spend time with Tom.'

'Yeah, they would. I'm just not sure how I feel about dragging them into things – having to lie to them about where I am. It's bad enough having to lie to Paul.'

'What about if Rob came to the house?' Clare grimaces as she suggests this, clearly not thinking it's advisable, but willing to play devil's advocate all the same.

'God! Can you imagine?! There's no way I'd be able to relax. Be my luck for Paul's parents to turn up or something.'

'Yep. Bad idea.'

'Besides, it wouldn't be fair to bring him into Paul's home. I couldn't do that to him. I know it makes no sense, but there are still some lines I can't cross.'

'I get that. And I think you're right.'

'I think it's best to keep my two worlds separate if I can. It's a sodding logistical nightmare though. And I'm desperate to see Rob again.'

'I know you are, Lucy. I do understand. Just wish I could do more to help.'

'You put up with me – I couldn't ask for anything more.'

'Yeah. Actually, I deserve a bloody medal for putting up with you,' Clare says, laughing.

'To go right alongside your Services to Vacuuming one.'

'You're just jealous because you haven't got one.' Clare sticks her tongue out at me.

'Nor ever likely to. I think I might be on for an Oscar though if my life carries on like this.' I smile a wry smile.

'Now that would be an interesting acceptance speech… "I'd like to thank my husband and family… blah blah blah… and not forgetting my lover…"'

'Hmmm. Red face and red dress to match the red carpet methinks.'

'*The Scarlet Woman*, starring the one and only…'

I groan. 'God, it's not funny though, is it? I really am *the other woman*. How is that ever going to be OK?'

'Don't think about it like that. You're not hurting anyone, just taking some happiness where you can. And Rob's doing the same. No harm no foul.'

'Easy to say…' I'm not convinced.

'Life's too sodding short, Lucy. Don't overthink it. As long as you're careful…'

'It's just so hard, Clare. Pretending all the time. It's exhausting.'

'Well, only you can change that – and you were pretending long before Rob came on the scene. And unless you're prepared to be honest with Paul and end your marriage, I don't see how that's ever going to change.' Clare shrugs.

'I know. God, it's a depressing thought. I just can't see how I could ever end things with Paul. It's still easier to be unhappy than hurt him.'

'I know you believe that, Lucy, but we're not responsible for other people's happiness.'

'I just don't get that. If I end our marriage, Paul gets hurt, so I'm responsible for his happiness, surely?'

'But you're living a lie – you're saying that Paul doesn't deserve real happiness, a chance to find someone who really wants to be with him. It's hard to explain.'

'I don't really understand. This is what I've always done, for as long as I can remember anyway. If my actions would cause someone pain, then I don't take them.'

'I do see where you're coming from. I wish I could explain it better. If you ended it with Paul, you wouldn't be hurting him intentionally, would you?'

'No, of course not, but I would be hurting him. So, if I can prevent that… then surely I would?' I'm trying to understand what Clare means, but it just makes no sense to me.

'I'll try and find an article for you on the subject. I think you've been a people pleaser for so long – it's all you know. But what about pleasing you, Lucy?'

'Thank you. I'll be honest, I'm struggling with the concept, but I'm willing to try and understand.'

Clare smiles at me. 'I just want you to be happy, Lucy.'

'I know. Thank you. Sorry,' I say with a grin, taking the conversation full circle in an attempt to lighten it once more.

Clare sticks her fingers back in her ears and starts to la la la once more.

I nudge her to listen. 'Changing the subject, have you spoken to Charlie lately?'

'No, I saw Zoe in Tesco's though and we had a bit of a natter about her. She's really struggling, isn't she?'

'Yes, poor thing. She's knows what she needs to do… not that easy though is it? She's terrified if she asks the question, she won't get the answer she wants.'

'I know. Can't go on like this indefinitely though. At some point something's got to give.'

'I think she's just clinging on to the hope that Rich stands up to his bloody mother.'

'Yep. He needs to show Charlie that she's the most important person in his life. His mum sounds like a right dragon.'

'He'll have to man up eventually though, surely? Or he's

going to lose Charlie.'

'I know. And they're so good together when the old bat's not sticking her oar in.'

'God, why are relationships so difficult? I thought they'd get easier as we got older – we'd all be sorted.'

'Wishful thinking, I'm afraid, my friend. We'll probably still be having conversations like this when we're ninety.'

'And running riot in the old people's home.'

'Oh yes! I'll be making patterns in the lawn with my mobility scooter.'

'Ha ha! And I'll still be internet dating – Grab-a-granny. com.'

'Secret-grab-a-granny.com more like!'

CHAPTER 49

Dinosaurs in the maze

October finally limps around. I'm aware that my SAD symptoms have as much to do with missing Rob as they do with the drawing in of the nights. Paul is getting ready for another trip to France and I'm looking forward to a few days where I don't have to act my socks off pretending everything's OK. The strain is making me feel I'm coming apart at the seams and I need to do a few repairs while Paul's away. Paul seems happier about making the trip this time. Maybe I haven't been hiding my mood as well as I thought and he's looking forward to a bit of time away from me too. I've done some guilty conscience ironing, and Paul has sufficient shirts to take with him.

Rob and I have been exchanging emails daily and I find I'm locking myself in the loo ten times a day to quickly check my phone. Every time Paul catches me looking at my mobile I feel a rush of blood to my head, even if I'm doing something completely innocent, which isn't actually that often to be truthful. I am continually chiding myself for taking risks and am paranoid about leaving my phone lying around, even though it's password protected. My nerves are as frayed as the hem on an overlong pair of flared jeans.

I'm sitting on the loo seat now, reading Rob's latest email.

Lucy, my love, how are you holding up? Better than me, I hope?! I'm missing you terribly and aching to be with you again. I've managed to clear my diary for parts of next week while you're on your own. Please, let's try and get together – even if it's only for a couple of hours. I could book somewhere a bit closer to you, cut down on the travelling for you if that helps? Or even a coffee somewhere. Or a walk with your dog. I just need to hold you again. Rxxxx.

Dearest Rob, I'm going round the bend to be honest. In fact, I think I've been right round and am about to lap myself! Right now I'd settle for five minutes with you. I'll have a think about what we can do next week – it would be wonderful if we could have some proper time alone. Until then, your emails will keep me going. Just! Your Lucy xxxx. I hit send and hug my phone to my chest, trying to feel closer to Rob somehow.

I reluctantly force my thoughts back to reality and vacate the loo, just remembering to flush before doing so. It's almost four p.m. and Paul will be finishing work very soon. I check on Tom in the playroom – he's happily battling with a Power Ranger in one hand and a Transformer in the other. I don't interrupt him as I'm more than happy to indulge in thoughts of Rob for as long as possible. I'm standing at the kitchen sink, staring unseeing out at the garden when Paul finds me.

'Penny for them,' he says, clicking his fingers by my ear and bursting into my bubble.

'What? Oh, hi. Probably not worth a penny - just wondering what to do for dinner.' I could hardly tell him what I was really thinking about, could I? 'I should really start thinking about it earlier, shouldn't I?'

'Yep. Maybe it's time to dig out the slow cooker again?

Nights are drawing in.'

'Don't remind me. I think I need to get one of those SAD lamps this winter. Might stop me being such a miserable cow.'

'Well, I didn't like to say anything... but... where can I buy one?' Paul asks with a grin. I know he's only joking, but I am miserable. 'Don't look so glum, you know I still love you, even if you are a miserable old bag sometimes.'

Another wave of guilt washes over me. 'I don't know why you put up with me,' I say with a sad smile. And I mean it. I really don't know why my husband puts up with me. I wish it was enough to galvanize me into taking action with my life, but it just paralyses me. I wish I knew how to get back what we once had, but those feelings simply don't exist anymore. I wish they did. But they don't. I think back to what Clare said to me about letting Paul go to find true happiness, but I know he'd be heartbroken if we split up. I simply can't do it to him.

'Well, I can't inflict you on anyone else, can I?' Paul says, ever the joker.

'Fair point. You must have done something awful in a previous life to have got lumbered with me – maybe you were Attila the Hun or someone like that.'

Paul laughs. 'Yeah, maybe! You, on the other hand, must have been an angel to be rewarded with a veritable god like me.'

'Yeah, yeah.' I suddenly feel very sorry for my next incarnation as I'm certainly no angel in this life. 'Anyway, why don't you go and play with Tom while I concoct something for dinner.'

'OK, just nipping out for a cigarette first.' Paul heads out the back door and soon I smell the hated smoke drifting in through the utility room and into the kitchen. It makes me grit my teeth, and my mood sinks once more.

I try to navigate my way out of the doldrums as I rummage through the freezer, looking for something quick and easy for dinner. I'm hoping to stumble across a 'something I prepared earlier' container lurking forgotten under the turkey dinosaurs. No such luck. Who was I kidding anyway? I have the best of intentions when it comes to batch cooking, but the reality rarely matches up. With a sigh, I pull out some fishcakes – at least they just need bunging in the oven. Tom will be happy with a couple of T-Rex and a Stegosaurus.

After finding some cheating potatoes in the fridge (four minutes in the microwave) and some steam-in-the-bag veg., I take up my position at the kitchen sink once more. It's too early to cook, and I'm aware that I should make Paul a drink and join him with Tom in the playroom, but I simply can't dredge up the enthusiasm to play happy families. I'm overcome with uncomfortable feelings of guilt and regret, and my head pounds under the weight of the pain and confusion. *What the hell am I going to do?* I ask myself, over and over. But there are no satisfactory answers. My head is the Power Ranger, my heart the Transformer, and there's a battle going on in which there can be no victor. I just want Rob to sweep me up in his arms and tell me everything's going to be OK. But that's never going to happen. It can't. It's impossible. On that battlefield his wife takes the spoils.

I'm losing myself deeper and deeper in my melancholy maze and starting to experience moments of panic that feel like hands squeezing my chest and throat. I can't go on like this, I know that, but I'm paralysed by indecision and fear. I have no idea what lies in the centre of the maze, or if I'll ever get there. In increasingly rare moments of clarity, when I'm honest with myself about the future, only Tom awaits me at the end of this tangle of paths. I don't want Paul and I can't have Rob. Both paths lead to heartbreak. Is it easier to break mine or Paul's? I know what I want. I simply have no idea how to get it when it's always been easier to hurt myself than another. I can't help feeling though, that this hurt might be more than I can bear.

CHAPTER 50

The bridge

I have no choice but to dig through my dressing-up box for my red crayon smile and carry on with the charade that my life has become. To me, when I look in the mirror, it looks maybe a little lopsided, maybe a little less bright. But nobody appears to notice as the days go by. The leaves on the horse chestnut tree in the garden are turning golden brown as their chlorophyll breaks down from reduced daylight and falling temperatures. And something similar is happening in me, turning me paler, inside and out.

I keep telling myself I just have to get through the next few days, until Paul leaves for France. Then I can shed my costume as the trees will soon be shedding theirs, revealing the bare naked truth of what lies beneath. I know it won't be pretty, but the relief will be immense, however short-lived. The trouble is that it's getting harder and harder to step back into character when the time comes. I honestly don't know how much longer I can maintain the façade. I have to act – to take action, that is. The irony is not lost on me.

Monday morning finally arrives and Tom and I wave Paul off early in the morning. I heave an internal sigh of relief and turn my attention to Tom. All I need to do is get him off to school and then I can relax. Thankfully, routine kicks in and soon I'm walking away from school with Clare. She hooks her arm through mine:

'So, tell. When are you seeing Rob?' she asks.

'Later this morning – just for a couple of hours.'

'No afternoon delight today then?'

'To be honest, Clare, I don't care what we do. I just want him to hold me tight enough to push the stuffing back in. I'm like one of those old teddy bears that's coming apart at the seams. Need some TLC to put me back together again.'

'Oh dear. You're really struggling aren't you?' Clare looks worried.

'Yep. Honestly, Clare, I don't know what to do. I know what I want to do, but I don't think I've got the strength to do it.'

'You want to end it with Paul, don't you?'

'Yes. But how can I? The whole prospect is terrifying. How do I turn our world upside down like that? I never wanted my child to come from a broken home like I did.' Tears are welling in the corners of my eyes.

Clare squeezes my arm. 'I know, Lucy, but Tom would adapt – kids do. Look at you – you're completely normal,' she says, pulling a mad face at me, trying to cheer me up. 'And Paul would get over it and meet someone else. You deserve to be happy. Everyone does.'

'It's doing my head in thinking about it. I just go round and round in circles, but I always come back to not being able to hurt Paul.'

'I know that, but how long can you go on like this? You'll make yourself really ill. Life is short – don't waste any more of it being with the wrong person. Surely it's better to be on your own and have the hope of meeting someone – the right someone – than be with someone you don't love?'

'Yes, it is. I know you're right, Clare. But it's not that easy. Where do I even start? How do I tell Paul it's over? I've done a pretty good job of pretending everything's OK until now – it's going to be one hell of a shock to him.'

'You've got to find a way of being honest with him, Lucy. He deserves that. Yes, it'll be hard and painful, for both of you, but I think you'll feel relieved too.'

'Just thinking about it makes me feel sick. And I honestly don't know how he'll react. I don't want him to hate me.'

'I don't think he could ever hate you, Lucy. It might seem like he does at first, but he'll come round, I'm sure of it.'

'The whole prospect terrifies me. I know you're right, though, I can't go on like this. Meeting Rob has proved to me that I want more, need more. I do want an honest relationship. I don't want to pretend anymore.'

'And you shouldn't have to. What are you going to do about Rob?'

'I honestly don't know. I don't want to be the other woman, but I'm not sure I'm ready to give him up.'

'You don't have to – why not just enjoy it for now?'

'God, what a bloody mess,' I say, with a sad smile at my friend.

'It'll get better, Lucy, I promise. And I'm here for you, no matter what. OK?'

'Thanks, Clare. Thank you for everything.'

We're standing by the cars now and Clare gives me a hug.

'Have a lovely time with Rob later. Try and relax and forget about the tough stuff for a couple of hours.'

'Thanks, Clare. I will. Have a good day and I'll see you on pick up.'

Alone in my car, I allow my thoughts to focus solely on Rob, and the thrilling prospect of being with him very soon. My smile is genuine as I start the engine, wondering as always what song the radio will deliver. The DJ's got his work cut out for him today, I think with a chuckle – good luck navigating this jumble of emotions. I recognise the song that's coming to an end as Tears for Fears' 'Woman in Chains' – hmm, glad that's ending, I think, as I wait for the next one, hoping for something a bit more uplifting. I'm not disappointed and drive home singing along to Steve Winwood's 'Higher Love'.

All I have to do is walk Alfie and get myself ready before setting off to meet Rob at about ten forty-five. The butterflies have started their fluttering in anticipation. I can't wait to see him. I think about Rob as I walk with the dog, about how my life has changed, how I have changed, since I met him just a few short weeks ago. This man who has brought both clarity and complication to my life. He has shown me what I could have with one hand, and snatched it away with the other. Bittersweet. I think that encapsulates my relationship with Rob. Pleasure and pain. Can't have one without the other. I just hope the pleasure is worth the anguish I will inevitably feel when the end comes. Which it must. Even if I manage to leave Paul, Rob still can't be mine. Our bubble must burst.

I try to switch off my thoughts for a few minutes as I walk, letting my senses take over for a while, allowing mindfulness to kick in. *Be in the moment, Lucy*, I tell myself, as I inhale the cool, damp morning air and appreciate my surroundings. The park is almost empty, save for a couple of other dog walkers. The only sounds are of birds, and the occasional bark of an excited dog asking for the ball to be thrown. *He's in the moment,*

I think with a smile. The ducks are still dozing along the edge of the lake, heads tucked in to their wings, and a pair of early-rising swans are cruising majestically through the water. You'd never know they were paddling furiously beneath the surface. I totally relate.

I'm nearing the end of the path, where the lake reverts to river and a small bridge allows you to cross after a quick game of Pooh sticks. There's a bench just before the bridge. I sometimes sit on it to think and to delay going home. I can see that it's already occupied today and I recognise the back of the occupier's blonde, sculpted bob immediately.

'We must stop meeting like this,' I say as I near the bench. 'People will talk.' It's Charlie.

'Hello, Lucy!' she laughs. 'Let them bloody well talk. They're probably already gossiping about my cancelled wedding anyway. Sod 'em!'

'That's the spirit,' I say, joining her on the bench after checking Alfie's close by. 'How're things?'

'The same. Stalemate.' She shrugs. 'Do you know what though, Lucy, I feel OK, stronger. I've made up my mind to talk honestly with Rich. I've realised that if he can't put us first, then why would I want to be with him? I deserve better than that.'

'Wow. I'm impressed. Well done you.'

'Thanks. I feel empowered now I've made the decision. And relieved. I was making myself ill wondering and worrying. If it's meant to be it will be. If not, it was never right and there's something better round the corner.'

'That's a brilliant attitude, Charlie. I'm so pleased. And full of admiration actually. I wish I could think a bit more like that.'

'You don't need to though. You're sorted, Lucy. I've always admired how together you are – how positive. You always light up a room when you come in.'

'Oh my god? Really? Is that how I come across? Wowzers! I've been feeling like a right miserable cow lately.' It's not the first time I've been told how *sorted* I appear and it always surprises me.

Charlie looks genuinely surprised. 'You're joking? Well, it doesn't show. Zoe and I once joked you must be on happy pills and were going to ask if we could have some of whatever you were on,' she tells me with a slightly apologetic giggle.

'Ha! Nope, just me practising to join the local amateur dramatic group.'

'Well, I'd buy tickets to see whatever you're in – are you honestly not happy? I'm gobsmacked.'

I shrug and smile sadly. I'm not ready to unburden myself to anyone else.

'For what it's worth, Lucy, my advice is change whatever's not working – you'll regret it if you don't. I'm already starting to feel resentment towards Rich, so I know I've got to do something before it's too late. Whatever the outcome. My mum's having Lewis and tonight's the night.'

'I really hope it's the outcome you want. I'll be thinking of you and keeping everything crossed. Let me know you're OK. And if I can do anything…'

'Thanks, Lucy. I'm going to be OK.'

And I believe her. I can see the strength shining out of her. I hope some of it lands on me.

CHAPTER 51

In laws and outlaws

It's eleven fifteen and I'm just pulling off the motorway, heading for a garden centre complex a mile or so further on. The smile I have on my face is real, and growing wider with every passing mile. In just fifteen short minutes, I'll be back in Rob's arms.

I'm early, as ever, but more than happy to wait: Rob's worth it. No waiting necessary though as, when I pull into the car park, I spot his car already parked, facing the entrance so I can spot him and vice versa. The grin reaches my ears as our gazes lock. And he's grinning broadly too. If it's possible to feel as though you'll burst with happiness, then that's how I'm feeling right now. In this moment, nothing else matters.

I pull into the space next to his, and Rob's out of the car and hurrying round before I've even taken my seatbelt off. And then I'm out and he's wrapping me into an embrace I wish would never end. I snuggle in tightly, breathing in his scent, his warmth, feeling his heart racing to meet mine. I'm safe. I'm loved. I'm home.

When we finally pull back from one another a little, Rob tilts my face up to his.

'Hello, you,' he says. 'I've missed you.'

'I've missed you too,' I tell him. 'Rather a lot actually.'

Rob's hands move to cup my face and he kisses me tenderly. The circuitry in my brain fizzes and my senses flare to his touch. Nothing has ever felt this right, this good. I think if I didn't have his arms around me, supporting me, my legs might have given way. I am literally melting in his arms.

'Thank you for meeting me today – I know it's not easy for you, and it's not ideal when we have nowhere to go...'

I put my finger to his lips and stop him: 'I would meet you anywhere, anytime, even if it was just for a hug hello and goodbye. Of course it would be nice to go somewhere private and have as much time together as possible, but whatever we can manage is just fine. I simply want to be close to you.'

'God, you wonderful, beautiful woman. I'm so happy I found you.' Rob squeezes me even tighter.

'I'm happy you found me too. I was pretty lost before.'

'I wish I'd found you sooner.' Rob looks wistful.

'I know. Me too. But the important thing is that we're together now.' I don't want us to slip into regret over what could have been. 'Let's just make the most of what we have now.'

'You're right, of course. Sorry. I didn't mean to bring the mood down. It's just that every time I'm with you, every time I think of you even, I wish our paths had crossed years ago. I find myself wishing my life had been different. Since I met you, Lucy, I can't help feeling that I've been living the wrong life.'

'I do understand and I feel the same. I've known I was living the wrong life for a while now, but meeting you has shown me what the right life can feel like. It's a painful truth to acknowledge, especially when we can't be together.'

'It's not fair, is it?'

'No, it's not fair. But life often isn't. God, listen to us – pair of old miseries! Let's go in search of coffee and cake. Everything will look so much better then.'

'Come on then. It's this way, I think.' Rob takes my hand and we head towards the entrance. 'It's not quite Claremont is it?' he remarks.

'Not quite. I'm not complaining though. As long as I'm with you.'

'It really is wonderful to see you again, Lucy. Having this to look forward to makes life more bearable. The empty times don't seem quite so empty now.'

'You too. It's hard though. Acting like everything's normal, when you're all I can think about. I miss you so much.'

We've made our way through the outdoor section of the garden centre and Rob holds open the door to the main centre for me, the perfect gentleman as ever. I've yet to find a fault in this man who already means so much to me.

'After you, m'lady,' he says, pretending to tug his forelock.

'Why, thank you kindly, my man,' I return. We laugh as we walk arm in arm to the coffee shop. It doesn't occur to me to worry about anyone seeing us together. Being with Rob just feels so right, so natural.

We find a comfy seating area in a quiet corner and Rob goes off to get coffees, returning a few minutes later with two steaming mugs and two different cakes.

'Orange and almond, or carrot? I wasn't sure which you'd prefer.'

'Ooh, orange and almond please, if that's ok with you. Or we can go halves. I'm easy.' I realise what I've said and feel myself blush.

'No you're not, Lucy. You're complex and enigmatic and fathomless. And I am in awe of you.'

'Even if I did kiss on the first date? And do pretty much everything else on the second? What a floozy!'

'Well, I'm not complaining. Quite the opposite, in fact. I need to sit down now. Are there any cushions?'

It takes me a second to realise what Rob's on about.

'Ha ha! Sorry, I shouldn't laugh at your discomfort.' I reach over with the smallest cushion I can find. 'Is this big enough?' I enquire, all innocence.

'Nope, you cheeky minx, gonna need a bigger one where you're concerned.'

We're both laughing as Rob plonks himself down on the sofa next to me. I bump against him: 'It's so good to be with you again.'

'You too. I want to hear about everything you've been doing. And about your son too, tell me about Tom.'

It's strange to hear him say Tom's name. I'd thought that Tom existed outside our bubble, but I suppose he's part of me and that makes him matter to Rob too. I'm touched that he's interested in my son. I'm also struck by the realisation that I don't know if Rob has children of his own, so I ask him.

'No, no children. We were never blessed that way. Elizabeth never really wanted them to be honest and I don't think she was disappointed when it didn't happen. I would've liked them though.'

'I'm sorry. You would've made a wonderful dad.' I put my hand on Rob's leg and stroke it with my thumb.

'I bet you're a wonderful mother. What's Tom like? Does he take after you?'

'He's amazing – although I'm biased obviously – he's smart and funny and thoughtful. He definitely takes after my family more than his dad's. He's my reason for getting out of bed every day – and not just because I have to take him to school. He gives my life reason, meaning. He's the best thing I've ever done. Something I got right.'

'He sounds wonderful. Like his mum.'

'He is. All I want is for him to be happy. I do worry that I'm getting it wrong sometimes, about letting him down.'

'I think all parents must feel like that at times though, don't you? Really, all children need is time and love at the end of the day, and I bet you give Tom those in spades.'

'I try to. I'm always telling him how much I love him. And we hug loads. I'm not always very patient when he wants someone to play with though. I do hear myself saying "in a minute" quite a lot.'

Rob laughs. 'I'd love to see the two of you together.'

I just smile. I know that will probably never happen and I don't want to acknowledge it aloud. I steer the subject back to Rob and ask him about his work.

'It's all deadly dull to be honest, Lucy. I'm seriously thinking about jacking it all in and doing something completely different. Trouble is, we've rather got used to the money and I'm not sure Elizabeth would appreciate downsizing things.'

The slight stab of discomfort I always feel at the mention of his wife digs me in the ribs. As much as I might like to, I can't pretend she doesn't exist. 'Is she happy?' I ask.

'I don't know. I think so, in her own way. She's always been pretty self-sufficient anyway. I never really felt she *needed* me. She keeps herself busy with one thing and another – friends, her horse, the golf club. I suppose more and more we live separate lives.'

'She sounds very different to me.'

'She is, Lucy. She has none of your passion and warmth. I don't think I realised quite how far apart we'd grown until I met you.'

'What keeps you together?' The question escapes my lips before I can stop it. 'Sorry, it's none of my business.'

'No, no, it's fine. I'd like us to be able to talk openly and honestly about everything. What keeps us together? Duty, maybe? The promises we made to one another. Finances, responsibility, a long shared history, I don't know. I do take my marriage vows seriously, Lucy, in spite of the fact that I'm here with you.'

'It's OK. I understand,' I tell him, squeezing his thigh to add reassurance.

'I just couldn't live without some sort of affection any longer. And there's been none for such a long time. I want to be wanted.'

'Well, for what it's worth, I want you. I want you very much. For however long we have.'

'You don't know how amazing those words are, how good they make me feel. I hope it's for a long time, Lucy.' Rob takes my hand and squeezes it tightly. Neither of us wants to convert the thoughts of how finite our relationship must inevitably be into words.

'What would you do if you gave up the law? Would that make you an outlaw?' It's a feeble attempt to lighten the mood once more.

Rob's groans. 'That was shocking – you should be ashamed of yourself.'

'I know. Sorry. Best I could do at short notice.'

'I don't know what I'd do to be honest. Maybe talk to my cousin about managing Claremont with him – take some of the responsibility off his shoulders. His heart's not really in the place the way mine is.' Rob shrugs. 'I can't see it happening though – Elizabeth would never agree to it.'

'That's a shame. Wouldn't she want you to do something you love rather than be stuck in a job you don't enjoy anymore?'

'It's complicated, Lucy. It's all about appearances to her, and I can't see her being happy telling people her husband's a glorified gardener.'

'Hmm. We do sound different. I think working at Claremont in any capacity would be wonderful.'

'And that's yet another reason why I wish I'd met you instead,' Rob says with a wistful smile.

'Regret is a horrid, useless emotion, but I have a whole heap too. Tom is the reason I can live with my regrets – the path I took ultimately led to me having him. I can't imagine my life without him now.'

'I can see that. Your face lights up when you talk about him.'

'It's hard though, pretending everything's OK. As much as I love Tom, I still feel empty and scared about the future. I don't want to ever do anything to hurt him, but I don't know how long I can go on like this.'

'Oh, Lucy, I'm sorry. I hope I'm not making the situation worse for you.' Rob looks concerned.

'You have nothing to be sorry for. No-one made me do this, and meeting you has brought me genuine happiness. I'll never be sorry we met, whatever happens next.'

'I'll never be sorry we met either. I haven't felt this alive in longer than I can remember. It may sound corny, but I feel like a man again. Being wanted by a woman is a pretty basic need for a man I think.'

I pause before answering, thinking uncomfortable thoughts about Paul and how he must feel. 'I guess actually I'm not so different to your wife after all – I must make my husband feel the way you've been feeling. I thought I was protecting him by staying in the marriage, but now I'm not so sure. I'm denying him the chance of real happiness, aren't I? Of meeting someone who makes *him* feel like a man again.'

'Maybe. Although I can't imagine any man not wanting to be with you, Lucy.'

'But that's because I do want you as much as you want me, isn't it?'

'I guess. What are you going to do? I wish I could help you.'

'Honestly? I have no idea. I don't think I've got the strength to end my marriage. I simply can't imagine what comes next. And there's Tom to consider. God, it's such a mess.'

'I know it's not much, but you can talk to me about it as much as you want - it might help to have a sounding board. And I'm here for you for as long as you want me.'

'Thank you. That means a lot, Rob.'

There's a pause in the conversation, both of us lost in our thoughts I think. My thoughts of an uncertain future are interrupted by the soft ringing of my mobile. I have kept it on low just in case of a problem at Tom's school. Digging it out of my bag I see that it's my mother-in-law. I immediately feel a rush of guilt.

'It's Paul's Mum,' I tell Rob, not knowing whether to answer the call. I decide to let it go to voicemail. 'I'd better listen to the message – they might need something. Sorry.'

'No apology needed. Go ahead. I'll get more coffee,' Rob says, getting up and excusing himself, obviously wanting to give me some privacy.

When Rob returns a couple of minutes later I'm smiling broadly. 'You'll never guess what she wanted.' I don't wait for Rob to have a guess. 'She wanted to know if they can pick Tom up from school tomorrow, take him to the park and out for dinner. She said she knows Paul's away and thought I might like some me time. I don't suppose...?'

'Yes! I'm absolutely, definitely free. Call her back now and say yes.' Rob's grinning too and suddenly the seriousness of our previous conversation is forgotten. For now, at least.

I return the call. We spend our remaining time together talking happily about the prospect of a whole, unexpected gift of a day and, when the time comes to part, it's easier knowing we will be reunited in just a few short hours.

CHAPTER 52

A rock and a hard place

That evening passes in a happy blur. Not for the first time I thank my lucky stars that Tom is such an easy child. There is no need to pretend, no pressure to feel anything that's not genuine. My unconditional love for this child is the one constant in my life. Right now, I can believe that no matter what happens next, we'll be OK.

Once Tom's asleep it's a relief to be on my own, rather than in a state of tension, worrying about Paul seeing through the charade of our marriage. I don't mind at all that I'm alone in the lounge, just the dog for company as he snores on the sofa next to me. I've realised that I'm often a mass of knotted tension when I'm alone with Paul, always worrying about needing to find excuses to keep him at arms' length. I wonder if this is how Rob's wife feels. It's a strange and discomfiting feeling, comparing myself with her. I can't imagine not wanting Rob. But she must have wanted him, desired him, once, just as I did Paul.

Paul had phoned for a brief chat earlier, and to say goodnight to Tom. He'd said he had a work dinner and would probably be out late, so best not to phone. 'No problem,' I told him. 'Have a good night,' I'd said. And all I felt was relief. Out of sight, out of mind, and nothing to get in the way of thoughts of me and Rob.

My laptop's open to my emails and I'm eagerly awaiting news from Rob on where we are to meet tomorrow. I try to concentrate on what's on the television, but it's pointless as I can't focus on anything but the prospect of a whole day of pure bliss with Rob. I decide to abandon the television and head upstairs to run a bath. As always, I leave the bathroom door open so that I can hear Tom if he stirs and so that Alfie can come in and pretend to be a bathmat.

I lie back in the scented bubbles and try to imagine life without Paul: what if we did split up? Would I cope? Would I really be any happier? I'm trying to be as honest with myself as possible as I contemplate life as a single parent. I know that the practical side of things would be tough, but the overall feeling I believe I'd have is one of relief. To put an end to the pretence. I think I could cope with the logistical stuff. Yes, I'd have to go back to work, which is a terrifying thought after so long as a stay at home mum, but my life would be real, honest. And I'd have hope again. Hope of one day finding true happiness with someone I could imagine growing old with. Someone I don't shrink from. Someone who helps me grow.

Then I think about Tom. It's more painful. But I tell myself that parents split up all the time. Mine did. And I'd make sure he saw Paul all the time. I'd never make it difficult for Paul to see his son. He'd still have two parents who loved him more than anything in the world. Would that be so bad? Surely it would be better than living in a house of cards, which could topple at any moment. Better, surely, to control the collapse, than wait for what feels like the inevitable uncontrolled explosion? Tom would be fine. But what about Paul? Mr. Black and White, the man who doesn't believe in the grey area in between.

The place I inhabit most of the time. Would he be OK? Would he hate me? Could I live with that?

Love and hate. I can easily imagine Paul switching instantaneously from one to the other. He will blame me, I'm sure of it. He will say I'm doing it on purpose. But I didn't fall out of love with him deliberately and I won't be hurting him willingly. I just can't see another way forward anymore. I can't pretend any longer that I can keep up the act. It feels like a little more of me dies on the inside with each and every day that passes. I have no other choice. I must find the strength to be honest with him. The thought still terrifies me and I know that avoidance will be all too easy, but I have to find the courage before it's too late.

Alfie chooses this moment to push the door open with his nose, a timely distraction from frightening thoughts. He stands by the bath for a moment, confused as ever by the bizarre human ritual, and then he flops onto the bath mat where he will snooze until I tell him to move. I'm grateful to him for snapping the chain of thought that was tying me up in knots. I reach over for the towel, dry my hands and pick up my mobile, eager to check for news from Rob. Thoughts of my ailing marriage are safely back in their box, although the lid is not quite down. I know that I will have to face them again soon. Rob hasn't let me down and there's a new email from him, standing out boldly in my inbox, a beacon to guide me home.

Lucy, so so good to see you again today. I realise I'm in danger of repeating myself, but you are the most beautiful woman I've ever met – inside and out. You're on my mind endlessly and I can barely get through the days for wanting you. When we're together, nothing else matters – nothing else exists. The prospect of tomorrow thrills me to my core, to hold you so close, to feel your skin against mine. You have the softest skin imaginable – have I told you that? It's like silk. I've never felt anything like it. I'm imagining you lying next to me now, the softness of your curves wrapped around me. Sometimes I forget to breathe when I think of being with you again. My Lucy, I am, your Rob xxxx.

Rob's words are like a salve on an open wound. The relief they bring to my troubled heart and mind is immense. I realise that I'm crying and smiling simultaneously. Happy or sad? Happy and sad. The oil and water emotions swirl and eddy, coming together and whirling apart. Suddenly, the maelstrom of emotions becomes too much for me, the chaotic jumble of feelings I have about two men meet like the crashing of a violent sea on immovable rocks. Somewhere in the middle of these two forces lies the sad truth: ultimately, no answers will be found here. While Paul may be the problem, Rob cannot be the solution. My heart is breaking on the rocks.

I don't know if I have the strength to face another painful truth, the inevitability of heartbreak. The confusion about my relationship with Rob has my head spinning now. On one hand, he could perhaps give me the strength and self-belief to leave Paul, but on the other he will still belong to another. Even if I do manage to end my marriage, I still can't be with Rob. I have already fallen hard for him and I know that my feelings for him will only grow in depth over time. The longer it goes on, the harder the inevitable separation will be. *Do I really want to put myself through that?* I wonder. The answer is too painful to contemplate right now; too much to bear.

I return my focus to Rob's email, just in time to see a new message flash up.

Hey lovely lady, thinking of you. Always thinking of you. And smiling. I've booked a hotel for tomorrow – a different one so you don't need to feel self-conscious about possibly seeing the same staff on reception. Sweet dreams, beautiful. See you in them. Rxxx. Details of the hotel are included as a postscript.

I choose to ignore the flash of feeling that this is kind of seedy. Meeting a married man in a hotel, essentially for sex. It doesn't feel that way when I'm with Rob, but that's how it would appear to the outside world, to everyone outside our bubble. But it's not just about sex, certainly not for me anyway. But would that matter in the final analysis? And if no-one ever knows about us, will there even be a final analysis? It will always be our secret. The turbulence of my thoughts is too much once more and I shake them away, choosing to focus just on the prospect of spending a day with the man who makes me feel really alive for the first time in so long. That is enough for now.

CHAPTER 53

Romeo, Romeo

It's another Tuesday. Tom is at school, Alfie's been walked and I'm getting ready to drive to the hotel to meet Rob. Clare has a key to the house and will be popping in to check on the dog and let him out a couple of times. She's excited for me once more.

'Have an amazing time, won't you? Lucky thing,' she says, when we meet on the school run.

'Thanks, Clare. And thanks for looking after the hound. I do feel a bit guilty about leaving him, and about Paul's parents having Tom after school.'

'Don't be daft. And Paul's parents offered anyway – they're probably thrilled to be spending time with Tom. Just go and enjoy yourself, forget all the crap for a while. If you don't maybe I will,' Clare says with a wink.

'Woah! It's bad enough sharing Rob with Elizabeth. Anyway, I'm sure you have hoovering to do?' I retaliate.

'This is true. Can't go a day without my Dyson.'

'Feel free to run the hoover round mine while you're there. You'd be in heaven with all the dust and balls of fluff.'

'Ooh! You temptress. I'm not sure I could cheat on my hoover with another though.' Clare realises what she's said. 'Oops! Sorry, Luce, I didn't mean to imply…'

I just smile at my friend. 'It's OK, Clare, I know exactly what I'm doing. Eyes wide open and all that.'

'Resisting the obvious smutty remark. I hope you appreciate the effort involved.'

I laugh. 'I do indeed. Now, get your mind out of the gutter. I have to go. I'll text you later, and thanks again. Bonios are on top of the fridge.'

'No worries. Have a lovely day.'

And now I'm in the car and as the miles pass in my rear view mirror, I make a conscious decision to be in the moment. I know rationally that I'm not driving towards my future, that this day is just about pressing pause on reality, but today that will be enough.

I think of Rob, driving towards our meeting point, approaching from the opposite direction, on a collision course with me. I wonder what he's thinking. If he has the same emotional turmoil going on in his head. I know what he'll be listening to at least and I can picture his smiling face as he sings along to Journey's 'Don't Stop Believin'', his fingers tapping out the beat on the steering wheel, just as I am on mine.

As I get closer to the meeting point, the sky, which had been pretty overcast, clears to a soft autumn blue – the kind of blue you buy baby boy clothes in. It's as if the universe actually approves of what I'm doing and any greyness in my mood is swept away with the clouds. I continue to follow the sat. nav. which guides me down a tree-lined country lane and through the gates of a pretty hotel that looks to date from Tudor times. There's a discreet sign directing me to a car park around to one side of the building and, as I turn the corner, I immediately spot Rob's car. I'm grateful once more for how thoughtful he is. He always foresees anything that might make me uncomfortable and pre-empts it.

And then I'm in his arms and I'm lost once more; real life problems forgotten, I feel safe and warm and loved.

'What a treat,' Rob says, 'seeing you two days in a row. I could get used to this.'

'Me too. Everything's alright with the world again now, isn't it?' I'm choosing to ignore the spiteful little voice that's whispering bitter nothings in my ear. *Don't get used to it. It can't last. It isn't real.*

'Yes, it is. I feel like I could conquer the world when I'm with you.'

'I just wish we could have more. I wish we could press pause on our real lives and be together for a night, or even more.'

'I do too. Who knows, maybe one day we can do just that.'

'That would be wonderful. I just don't see how… anyway, let's get inside shall we? I can't wait to see the rest of this beautiful old building.' I know I'm changing the subject, but I don't want to think the painful truths right now. I just want to shut the world outside and lose myself in Rob for a few hours.

We walk the short distance across the gravel drive and step into the reception area, where we're greeted by a friendly-looking young man on reception, and the smell of wood smoke. There's an open fire burning in a cosy-looking snug just to our left. I don't know why, but I feel less self-conscious being greeted by a man than I had by the two women at the previous hotel. We're obviously expected as he greets Rob by name:

'Mr. Clare, welcome to Holly Lodge. Your room will be ready shortly. I have taken the liberty of arranging for morning coffee to be served in the snug.' He gestures to the room with the fire in. 'I'll come and get you just as soon as your room is ready.'

Rob thanks him and I smile my gratitude. Soon, we're settled on a comfy sofa – the cushions sighed along with me as I felt myself relax - choosing to reject the wing-backed chairs in front of the fire. A tray of coffee and shortbread has been placed on a low table in front of us, and we're alone. Rob is just looking at me and smiling.

'God, it's so good to be with you again. I dreamt about you last night.'

'Oh dear. Hope you didn't wake up screaming?' I still find it hard not to say something self-deprecating in the face of a compliment.

'If I did, it was with pleasure. I don't think you realise quite how lovely you are, Lucy. If I could wake up next to you in the morning, I'd be the happiest man alive.'

I start to say that he hasn't seen me without make-up yet, but I stop myself. I shouldn't devalue what's he's saying to me. I just smile instead, and reach over to hold his hand.

'Do you think the guy on reception knows why we're here?' I ask.

'Probably. Does it bother you?' Rob looks concerned and squeezes my hand.

'Sort of. A bit. But actually, less than I thought it would. And less than the first time. All I care about is being with you. And if that means a bit of tittering behind my back, I can live with it.' It's actually a revelation to myself, how unembarrassed I feel about checking in to a hotel for what is clearly a lovers' tryst. I giggle at the Shakespearean-sounding phrase that's flashed into my mind. Rob looks at me quizzically.

'What's tickled you?' he asks.

'I just thought of this as a lovers' tryst. It struck me as funny.'
I shrug.

'Well, we're no Romeo and Juliet, but the obstacles in our
way are just as real, aren't they?'

'Yep,' I agree with a sigh. 'Maybe we could somehow pair up
Paul and Elizabeth? That would be ironic, wouldn't it, if they
were both on Secret Affair and met each other?'

Rob laughs. 'That would be hilarious. I can't imagine
Elizabeth being on there, sadly. What about Paul? Do you
think he'd ever do something like that?'

'No, I don't think so. He's always said that I'm his dream
woman. I can't imagine him ever cheating on me. I have wished
that he would though – at times. Then I could end the marriage
without all the associated guilt. I know that's cowardly, but it's
the truth.'

'It's not cowardly, Lucy, just honest. You don't want to
hurt him.'

'No, I don't. But I'm hurting myself by staying in the
marriage. It's a mess.'

'I'm sorry. I wish I could help you, I really do. I hate to see
you sad.'

'You do help. You've made me feel alive again, to feel hope.
I know it's not ideal, but I'm still thankful we met.'

'As am I.'

It's not long before our room key arrives and we head
upstairs. The room is panelled in dark wood, with beams on
the ceiling, but the focal point is a beautiful four-poster bed,
generously bedecked with throws and cushions. I immediately
flop down onto it.

'Take me, I'm yours!' I say with a grin, throwing my arms wide.

Rob needs no further encouragement to join me on the bed, and then we're kissing, and laughing, tickling and caressing. And it feels so damn good. This is what true happiness feels like. Born out of betrayal and deceit, this happiness is the most honest I've ever known.

Soon we're breathless and our kisses slow and become tender. Rob's hands are in my hair, caressing my neck. I'm molten to his touch and my body fluid as his hands begin to explore. We undress slowly, taking our time, savouring every new discovery as skin is gradually exposed. Rob kisses each part of me as it is uncovered. The build-up is slow and tantalising, neither wanting to rush. My senses are so heightened to Rob's touch as his fingers, his lips, his tongue travel the length of my body, that I find myself holding my breath, my every focus on the pleasure centres firing in my brain.

Then, with our naked bodies entwined like the tangle of clothes on the floor, Rob takes my face in his hands, his eyes meeting mine. His brown eyes are dark with desire as he moves his hands to take the weight of his body. I move with him, and then he's inside me, his eyes never leaving mine. We are home.

CHAPTER 54

Sugar rush

I'm home again. That is, I'm back in the house I share with Paul and Tom. The highs of my day with Rob, like a sugar spike, have crashed, leaving me feeling low and unutterably sad. I'm left wondering again if the pleasure is worth the pain? But the pleasure is so exquisite and I fear I'm already too addicted to Rob. I'm not sure I could stop, even if I wanted to. And I don't want to, I know that, but as with any drug I know I'm going to need a bigger fix as time goes on. Rob can't give me that.

Our day at Holly Lodge, cocooned in our little bubble, had been so perfect. The rest of the world simply didn't exist for those hours spent together. Everything with Rob feels so right, so natural. It's hard to believe we've only met four times and spent so little time together. We're like two halves of the same whole. All our lives we've been trying to find the match to our halves. Paul was never a fit for me, just as Elizabeth is not for Rob. We've tried to make them fit, but it's an impossible task. For Rob is the other half of me, just as I am to him. We were meant to meet, somehow, somewhere – to find one another. It's a cruel twist of fate that we found one another too late.

It makes me wonder why we met? When we can't be together, not really. Just a few snatched hours when our real lives allow. It feels almost like a punishment, a tantalising taste of what could have been. I wonder if Rob has come in to my life simply to make me realise that I can't continue on my current path; that I must find a way out of my marriage. It must surely be better to be alone, than with the wrong person? But the whole prospect scares me to death. I push the thoughts out of my head because all I'm doing is going round in circles.

Instead, I relive every moment of the day, from the time I pulled into the car park that morning to the heart wrenching moment Rob and I said goodbye again. Rob had fallen asleep quite soon after we made love the first time. I lay curled around him, listening to his breathing, frightened to move for fear of disturbing him. I didn't mind that he slept. I was happy that he felt relaxed enough with me to do so. I ignored the fact that my neck was starting to hurt from the position I was lying in – why is it in films and on TV that couples always look so damned comfy lying together like this? I wondered. It always made my neck hurt and I'd probably have a headache for days now. But I still couldn't move. Couldn't disturb this beautiful man beside me.

'Sorry, Lucy, I think I was nodding off there for a minute.'

He's awake again. I don't tell him that he's been sleeping for some time, or how uncomfortable I've been. I quickly shift my position. 'No need to apologise,' I say instead. 'I choose to take it as a compliment.'

'Oh, believe me, it is,' Rob tells me. 'I feel so relaxed with you. I can't remember the last time I felt this at ease. If I ever did.'

'I know what you mean. I was just thinking the same thing.'

'You are the piece of me that's always been missing, Lucy. I think I've been searching for you my whole life – even if

I didn't really realise it. You make me feel whole. Does that sound really naff?'

'No, not at all. It probably should, but I feel the same. I just fail to understand why the universe has put us in each other's path now, when we can't be together.'

Rob hugs me to him. 'I know. It's not fair.'

We lie like that for a while, neither of us speaking, each lost in our thoughts of the injustice of it all. Eventually, Rob breaks the silence and asks me if I'm thirsty.

'Mm, a glass of water would be nice, actually. I'll get it.' I unwrap myself from the tangle of bodies and sheets and pad over to the table where a carafe of water and two glasses sit. I can feel Rob's eyes on me as I walk, and I feel no embarrassment at all. I feel beautiful and powerful in his presence, unselfconscious and sensual. I pour two glasses of water and carry them back to the bed.

We sit in bed, propped up on pillows, leaning into one another, just talking. About everything, and nothing. About highs and lows, hopes and dreams; learning about one another.

'So, where did you and Elizabeth meet?' I ask. As much as I'd like to pretend she doesn't exist, this woman is a big part of Rob's life.

'At university in Oxford. We were both studying law. She was beautiful and brilliant, but kind of aloof and unattainable. I think I saw pursuing her as a bit of a challenge – you know, see if I could melt the ice queen's heart.' Rob's smile is wistful and tinged with sadness.

'Well, you obviously succeeded – she married you.'

'Yes, she did. But that heart of hers didn't stay melted for long. I sometimes wonder why she did marry me. I think that maybe I ticked all the boxes on paper, but that she really just wanted the appearance of a perfect marriage. She's never been a tactile or particularly passionate partner. Not like you at all. Within a year, really, looking back, she lost interest in a physical relationship. Sex was something she saw as a duty, to be endured rather than enjoyed.'

'I'm sorry, Rob. You deserved better than that.' I think of Paul as I utter the words.

Rob shrugs. 'Eventually I just stopped trying. I threw myself into my work, provided for Elizabeth, gave her the life she wanted. But it wasn't the life I dreamt of. Being with you has been a little snapshot of what life could have been, could be…' Rob lets the words hang.

I have no words; my heart is hurting and tears are welling in my eyes. I reach over and place my hand over Rob's heart. He places his on top. I can feel the rapidity of his heart like a thousand butterflies trapped in a net. His emotional energy flows into me, charging my own heart. There is only one thing I can do, have to do. I can show this man the passion he inspires in me, take him to the dizzying heights he takes me, and hold him there as long as I possibly can. For I know that when we fall back to the earth together we will surely break.

And now, I'm hugging Tom as tight as he can bear. He's the only reason I could stand to leave Rob when our day had to end. Tom's little arms are squeezing me tight, gluing me back together. I'm trying hard not to let the tears come as I breathe him in, fighting the rush and rollercoaster of emotions threatening to send me over the edge. Reminding and reminding myself that this little boy is a reason to keep going, whatever else happens, Tom is my constant and I am his.

'So, did you have fun with Grandma and Grandad?' I ask, finally releasing him from the bear hug.

'Yep. They bought me a new skateboard and took me to the park – you know, the one with the ramps? Only the little ones though. Because I'm only a beginner.'

'Wow! What a lucky boy. How was it? Did you fall off?'

'Nope. Well, nearly. I didn't go very fast. And Grandma made Grandad hold my hand anyway. Grandma thinks I'm still a baby.'

I laugh at the face Tom pulls. 'Well, you'll always be my baby – even when you're a grown up.' I tell him. 'And I'll always love you more than anything or anybody in the whole wide world. So there nur.'

'I love you too, Mummy.' And there they are. The words that make everything alright with the world. For a while at least.

CHAPTER 55

Star-crossed lovers

Tom is now sleeping soundly, his black and white cuddly dog in the crook of his arm. I sit for some time, just watching him sleep in the soft glow of the nightlight. Alfie is snoozing in the doorway. The house feels peaceful. I feel calm.

Standing up, I lean over and kiss Tom's forehead. 'Sleep tight,' I whisper, before heading back downstairs.

I'm grateful that Paul is away. I need time and space to corral my thoughts. I pour myself a glass of wine and look for a CD to listen to, settling on London Grammar as the right music for my mood. Kicking up the recliner on my end of the sofa, I settle back with a sigh. Alfie takes advantage of Paul's absence and stretches out next to me, spilling over onto his usual seat.

I try to analyse my feelings. I'm surprised at the lack of guilt I feel. I'd thought when I embarked on my Secret Affair journey, that I'd be overwhelmed with feelings of contrition and self-reproach. It hasn't happened like that at all. *Does that make me a bad person?* I wonder. I suppose in the eyes of the world it does, doesn't it? A cheat and a liar. But when I'm with Rob, everything feels right, with me, with the world. A sigh escapes my lips. I take a glug of wine.

I sit like that for some time, I don't know how long, with my thoughts pin-balling around my head, bouncing from Rob to Paul to Tom. I realise that I haven't spoken to Paul today, and think for a moment that it's strange for him not to have phoned, at least to say goodnight to Tom. I feel bad that I didn't make the call myself when putting Tom to bed. I assume that he's just been busy with work and socialising. He's well-known for being the last man standing at the end of the night. As much as I'm enjoying his absence, I decide the right thing to do is to phone him, just to let him know that all's well.

There's no answer from his mobile. I check the time. I hadn't realised how late it is, it's gone ten here. I wonder if he's asleep, but it's still relatively early for Paul, so I dial the number of the hotel and ask to be put through to his room. The phone goes unanswered and the concierge comes apologetically back on the line. I thank him and hang up. Paul must be propping up a bar somewhere and just didn't hear his phone. I reassure myself that he will see the missed call and at least know that I'd tried.

I let my thoughts return to Rob and get up to find my laptop. Alfie stirs and starts to get up to follow. 'Stay,' I tell him. 'I'm coming back.'

I want to email Rob, to tell him what a wonderful time I had. I'm not expecting to hear from him as he told me he and Elizabeth had a social engagement. He said he wasn't looking forward to it, that it was all about appearances and he hated all the pretence. I can't help feeling jealous that she's the woman on his arm tonight, even though I know he would rather be with me. I'm reminded once again of the agony and the ecstasy of my relationship with Rob. The realisation that it can only ever be like this is almost too painful to bear.

I'm surprised and delighted to see Rob's name amongst the unread messages.

Lucy, a snatched moment to say thank you for the most perfect and blissful of days. I wish with all my heart that it hadn't had to end. I wish with all my heart that you were the woman on my arm tonight. I am in love with you, Lucy Shaw. One hundred percent, head over heels in love with you. Rob xxxx.

I taste the salt of my tears before I even realise they're streaming silently down my face. Rob's words bring joy and sorrow in equal measure, but the more I think about them, the more the scales tip towards the side of sorrow. For what use is his love if we can't be together? I wipe my hands across my face. I want to reply to Rob. I'm not sure I can find the words.

I type into the subject bar the words *Star-crossed lovers*. *Rob*, I begin, pausing as I try and work out what I want to say. *I love you too. Hopelessly and completely. And it's breaking my heart. I don't know what to do. How do we reconcile what we feel for one another with the reality of the situation? When we're together everything is right with the world, but it's not real is it? How can it be when we are tied to others? I'm so confused. I can only see more pain and heartbreak if we carry on, but the thought of giving you up is more than I can bear. Lucy xxxx.*

It might not be what Rob wants to hear, but I must be honest with him. And with myself. The longer we go on, the deeper our feelings grow, the harder it will be to finish it and the greater the pain. The honest part of me thinks the sensible thing to do would be to end it now. Head and heart. But the heart wants what the heart wants, doesn't it? It's not easy to defy it. I try telling my heart that it's about self-preservation, about living to fight another day. But the heart is deaf to logic, isn't it? How do I make it understand that I'm just trying to protect it, to keep it from breaking irrevocably?

I'm grateful to have my thoughts interrupted by a beep from my mobile phone. My first thought is that it's Paul, having seen my missed call. I'm relieved, however, when I check the screen to see it's actually a text message from Clare:

You still up? How are you feeling after your play date?!

I can't help laughing at her choice of words. *Yes, I'm up. And down. Very up and very down.*

Oh no! Why? What happened?

Nothing. Everything. I fell in love with a married man. He fell in love with me. Our hearts got broken. The end.

God, Lucy. Are you OK? What are you going to do?

Honestly? I have no idea. The sensible part of me thinks I should end it now. It can only end in heartbreak can't it? I can't bear the thought of giving him up though. Of never seeing him again.

I am sorry. Can I do anything?

Just be there for me the way you always are. Keep me from falling apart.

Always always, you know that. You were afraid this would happen though.

Yep, I knew the risks. Didn't think I would fall so hard and so fast, mind you.

Do you regret it, meeting him?

No, not for a second. Rob made me feel alive again. I'll always be glad we met.

It sounds to me as though you've made your mind up to end it.

I think I have. I don't think I could survive otherwise. God, Clare, how can I go back to life the way it was before Rob? Just the thought of it depresses the hell out of me.

Then don't. Be honest with Paul. I'll be here for you every step of the way.

294

I know you're right. And I want to. God, why am I so rubbish at putting my happiness first?

It's time to change that, Lucy. You have to know you deserve to be happy.

I do. At least I'm trying to. Thank you, Clare. I'm so sorry you have to put up with all my nonsense.

It's not nonsense, it's life. And that's what friends are for.

We say our goodnights and I feel a little calmer once more. I know what I have to do, and it's going to be the hardest thing I've ever had to do. Make that hardest things.

CHAPTER 56

Resolution

I sleep fitfully that night. I am terrified by what lies ahead. By the morning though, I seem to have wrestled my way to some sort of acceptance. I have finally realised that life can never go back to what it was before. Before Rob. But equally, Rob cannot be the excuse or the reason to end my marriage. He is the catalyst, of that there is no doubt. If I hadn't met him, I might never have made it to this crossroads. I would still be trekking the rocky path of my marriage, unable to find a better way. But I must walk this new path alone.

I am starting to feel a new inner strength, a resolve I thought I would never have. Having made up my mind about what I must do has brought a sense of relief already. I am filled with dread, of course, at the prospect of the most painful of conversations I must have with Paul, but I am focussed on the feeling of relief which can only be intensified when the deed is done.

I just have to hang on to my resolve for another day. The task of getting Tom up and ready for school distracts me temporarily. I do have a wobbly moment when Clare gives me the biggest of hugs and whispers, 'I'm here for you. Stay strong.' I smile at her gratefully, unable to get any words out past the lump in my throat.

Clare chats animatedly to the children as we walk up the

road to school, disguising my emotional state. I use those few minutes to compose myself once more and soon we're waving Tom and Chloe off into the playground. As we turn to head back to the cars, I spot Charlie waving at us. We wait for her to catch up with us.

'Hello you two,' she begins, and I notice at once how different she looks from the last time I saw her at the park. 'Thanks for waiting. I just wanted to share my news. I'm getting married! Again!' Charlie beams at us.

'Oh my God, Charlie, that's fantastic news. I'm so, so happy for you,' I say taking her hands.

'Yes, that's wonderful,' Clare agrees.

'Thank you both. I couldn't be happier.' Charlie is glowing.

'So, what happened?' I ask.

'I finally plucked up the courage to have it out with Rich – we couldn't go on as we were. I just made it clear to him that he had to put us first. That I deserved better.'

I'm full of admiration for Charlie. 'Wow, well done you. What did he say?'

'That I was right and he was sorry. He said he didn't want to lose me and he knew he had to get out of his mum's shadow. He said he'd seen his dad kowtow to her his whole life and just followed suit. He phoned her there and then and told her that I came first and that if she wanted to be invited to our wedding that she had better bloody well pull her head in!'

'Oh my God,' Clare and I say in unison.

'I know!' Charlie is elated. 'You will both be at my hen night won't you?'

'Absolutely! Wouldn't miss it for the world.'

Charlie grins at us both before heading off to spread the good news, and Clare and I walk slowly back to the cars.

'God, she's so brave,' I say to Clare. 'I wish I was that brave.'

'You are. You will be.'

'I hope so. I do feel a sense of relief just having made the decision. Going through with it still scares me to death though.'

'I know, and that's understandable. But you know it's the right thing. Stay strong.'

I keep those two words uppermost in my mind as I drive home, and as I walk the dog across the field; as I keep myself busy until it's time to pick Tom up again. 'Stay strong, Lucy,' I tell myself when I phone Paul's mum.

'Hello,' I say. 'I was just wondering if you could do me a huge favour? Could you possibly have Tom for a couple of hours on Thursday evening?'

Of course, the answer's yes, they'd love to. And I am a step closer to fulfilling the promise I have made to myself to talk to Paul. I keep reminding myself that the sky didn't come crashing down on Charlie's world when she faced her fears and spoke to Rich. *Stay strong, Lucy.*

Paul phones at lunchtime. 'Hey,' he says. 'Sorry I missed your call last night. Out with the boys, you know, didn't hear my phone.'

He sounds odd. Off, somehow. I can't put my finger on it.

'No problem. Just wanted to let you know all was well here. Tom had a lovely time with your Mum and Dad – they got him a skateboard. He was mortified that he had to hold your dad's hand going down the slope.'

'I can imagine. Anyway, I'll be home tonight, so he can tell me all about it.'

It's a brief phone call. I'm grateful. I put the strangeness down to my own emotional state. I'm anxious about his return and the prospect of pretending that everything's OK for one more night. I don't want to have the conversation I'm intending to have with Tom in the house, but the idea of carrying on the deceit doesn't sit well with me now that I have made up my mind. It can't be helped though. I don't know how Paul is going to react and I cannot risk Tom being caught in any crossfire.

After I've hung up the phone, I realise I've been putting off looking at my emails. Rob will no doubt have seen my reply from last night, and I'm afraid to face his response. The phrase 'rip off the Band-Aid' springs to mind. Band-Aids in my case. Maybe the best thing to do is to rip them both off at once. It's going to hurt like hell, but better once than twice. *How the hell did it come to this?* I ask myself. *How did my life go so badly wrong?* I take a deep breath and login to my email account.

Hey you, the message from Rob starts. *I understand. Everything you said makes sense, Lucy. To my head. My heart thinks otherwise. I just want to hold you in my arms right now, and never ever let you go. I don't want to give you up, but I love and respect you too much to pressure you. Whatever your decision, Lucy, I will abide by it. I'll never be sorry we met though, whatever happens. You will always have my heart. I will always be your Rob xxxx.*

The familiar lump is back in my throat, the salty wetness on my face. This excruciating pain I feel at the thought of saying goodbye to Rob is almost more than I can bear. How much worse will it be down the line if I don't put a stop to us now? I take a deep breath and start typing.

Hey you, I echo. *Thank you for understanding. For not making this harder than it already is. Meeting you has been one of the best things ever to have happened to me. I still can't quite believe how hard and fast we fell. I wish things could be different, but facing the heartbreak now is the only way I think I can survive letting you go. You brought me back to life, Rob. I thought I was dead inside until your touch brought me back to life. For the first time in so long, I felt real, honest emotions. I have been acting my way through life, pretending everything is fine. With you I didn't have to pretend. With you it was real. I will always be grateful. I hope you find true happiness, Rob. I wish it could have been with me. I will always be, your Lucy xxxxx.*

I hit send before my courage fails me. I feel numb. I sit and stare at nothing. It's not fair. I picture Rob reading my message, imagine him feeling what I'm feeling, wondering how life can go on as it did before. I haven't told him that I intend to end my marriage. I can't see how that would help matters. He would still be trapped in his loveless, duty-bound marriage, and I don't want to be the other woman. Not anymore. Not once I'm free.

I reach out to Clare, needing the support of my friend. I text her. *I just ended things with Rob. Life sucks.*

As usual she texts straight back. *Oh, Lucy, I'm sorry. I think you've done the right thing though. Hugs.*

Thank you. It doesn't feel like the right thing. It feels awful.

I know, but imagine how much harder it would've been further down the line.

I keep telling myself that. It doesn't help.

Give it time. It's raw right now. Stay strong. You'll get through this.

Thanks, Clare. Those words again. *Stay strong.* My new mantra. I don't want to be strong. I want to collapse. Give in to the maelstrom of emotions that is raging just beneath the surface, to rail at the injustice of it all. *Stay strong, Lucy, for just*

300

a little while longer.

I draw on my ever-decreasing reserve of strength and resolve, and paint the crayon smile back on my face for what I hope is the last time. I am entering the final act. One player has left the stage already and I'm soon to drive a dagger into the heart of another. I just want it to be over now. I want the performance to be over and the curtain to fall.

CHAPTER 57

Exit stage right

It's Wednesday evening. Tom is bathed and in his pyjamas, waiting up for his Dad to get home, oblivious to the fact that his little world is about to be turned upside down. It's the worst part of what is going to happen by far. I keep telling myself that he will be better off being loved by two happy parents, that he will adapt, he'll be fine. I quash the little voices that ask if I was OK as a result of my parents splitting up? I will make sure that my little boy is OK. He will always know that he is loved and wanted and cherished. And I will hug him every single day of his life. He will never have to doubt how much he is loved. I will tell him how amazing he is, how he can achieve whatever he wants in life, to strive for his dreams.

As the time approaches for Paul to get home, my levels of anxiety rise. I don't know how I'm going to get through this night. When the front door opens, I'm grateful that Tom can be the one to greet him, his joy at seeing Paul genuine. I'm afraid that my acting skills would let me down; I would become transparent. I stand in the hall watching the reunion between my husband and our child and it causes a physical pain in my chest. Paul looks over at me.

'Hey you.'

'Hey you. Welcome home. Good trip?'

'Yes, thanks. You OK?'

'Yep. All good.' Inside I'm screaming. I just want it all to stop. These banal platitudes coming from both our mouths. Nothing is alright anymore. Nothing ever will be again. I can't do this. I can't go on. Make it stop.

Paul moves towards me. I want to back away. I don't want him to touch me. I force myself to stand still. He leans in to hug me and kisses me on the cheek. And I know in that moment, without a shadow of a doubt, that he is having an affair.

'New aftershave?' I ask him. I already know the answer. And I already know that he is about to lie to me. Paul has never bought himself an aftershave in his life.

'Um, yep. Fancied treating myself. From the Duty Free. I got you a perfume too.'

'Lovely, thank you,' I hear myself saying. I know now why he didn't answer his phone when I called. I know now what I felt instinctively over the phone. And all I feel is relief. He doesn't need to know that I know. There is nothing to be gained. The guilt is still mine. I drove him to this, after all. I rejected him. And he looked for affection elsewhere. Just as Rob had.

I feel strangely calm now. I still feel like the villain of the piece, but it's somehow easier knowing that Paul too has broken our marriage vows. The charade is playing itself out at last, and the relief washing over me is immense. I know that I can't wait another day though. I have to put an end to this tonight.

While Paul puts a now sleepy Tom to bed, I pour us both a drink and wait in the lounge for him. I hand him the whisky glass. 'We need to talk.'

A look of panic crosses his face. 'You know, don't you?'

I smile at him. 'It doesn't matter, Paul. I don't blame you.

303

If I'm being completely honest, I'm only surprised it didn't happen sooner. I didn't leave you any choice.'

'I'm sorry, Lucy, I'm so sorry.' Paul looks distraught.

'Don't be. I'm sorry that I couldn't be the wife you needed, deserved. And…' I know I need to be honest with him about Rob, he deserves that much – 'there was someone else, briefly. It's over now. But it made me realise that I couldn't go on like this.'

'You were my dream woman, Lucy. You still are in so many ways. But I needed more, I needed to feel like a man again. I needed someone to want me.' Paul is crying. I reach over and take his hand.

'Believe me, I do understand. And I'm so sorry.' All I want in this moment is to comfort this man, the father of my child. I want to carry the burden of blame, to take responsibility. The sense of relief has brought with it a strength I didn't dream I could possess. I can make this alright for us, for Paul and for our son. 'It's going to be OK,' I tell him.

We talk into the wee small hours. We remember the happier times. We laugh together and we cry together. We vow to protect our son, no matter what. And we hold one another when we finally crawl exhausted into bed. We stay like that until I feel Paul's breathing slow as sleep finally claims him, and then I carefully roll away, lying on my back staring unseeing at the ceiling. It is done. And the world did not end. The sky did not come crashing down around me. There is still much to talk about. The practicalities still terrify me and the future looms uncertain, but all that can wait. The hard bit, the painful bit, is over.

Sleep doesn't claim me - my mind won't allow it. I cannot

order the chaos of thoughts and emotions: relief, regret, sorrow, hope, all jostle for my attention. I allow myself to think of Rob, but the wound is still too raw. A part of me wants to tell him that I'm free now. That we could be together. If he could just leave Elizabeth... But I don't want to be a marriage wrecker. I have too much guilt and regret already, without adding that to the mix. Finally, the overwhelming sense of relief claims me and sleep finally comes just before the dawn.

When I wake the next day, Paul's side of the bed is empty and I experience a moment of panic and disorientation. The clock beside the bed tells me it's ten-thirty. I've slept right through the alarm. I jump out of bed and run to Tom's room. Empty. I check Paul's office. Empty. I run downstairs. Paul looks up from the sofa in the lounge, where he's sitting with his laptop.

'Hey, sleepyhead. I thought I'd let you sleep in.'

'Tom. Is Tom OK?'

'He's fine. Went off to school happy as Larry.'

'Oh. OK. Thanks.' I feel the panic subside.'

'It's OK, Lucy. Everything's going to be OK. And honestly? I'm relieved that we finally faced facts.'

'Me too. I was just so afraid of hurting you. And of you hating me.'

'I could never hate you, Lucy. Yes, I wish things had worked out with us, but that's life. We made an amazing little boy together and no one can take that away from us.'

'What happens now?' I ask him.

'I've been thinking about that this morning. I think I might have a solution. They've asked me if I'd consider moving to France full-time – I could come back at least every other weekend to be with Tom. What do you think? It would mean you and Tom could stay in the house.'

I'm a little taken aback at how calm Paul is about the whole thing, but grateful all the same. I suppose I shouldn't be surprised – he always was the black and white one. 'I guess that could work. How do we tell Tom though?'

'Just tell him that Daddy has to go away for work. He'll adjust. As long as he always has one of us around, he'll be fine.'

'Is it serious then? With this woman in France.' The question that had been at the back of my mind comes to the fore.

'I think it could be. Now.'

'I'm happy for you,' I tell him, smiling. And I am. If Paul is happy, my guilt is assuaged. 'God, look at us being a right pair of grown-ups!'

Paul laughs. 'I know. Who'd have thought it?'

I'm grateful to Paul for making this easier for us and I tell him so.

'So, this guy you were seeing – is he out of the picture completely?'

I feel the familiar wrench in my gut when I think of Rob. 'Yes. That's over.' It's strange to be talking about these other people we've been seeing. I never imagined it would happen like this, but I'm thankful that it has. 'I suppose I'd better have a shower and get dressed,' I say after a while.

'OK,' Paul says. 'I'm sort of working - just answering emails really. Thought we could go out for dinner tonight and talk about what happens next.'

'That sounds very civilised – thank you for being so grounded about all this.' I head back upstairs, my step lighter than it's been in a very long time. When I get back to the bedroom, I check my mobile phone and find a text from Clare.

You OK? Saw Paul on the school run. Let me know.

I feel bad for worrying my friend yet again and quickly tap out a reply. *Sorry, I'm OK. My marriage is over though.* I wait for her reply, knowing that she'll be straight back to me.

Holy moly. What happened? Thought you were doing the deed tonight.

I was. It just sort of happened. Paul's been seeing someone in France.

Nooooo! OMG! Really?!!

I can't help laughing as I picture Clare's undoubtedly gobsmacked face. *Yes, really. It's all good though, honestly. I'm so relieved.*

I'm stunned. Glad you're OK though.

Thanks, Clare. See you later.

Twenty minutes later and I'm showered and dressed and ready to face the rest of this most bizarre of days. Paul and I walk Alfie together for the first time in ages. Ironically, I feel closer to him than I have in such a long time. The communication we lost so long ago returns and we talk like old friends. It feels good, and it feels as though we will be able to have a special friendship moving forward. We're reminiscing about the early days of our relationship. There is no bitterness on either side, just an affection that I believe will endure; a desire on each side for the other to be happy.

We pick Tom up from school together and drop him round with Paul's parents. Over dinner, we talk practicalities. It should be strange, but it's not.

'So, obviously, I'll still pay the mortgage etc. here – nothing need change for you and Tom. I'll live at Sylvie's. Maybe I can stay at the house when I come back to see Tom? We can work that out anyway. There's always my parents'.'

'No, no, you should stay at the house with Tom. It's still your home. It would be better for Tom. I can always disappear those weekends if need be.' I wanted this to be as easy for Paul and Tom as possible, although I had no idea where I would go. Clare's husband might have to get used to seeing a lot more of me.

'OK, thanks. The main thing is that we do what's best for Tom.'

'Absolutely,' I agree.

'Right, so I'll arrange to transfer to the Paris office. I can move into the spare room in the meantime if you want?'

I think for a moment. 'I'm not sure. How would we explain that to Tom? Can we just play it by ear? See what feels right until we've spoken to him, explained what's happening.'

'Sure. I think it will all happen pretty fast now though. No point prolonging things.'

And so that's that. Just like that. Marriage ended, logistics sorted. Life will go on. I just wish it could have gone on with Rob.

CHAPTER 58

Everything is changing

Fast forward three weeks. It's almost November. It's all happened very quickly. With the decision made, Paul wasted no time in arranging his transfer and now Tom and I are waving him off. His car is loaded with clothes and a few treasured items he wanted from the house. I have hidden a present in one of his suitcases – a favourite photo of Tom which I had framed for him. I still can't quite believe what's happening and I would be lying if I said I wasn't scared.

We'd talked to Tom about what was going to happen and he seems to be taking it in his stride. In his mind, I think it just means a present every time Paul comes back to visit. He's waving animatedly now as Paul's car pulls off the drive. Paul waves out of the car window and I have to suppress a sob, putting my hand to my mouth to stop the sound escaping. This is really happening. The finality is terrifying, but I know that it's the right thing. I know it will get easier.

We carry on waving until Paul's car disappears from view. I'm frozen to the spot, not knowing what to do next. Tom pulls on my arm.

'Come on, Mummy. Will you play battles with me?'

'What? Yes, of course. Come on.' I take his hand and we head back indoors, closing the front door. 'You go into the playroom – I just need a minute.' I lean back on the door. I'm still struggling to accept what is happening. It's all happened so fast. Suddenly I'm doing this on my own. Paul will be in another country most of the time. It's not that I regret what's happened, it's just a huge adjustment and it's scary as hell.

Tom calls me from the playroom. 'Mummy, are you coming? You can be Optimus Prime if you want.'

'Coming,' I call, taking a steadying breath. *Stay strong, Lucy, stay strong. You can do this.* Not for the first time in the last few weeks, Rob flashes into my mind and I wish he was still in my life. It's been so hard not having contact with him. On more than one occasion I've been tempted to contact him, desperate to feel close to him again, to draw strength from him. Somehow I've found the strength to resist, reminding myself that he's not the answer. However hard this is, however frightened I feel, a married man is not the answer.

And so Tom and I drift into a routine not that dissimilar to our old one a lot of the time. For the first few days, it's just as though Paul's away with work, as he has been in the past. Then a few days turns into a week. Then two. He comes back on the second weekend and we do things as a family, playing it by ear as I hoped we would. Paul seems happier and more relaxed. I do feel a twinge of sadness now and then, but still the over-riding feeling is one of relief. Tom seems unaffected by the split. Happy Paul, happy Tom. Happy Lucy? Well, not quite, but I suppose time will heal my wounds. I still miss Rob terribly and he continues to haunt my waking hours and my dreams. I still wish things could have been different.

Clare has been my rock, as ever, clucking round me like an overprotective mother hen. I don't think I could have got through these last weeks without her to be honest. She's even sacrificed vacuuming some days when I've really been struggling to accept my new reality.

'It'll get easier, Lucy. I promise. Don't forget you're dealing with the end of two relationships. It's a double whammy.'

'I know. Never was one to do things by halves.'

'You're not kidding,' she agrees. 'But you've done the right thing. You know that don't you?'

'Yes, it's bloody hard though. I wasn't expecting to feel quite so alone. I suppose I thought Paul would still be around, not hundreds of miles away in another country.'

'Well, no, didn't see that one coming, but it's not the other side of the world – he can be back in a few hours. Doesn't it freak you out that he's living with another woman?'

'Funnily enough, no. I'm glad he's happy. That's all I ever wanted. Maybe I'm a bit jealous – not that's he's got someone, but that I haven't.'

'You'll find someone. Give it time.'

'I'm not even thinking about that – I'm still completely hung up on Rob. I can't imagine ever wanting anyone else. Not the way I want him.'

'You will. One day.'

'Hmm. Maybe.' I'm not convinced.

'Have you heard from him?'

'No, but I don't really expect to. He'll respect my decision too much to disrupt my life. It would have been so easy to carry on seeing him, Clare, even after my split from Paul, but I don't want somebody else's man.'

'Quite right too. You deserve better than to be just someone's bit on the side. I have total respect for you on that one – I know it can't have been easy.'

'It wasn't. It broke my heart. I am proud of myself though, for standing on my own two feet.'

'So you should be. You've got this. And you've got me.' Clare pulls a mad face and we both laugh.

Paul's parents have been great too, however much they might disapprove of the split. They have taken to picking Tom up from school once a week and treating him. I guess we're all trying to compensate for Paul's absence. Paul tries to Skype Tom every night before bed; it's becoming a part of his bedtime routine, like brushing his teeth and having a story. Sometimes I do wish Paul was here to share the load, but when I climb into bed alone I remember how much I'd started to dread being alone with my husband. I wish I wasn't alone, but it's Rob I yearn for, not Paul.

Clare has taken it upon herself to share my news with the other mums and they've been lovely and supportive, taking me to one side at school and telling me how sorry they are. Charlie was upset when she found out.

'Lucy, I'm so sorry,' she said. 'I was being a total drama queen and you were going through this. You were so lovely to me when I was struggling. I wish I could've done the same for you.'

'Don't be daft. What you were going through was very real. I'm just glad it all worked out for you in the end. What happened with me and Paul had been brewing for a long time and it was a relief when the end came. Please don't let what's happened cast a shadow over your happiness. You and Rich were made for each other.'

'Thanks, Lucy. I hope you'll still be at the wedding? And the hen? It wouldn't be the same without you.'

'Of course I will. I can't wait. Have you got a singles table you can put me on at the reception?' I joke.

In truth, I'm a bit anxious about the wedding. It will be my first real outing as a newly-single woman and it's an uncomfortable prospect. All my friends are happily married and I'm going to be the odd one out. Clare has already offered to share Greg, informing me that he's more than happy to have a woman on each arm, saying his street cred will soar. 'I didn't like to tell him that he didn't have any street cred to start with, bless him,' she'd said.

I console myself with the thought that at least the hen night will be couple-free. Part of me is looking forward to having a few drinks and forgetting my troubles for a few hours, although I know the night will be tinged with sadness in the light of my failed marriage. Tom will be spending the weekend with his grandparents, giving me time to recover from any hangover I might have on the Sunday.

CHAPTER 59

Toast and coffee

The Saturday of Charlie's hen night has arrived and Clare has taken me under her wing once more. When the doorbell goes at five thirty, I open the door to find Clare standing there holding out a bottle of bubbly with one hand and a bulging holdall in the other. Greg has dropped her off.

'Here you go,' she says, handing me the bottle. 'Get it open. Let's get this party started.' She instructs.

I laugh as Clare bustles in. 'Yes, Miss! Right away!' It's clear that she's already started the party ahead of me.

Clare dumps her bag on the sofa as I head into the dining room to hunt for some rarely used champagne flutes. Alfie jumps when the cork pops from the bottle.

'Cheers!' Clare and I chink glasses and take a sip of the bubbles. 'Here's to a great night.'

'Thanks for coming round to get ready. I'm not sure I could've summoned up much enthusiasm otherwise. I don't want to be a party pooper or let Charlie down, but...'

'It's OK, I understand. And I won't let you poop this party, you poop-head.'

'Nutter. Poop-head indeed. You do make me laugh.' For the umpteenth time in recent weeks, I thank my lucky stars I have a friend like Clare.

'You should be used to my face by now,' she replies, pulling her best mad one.

I defy anyone to stay sad in the presence of this woman, and I am no exception. Taking a good swig of champagne, I raise my glass in another toast. 'To you, Clare, the best friend I could ever wish for. Thank you, for everything.'

'Aw! Stop it. You'll make me cry,' she's only half joking now.

'Nope. No more crying. There have been enough tears of late to last several lifetimes. Tonight we celebrate. To Charlie and Rich!'

'Charlie and Rich!' We clink glasses again and top them up from the bottle which Clare is now brandishing around.

It's turning into a bit of a toast-fest, causing us to drink rather more and faster than we otherwise would have.

'And to you, Lucy, for being my bestest friend and for finding the courage to pursue happiness.'

'No, to you, Clare, for nagging me to death until I did so.'

'Nah! You deserve all the credit. I was just playing Devil's avocado.' We're both giggling now and starting to show the effects of the champagne.

'To avocados! And the Devil! And what the devil am I going to wear tonight?'

'To clothes!' Clare says, filling her glass once more before splashing what's left in the bottle into mine.

'Why are we toasting clothes?' I ask.

'No, to clothes – I mean, let's go and look in your wardrobe for something suitably slutty for you to wear.'

'I'm not sure I own anything slutty anymore. Certainly not anything that will still fit, anyway.' We're heading up the stairs now. I know that Clare is tiddly because she doesn't mention the state of the carpet.

Alfie is plodding up behind us, obviously thinking someone needs to keep an eye on us.

I flop down on my bed and Clare opens one side of the wardrobe. The wrong side. Paul's side. It's pretty much empty, save for a couple of shirts that need ironing and his dinner jacket. Everything that's happened hits home like a punch to the chest; the empty wardrobe a stark metaphor for my life right now.

'Oh God.'

'Oops. Sorry, Luce. I'm so sorry.' Clare looks horrified and sits down next to me on the bed, putting her arms around me.

'It's not your fault, Clare. It just scares me sometimes. I made this happen – I wanted it to happen. It's still hard though, being on my own.' I smile sadly at my friend, feeling suddenly sober once more.

'I've ruined the mood again though. How can we get you back up?'

'I dunno. Drugs?' is my helpful suggestion.

Clare laughs. 'Great idea. Know where we can score some… er… I don't flippin' know. I've never even smoked weed.'

'No, me neither. We could go round the rec. and ask the local yoofs.' I can't help smiling at the idea of two married women tottering up to the teenagers in the park to enquire about something to get high on.

'Now you're talking,' Clare nods vigorous agreement. She's still clearly feeling the effects of half a bottle of bubbly on top of whatever she had before she arrived.

'Right, sounds like a plan. Maybe we should get ready first though.' I can't ruin the night for Clare by being a misery. I know she's been looking forward to Charlie's hen night for ages.

Leaving her sitting on the edge of the bed, I close the doors on Paul's side of the wardrobe and open mine, riffling through blouses, skirts and dresses for something suitable. I pull out a body-con dress in dark emerald green which is an old favourite. I haven't worn it since I had Tom, too conscious of the lumps and bumps gained during pregnancy.

'Ooh, that's nice,' Clare pipes up from behind me.

'Hmm. Don't think I can get away with it anymore.'

'Course you can. That's what control undies were invented for anyway. Besides, have you looked in the mirror lately? You look bloody amazing.'

I close the door that has a full-length mirror on the outside and look at my reflection, realising that I haven't really looked at myself in a while. I turn sideways and am surprised to see that my stomach looks pretty flat. I've lost quite a lot of weight, but with all the stress and upset of these past weeks and months, I simply hadn't noticed. Only now am I realising how loose my jeans are - they're sitting on my hips instead of my waist.

'Holy hell. I'm not that fat.'

'You're not fat at all, dopey. Now, try that green dress on. I bet it'll look amazing.'

I do as instructed, and am pleasantly surprised when I take another look at my reflection. The right pair of magic knickers and a high heel and I think I'll look OK.

Clare attempts a wolf whistle to show her approval. 'Gorgeous! Got some black heels? Zoe's had black sashes made for us all – they've got our names on the front and 'Charlie's Angels' on the back. Or the other way around. Anyway,' Clare finishes her sentence with a wave of her hand, throwing what little champagne was left in her glass over the bed. 'Bugger.

Got any more fizz?'

I can feel my mood lifting once more, boosted by my new svelte figure and my lovely, tiddly friend. 'I'll go and look,' I tell her and I head back downstairs to check the fridge. Alfie looks at me as I leave the room, but decides that his services are needed more in the bedroom. Returning a couple of minutes later, with more champagne, I find Clare flat out on the bed with Alfie lying next to her licking her face. I can't resist grabbing my mobile and taking a couple of photos and a short video.

I leave Clare like that for a few minutes and go and sit in Tom's room. Picking up his cuddly dog, I hold it to my chest. My life has been turned upside down, but I still have Tom. I still have a reason to get up every day, a reason to keep going. I take a deep breath and head back to my room with a renewed determination to get the evening back on track.

Clare is still sparko on the bed. Alfie has given up trying to revive her. 'Oy! Sleeping beauty!' I say, giving her a little shake. 'Time to wake up. The stripper's arrived.'

Clare opens one eye and looks at me blearily, gradually heaving herself back to a sitting position. 'Has he brought the drugs?' she asks.

'Yep, drugs galore. They're in his pants.'

'Shplendid,' she slurs.

'Uh uh! No drugs for you just yet. You're going in the shower while I make some coffee. I think you peaked too soon, my friend,' I tell her.

'Don't be a poopy-parter,' she says.

'I think you mean party-pooper. And I'm not. I'm trying to make sure you actually make it to the party. Come on, I'll get

318

you some fresh towels.'

With Clare finally in the shower, I head back to the kitchen to make a pot of strong coffee. While I'm downstairs I hunt for some suitable music to play while we get ready, settling on disco anthems. I'm hoping that the shower will revive Clare a bit, or she's not going to stay the course.

Clare's sitting on the bed with a towel wrapped round her when I go back upstairs with the coffee. She's looks much more with it. I hand her a mug.

'Thanks, Luce. Sorry. I think I may have started drinking a bit too early. Not used to it these days. Can't remember the last time I had a proper night out.'

'No apology needed. I think we've both needed a girly night out for a very long time.'

I sit down on the bed next to her and we clink coffee mugs. 'To us,' I say. 'And a bloody good night.'

CHAPTER 60

Charlie's Angels

The coffee and shower perk Clare up and we start to look forward to the night ahead once more. It's a long time since either of us has had a girly night out, let alone one where we get ready together. It's something of a ritual when you're younger, and single… Single. That's me. Well, separated at least. I still can't quite get my head around it. My husband is living with someone called Sylvie. In another country. It's all a bit surreal.

Shaking the thoughts away, I focus on getting ready. I'd almost forgotten how much fun it is getting ready with a girl-friend. Clare is currently singing into a hairbrush along with Donna Summer, and dancing round the bedroom, followed by an Old English Sheepdog who seems to think it's all rather good fun. Either that or he's trying to round her up. Grabbing my hair-straighteners, I join in with the chorus: 'I'm going crazy just to let you know/You'd be amazed how much I love you so, baby/When I get my hands on you I won't let go/This time I know it's for real…'

I feel happier than I have done in weeks as I put the finishing touches to my make-up, and hunt for the perfect jewellery to go with my dress. The woman who looks back at me from the mirror looks like someone I used to know. Someone who was happy and bubbly and funny. It's nice to see her again. I wonder if she's back to stay? I hope so. I've missed her.

Clare comes and stands next to me. 'You look fab,' I tell her.

'You're too kind. You look pretty amazing yourself. I haven't seen this Lucy in a long time.'

'No, me neither. I was just thinking that I hope she stays around for a while.'

'No reason why she shouldn't. She's footloose and fancy free again.'

'Hardly that, but I do feel like a great weight's been lifted.'

'Good. Let's make tonight a celebration of the return of the real Lucy.'

'Deal. Now, what's the time – it must be getting on. Taxi's due at half seven.' I look at the digital clock on the bedside table. 'Damn. It's almost half past. I need to let the dog out to pee.' Calling Alfie to follow me, I hurry downstairs and let him out into the back garden. While he's out there, I turn on the TV. Clare looks puzzled.

'What? I always leave the television on for him. It's company.'

'OK. Does he have a favourite channel?'

'Yeah. He likes the holiday programmes. Not the news. Talking, but nothing too heavy.'

'Right…' Clare clearly thinks I'm mad. 'Going with it…'

I laugh. 'OK, it might be mental. He might not give a damn if the tele's on or not, but it makes me feel better about leaving him.'

'Lady, you have some serious issues with attachment and guilt. Have you thought about seeing a therapist?'

'Many times, trust me. But you're cheaper,' I say, sticking my tongue out at her. Alfie has wandered back in, so I go and lock the back door just as the bell sounds at the front. Taxi. We're off. Watch out world.

Charlie's hen night is taking place in a lively bar/restaurant renowned for its cocktails and party atmosphere. Zoe has done the organising and is renowned for her wicked sense of humour and attention to detail, so I'm confident we're in for good night. When we arrive, she greets us at the door with our sashes.

'Names go at the front,' she informs us.

'Just call me Obtuse then,' I say having examined mine.

'What?' Zoe and Clare ask, in unison, each looking at me as if I'm mad.

'It says "Charlie's Angles" – not Angels. Look,' I tell them, holding up the offending article.

'Oh for goodness' sake!' Zoe exclaims. 'Only I could employ a dyslexic printer.'

Clare's laughing. 'Can I be Acute?' she asks.

Zoe looks daggers at her. Clare and I stifle our giggles.

'Don't worry about it, Zoe, I'm sure no-one else will notice,' I try to reassure. 'And if they do, you can put them *right*.' I can't resist.

'Or *straight*,' Clare chips in. We both give in to the giggles.

Zoe's facial expression tells us we've gone far enough. 'Sorry, Zoe,' we say together.

'Just bugger off, the pair of you, before I stab you with a protractor,' Zoe says, and directs us over to our table, where Charlie is already surrounded by friends and family. There's a lot of girly screaming going on, which would normally have me running for the hills, but I'm determined to throw myself into this night with as much abandon as I can muster. The screaming goes up a few decibels when the other mums see us and there are hugs all round, and an intoxicating heady mix of perfumes threatens to overwhelm us.

By eight o'clock, everyone's arrived and is seated at a long table that Zoe has bedecked with cock confetti and balloons. In fact, pretty much everything is phallic, from the cocktail stirrers to the lipsticks we're all gifted in the goodie bags. Clare and I have seated ourselves at one end of the table, away from the main action. It's not really our cup of tea, but we're doing our best to embrace it. Clare is currently sucking a bright pink cocktail through a penis-shaped straw. I grimace at her. She shrugs.

'When in Rome.'

'I guess,' I say, looking dubiously at the glass of pink liquid in front of me. 'What even is it?'

'No idea. Tastes good though.'

I take a tentative sip and she's right, it does taste good. I shrug. 'When in Rome.'

Dinner is finally served at around nine, when everyone around the table is more than a little squiffy. The screams intensify when it becomes apparent that it will be served by butlers in the buff: strapping young men wearing nothing but bowties and short aprons. Clare looks at me with a slightly disappointed expression.

'Why doesn't Greg look like that? You do realise, don't you, that you could actually take one of these hunks of British beef home with you?'

'How do you know they're British?' I ask, perplexed.

'Er, missing the point much? You are young, free and single, Lucy, you can do what – make that who – you like.'

'Who I like is Rob. Who I like I can't have.' I stick my

bottom lip out like a spoilt girl denied a pony.

'Well, you know what they say – to get over one man, you need to get under another.'

'No thanks. I'll do my getting over him the old fashioned way – moping and pining and crying into my pillow.'

'Ugh. Boring. Well, maybe I can try the other way on your behalf?'

'You are joking, I assume?'

'Yes. Of course. Sort of. No. Oh, I don't know. Ignore me, it's the alcohol talking,' she says, taking another sip through the cock straw.

I giggle. 'Sorry, Clare, it's kind of hard to have a serious conversation with that thing in your mouth.'

Clare takes that as her cue to suck provocatively on the straw, just as one of the nearly naked waiters appears with our starters. Clare goes as pink as the cocktail. He grins at her as he places a bowl of soup in front of her containing cock-shaped croutons.

'Cock-a-leekie, I presume?' she enquires of him.

He just smiles and then proceeds to withdraw an enormous and undeniably phallic-looking pepper grinder from his apron, at which point Clare and I both burst out laughing.

Clare engages the young man in conversation while he grinds pepper over her bowl: 'So, dish of the day, are you British?' she enquires, all innocence on the outside, but kicking me under the table at the same time.

I'm stifling a giggle and trying not to look at the muscles rippling in his torso as he moves.

'No, I'm from Australia,' he tells her.

'Oh, *down under*,' she says in a way that makes it sound just plain rude. 'Well, I understand they have some of the best beef in the world,' she says, sneaking a wink at me.

'We sure do. Like a nice bit of rump, do you?' he asks with a grin. He's on to Clare and clearly willing to play the game.

'Oh, yes, can't *beat* a bit of rump. Unless you ask me nicely.' Clare has gone into full-on seductress mode and I'm trying not to laugh. My stomach's hurting from the effort. Either that or my magic knickers are just too tight.

'So, what's your name, big boy?' she asks him. I'm close to losing it at this point. How Clare is keeping a straight face I have no idea.

'Roger.' That's it, I'm gone, and Clare finally screams with laughter.

'Roger!' she shrieks.

He just grins at us. 'Ladies,' he says, moving away to serve other guests.

'Oh my god,' I say, trying to get my breath back. 'Oh, Clare, I haven't laughed this hard in ages – thank you.'

'Don't thank me, thank Roger. Do you think he really is called Roger?'

'I doubt it, but I really don't care. That was brilliant.'

'Did you notice his bum as he walked away?'

'Hard not to, to be honest. He is a fine young specimen.'

'And a very good sport.'

'Yes indeed.'

'I'd certainly like to play a round with him.'

'Enough! My sides and this dress can't take it.'

Clare toys with her soup. 'I hate pepper.'

CHAPTER 61

Roses for remembrance

The remainder of the evening passes in much the same way, with laughter and innuendos aplenty. Food is consumed along with a great deal of alcohol, and the butlers are the butt of many a one liner, all of which they take in good spirits. Clare is in top form and has somehow managed to carry on drinking steadily all night. I slow down and switch to sparkling water for the last hour or so, not wanting to be too hungover the next day when Tom comes home. Unlike Clare, I no longer have a husband at home to take over the childcare until normal service can be resumed.

I can feel myself starting to sober up and I sit quietly, observing the antics around the table. I start to feel kind of removed from the party, like an observer. At the other end of the table I watch as Charlie opens the many gifts she's received. She looks radiant - the happiest I've seen her in such a long time. She will be the most beautiful of brides. I'm so very happy for her.

I'm suddenly feeling very tired though. I'd really like to make my excuses and leave. I just want to be on my own for a bit. I feel as though I'm coming down from a massive high, and that my emotional state has become terribly fragile.

'Just nipping to the loo,' I tell Clare. She's sharing a joke with Sarah and acknowledges with a nod.

Once in the Ladies, I lean on a sink and take a few deep breaths. I can feel the prickle of tears in the corners of my eyes. I can't, won't give in to them. I won't do anything that mars Charlie's special night. I turn on the cold tap and run the water over my wrists for a while. I must compose myself and return to the party. But I wish I was at home, sitting in the dark, and letting the tears flow. More than that, I wish I was anywhere with Rob. I wish I was wrapped up in his strong arms, with him telling me everything's going to be OK.

The door suddenly swings open, and in sways Clare.

'There you are. You've been gone ages. You OK?' she asks, sashaying over to the mirror to check her make-up. 'Oh my God,' is all she says when she sees her reflection.

'I miss him, Clare, I miss him so much.'

'Paul?'

'No, not Paul. Rob. I miss Rob.'

'It'll get easier, I promise. Just give it some time,' she says, giving me a boozy hug and planting a kiss on my cheek. 'I love you, Lucy. You're my best friend, you know that right?'

I can't help laughing. Clare is a very happy drunk. 'I love you too, Clare. And you're my best friend too. In the whole wide world.'

'I think I'd like to go home now.' Clare's words are music to my ears.

'In that case, I'll make our excuses and call a cab.'

And now I'm home. I dropped Clare safely back with Greg en route. Alfie greets me at the door like a long lost friend.

'Hello, boy. Did you miss me?' I let him out in the garden and reward him with a treat upon his return. The house feels empty, quiet. 'Time to mope for a bit, I think,' I tell him, kicking off my shoes and curling my legs under me on the sofa. Alfie jumps up next to me, putting his muzzle across my lap. I stroke his head absent-mindedly. I just want to wallow for a while, indulge myself in thoughts of Rob. I miss him so much it's like a physical pain and I can't imagine a time when it won't hurt like this.

I don't know how much time passes like that, but I suddenly realise that I'm stiff and cold. Bedtime. I fill a glass of water and swallow a couple of paracetamol to pre-empt any potential hangover, and head upstairs. I want to just fall into bed, but I force myself to remove my make-up first. Sleep claims me quickly when I crawl under the duvet.

Sunday dawns bright and clear. Brighter and clearer than my head at least. Considering how much I drank last night, though, I don't feel too bad. Tom isn't due back until teatime and the day stretches ahead of me like an uncharted map. I don't know what to do with the time. I still feel desperately sad.

Padding downstairs, I make tea and toast, both of which help a little. A hot shower follows and I begin to feel more than vaguely human. Alfie looks at me expectantly as I get dressed, daring to hope that a walk is on the cards when I pull on jeans and a jumper. 'Yes,' I tell him. He knows what that means and he starts to jump about excitedly.

Soon, we're in the car. 'Long journey,' I tell him. 'Lie down.'

I switch the radio off for once, not daring to hear what the DJ might play, and pull off the drive. Forty-five minutes later and I'm parking the car once more, in the gravelled car park of Claremont House. It feels like a pilgrimage. I'm not sure exactly what I'm expecting, or why I'm here. I just know I have to do something to feel closer to Rob. I'd seen from my previous visit that dogs are allowed on leads in the grounds.

Alfie pulls on his lead, eager to explore this new place.

'Come on then,' I say, heading for the gate. It's even more beautiful than I remember and the feeling is bittersweet when I remember being here with Rob. My spirits soar at the breath-taking beauty of the formal gardens and the rolling parkland beyond, whilst my heart simultaneously plummets with the pain and remembrance of loss.

My feet know the way of my heart, and before long the folly comes into view, its stone columns reaching for the sky like a parched face tilting up towards long awaited rain. The place where I first kissed Rob, and my fate was sealed. There's not another person in sight, although I saw a few visitors milling around near the house. I'm grateful for the solitude.

We reach the folly and I walk around it's perimeter before sitting down in the exact spot I had the first time. I'm curious to find a single rose has been placed here. It looks a little sad and wilted, but the sunset hues are still vivid. Picking it up, I cup its head, lifting it to my nose to see if its perfume matches its beauty. I close my eyes and inhale. The soft, sweet scent it gives up brings a smile to my lips.

I cradle the rose in my lap and sit quietly, lost in my thoughts. It's only when Alfie becomes alert that I see someone coming towards the folly. I don't want an intrusion on this, my act of remembrance, so I prepare to get up and leave if necessary.

As the figure comes closer, I think I can make out one of the Estate's bottle green T-shirts – the ones worn by the gardeners. I look away. Hopefully they'll just keep going to whichever bit of garden they are to tend. But the figure keeps on coming. Closer. And it's him. It's Rob. And he's running towards me. I get to my feet, unable to believe my eyes. And then I'm in his arms.

The world stands still for a few minutes as we just hold one another. Eventually, Rob speaks.

'I can't believe it's you. You're really here. And you found your rose.'

'My rose?' I ask, confused.

Rob holds up a yellow rose that I hadn't noticed in his hand. 'I've left a fresh rose here every day for the last twenty-two days – ever since I moved to Claremont.'

'Moved to Claremont?' I'm feeling stunned and confused.

'Yes, Lucy, I live here now. And work here.'

'But...?' I don't understand.

'I've left Elizabeth. After you, I just couldn't go back to my old life, to living a lie. I think she was actually relieved.'

'But... why didn't you tell me?'

'How could I? You're still married and I respect you too much to be a home-wrecker. I couldn't ask you to choose.'

I can't believe what I'm hearing. 'Rob, my marriage is over. I couldn't live a lie any longer either. But I thought...'

'You thought you'd still be the other woman and didn't want to break up my marriage!'

'Yes! I can't believe this is happening. I thought I'd never see

330

you again. These last weeks have been agony. I've never known pain like it.'

'I know, Lucy, me neither. But everything's going to be OK.'

There they were. The words I'd dreamt of hearing from the lips of the man I longed for. There was only one thing left to ask.

'I don't suppose you'd like to come to a wedding with me?'

THE END